WITH O'LEARY IN THE GRAVE

With O'Leary in the Grave

JAMES CARRICK

HEINEMANN : LONDON

William Heinemann Ltd

15 Queen St, Mayfair, London W1X 8BE

LONDON MELBOURNE TORONTO

JOHANNESBURG AUCKLAND

First published 1971
© Anthony Bradley and Peter Whittle 1971

434 10935 5

The lines from W. B. Yeats's poems 'September 1913'
and 'The Lake Isle of Innisfree' are from *The Collected
Poems of W. B. Yeats*, and are used by permission of
Mr. M. B. Yeats and Macmillan and Co.

Printed in Great Britain by
Northumberland Press Limited
Gateshead

Author's Note

This book is based on something that actually happened, and it follows history to a point. Beyond that point it carries the story into what might have happened if the events described had taken another turn. There are some real people named in this book. They are there to set the time and the scene and, while they may have been moving figures at the time, their influence is not felt in this story. The cast is fiction. Too many of the facts are sadly true.

Romantic Ireland's dead and gone,
It's with O'Leary in the grave.
                    — W. B. Yeats

1

Around four o'clock in the morning the first light of day began to wash across the empty wastes of the sea. A lone seagull came down from the east, its wings silver in the morning light. The seagull circled slowly around the ship three times and then turned and headed off in search of more prosperous pickings.

Below deck Nealis stirred uneasily in his bunk. The ship was pitching and rolling the way it had all night and he wanted some air. He got out of the bunk and fumbled for his clothes. As he dressed he lit a cigarette. Then he stumbled up to where the deck passengers huddled into themselves on the benches, or stood looking over the side of the ship and shivering in the wind. Nealis went aft and stood looking at the long white wake, turning up his coat collar against the wet morning wind.

The boat that runs nightly between Liverpool and Belfast provides one of the main routes for much of the human flotsam that flows backwards and forwards across the Irish Channel. She is not a big ship, but she is a strong ship, for the seas that run between the two countries are capable of great ferocity. On wild nights the boat is tossed about like a piece of driftwood, but she swoops and surges through the heaving turbulence with a power that seems incredible in so small a vessel. The boat slips away from her berth in the late evening and starts her run up the black reaches of the River Mersey on her way to the open sea. Upriver it floats by the moorings of weather-beaten, rust-pocked cargo ships, international travellers whose worldliness casts disdain on the little ship. Small tugboats puff their way up and down the river, and behind the breakwater the big ocean liners point their bows inland and stare, supercilious as duchesses, at the lights gleaming ashore. The little Irish boat puts her head down and butts her way on past them all, remorseless as a beetle.

By the time she reaches the harbour bar, night has fallen and the land lights have mostly disappeared. Away on the port bow the coast of Wales stands black and shapeless against the glooming sky. The passengers now feel that the voyage has properly begun. Some of them get out flasks of tea or coffee while others head for the bar. The bar stays open until around dawn, for many of the travellers prefer to while away the hours in drink and talk rather than in sleep.

The sailors who man the ship are cheerful, cynical men who view life as a pageant that passes nightly across the Irish Sea. Occasionally they are called into the bar to help separate men who have lost their tempers in drink and who, if left alone, might cause damage to each other.

The boat from Liverpool is that sort of roistering ship.

Her passengers are generally drawn from the ranks of emigrant Irishmen. These are the men who leave home, wives and families to cross to England where jobs are more certain and the pay is better. In England they spend their time labouring on building sites, carrying hods of bricks up interminable ladders. They are a raucous, beefy race; unfashionably dressed and temporarily affluent, they are eager to get their money spent so that they may exchange the awful responsibility of having money for the uncomplicated pleasures of being poor.

These are in the majority, but on any night there will be others on board the Irish boat. There are the lean men who have given up the struggle to keep themselves in England while sending money home to keep their families; and the quiet men who are returning home because they have found out that the El Dorado they sought does not exist; and the quiet priests who sit and read their breviaries in the second-

2

class saloon; and the flaunting women returning to their towns and villages to parade a new-found sophistication.

For all of the Irish who cross to Liverpool the boat is more than a means of transport; it is an umbilical cord that links them to their motherland with bonds forged of nostalgia for a past that never was.

It was fifteen years since Nealis had first made the crossing. Now he stood in the stern of the boat, a seasoned man of thirty-four, and thought back to that other, unproved, nineteen-years-old Nealis. That earlier Nealis had boarded the ship at Belfast clutching a cheap cardboard suitcase in his right hand. The suitcase had contained two shirts, shaving kit, three pairs of socks, a vest and a pair of drawers. The drawers had a hole on the left buttock. Now the drawers he possessed were unbroken and—a slight intimation of progress—he had learnt to call them underpants.

The years between had taken the raw material that was Nealis and forged him into something other than he had set out to be. His dream when he had boarded the boat at Belfast had been to make enough money in England to return within five years and set himself up with a small farm. That had not happened.

Six months after stepping off the boat at Liverpool he had found himself at an Army camp, a gunner in the Royal Artillery starting out on two years' National Service. Six weeks after starting his basic training he had applied for a transfer to the Military Police. He got the transfer because of his height and physique and, after training, the Military Police sent him to Cyprus.

Service with the Military Police taught him things about himself that he had never known.

Long monotonous nights, spent cleaning boots and equipment, nurtured in him pride in his personal appearance that must always have been lying just below the surface; the hard grind of the physical training brought him a new consciousness of his body until he began to glory in the smooth working of sinew, nerve and muscle. He also learned to kill and

3

maim, quickly and easily. When a Greek terrorist cut loose with a sten gun in a crowded street in Nicosia one day Nealis drew his pistol and shot him in the head. There are two things a soldier must learn about killing. One is the actual mechanical process that starts with an action by the soldier which ends in the death of another man. The second, and harder lesson, is to learn to accomplish this without pain to oneself. As the Greek slumped to the ground, Nealis was mildly surprised to find that he had learned this second lesson well. He put his pistol back in his holster and walked into the centre of the excited Cypriot mob to take charge of the situation. He felt nothing beyond the need to keep the crowd under control and gather up the sten gun before somebody else got to it.

It might have ended there for Nealis, for the man's brother was watching from the crowd. He was a small man and he made his way over to where Nealis was standing, his eyes blazing with hate. As he pushed his way through the crowd he said, 'That's my brother, that's my brother he has killed. That is my brother.'

There was a quick upsurge of sympathy among the people who heard him. 'It is his brother. It is that man's brother who has been killed.' The whisper passed among the small crowd, and the quick cement of sympathy bound them together in a solid wall of faceless hostility. The man came up behind him moving slowly through the parting crowd, and as he did so he drew a knife. It was a flat-bladed knife, the sort fishermen use for gutting their catches. The point came up, glittering in the sunlight.

The man was about four feet from Nealis when a voice barked out: 'Drop it!' The man lunged forward as Nealis half turned to see what was happening. As the man moved, a burst of gunfire ripped across his body in a small crescent as twelve bullets found a home in his stomach.

Sergeant Simmons, Nealis's immediate superior, thrust forward, sten gun held across the body in the ready position. 'Never turn your back on any of these bastards,' he said.

His voice was deep and carried the unmistakable inflections

of Ulster. He came from Belfast and Nealis thought of him admiringly as a tough, professional soldier.

Nealis searched his mind for the right response to make to the man. 'Thanks, Sarge,' he said, 'I would have bought it there if you hadn't ...'

'Never mind that,' Simmons said, 'just remember that you never turn your back on these treacherous bastards.' It was a lesson in tactics which Nealis was to remember long afterwards.

After the Army, Nealis wondered about the future and then went back to Liverpool. He spent four months totting up figures in a drab little office near the docks, and then he answered a recruiting advertisement for the Liverpool City Police.

Nealis had done well at his job. Buoyed up as he was by a total belief in himself and an equally total disbelief in everybody else, he made a good policeman.

Cases had come and gone, men had gone to prison, been released and been returned again as he went about his task of building up a reputation as a steady and efficient police officer. It was the official notice of his promotion from Detective Sergeant to Detective Inspector that had turned his thoughts to Ireland.

It had all started there, fifteen years ago. Along the way Nealis had picked up a reputation as a tough operator. He had also picked up a wife. That was a constantly nagging pain—one of his mistakes. Apart from that, though, the callow boy was now a proven man; a hard, inquisitive man who had made his mark. When he heard of the promotion Nealis began to nourish an impulse to go back and see what he had left behind. He was not, he told himself, trying to recapture his youth. There was nothing in his youth that was half so good as what he had now. Even counting the estranged wife.

So why not go back and see? Why not take a nostalgic look at his home town? He would walk around the streets, looking at the dingy little houses and the shabby, no-hope people. He had been one of them, and while he was one of them no longer there was a certain feeling of kinship within him.

If he saw anybody he knew he would take them into the nearest bar and buy them a pint and talk long yarns about the old days. He would walk the old neighbourhoods, picking out the sights and scenes that he had once known. Breathing in the city smells that had stayed with him in all his long years of absence. He knew now that a man never loses the taste and feel of his birthplace and that going back can be the purest form of spiritual regeneration.

So, as the little ship thrust her way forward through the lightening sea, Nealis stood in the stern and watched the newly-risen sun dappling the waters. The boat was much nearer to land now and passengers began streaming onto the decks to strain their eyes for the first sight of the coast.

For many of them it was a sight that would herald the curing of all the ills that had befallen them. Some of those who sought the coastline were going back to Ireland to stay: for them the voyage had ended. It was different for Nealis; he was just going back to see where it all began.

2

The train ride northwards to Londonderry was a journey of the most exquisite nostalgia for Nealis. He had been savouring the emotion, tasting it almost, from the moment he stepped aboard the ferry in Liverpool. Each fresh landmark had its own memory as the train headed up through high, green rolling country, away from Belfast. There was peace here, he felt, a deep and timeless peace that men could never interfere with. In the fields men worked and cows grazed. Sheep meandered alongside the railway track, fleeing with neurotic persistence at the approach of each train, and languorous mountain streams burbled in the morning sun. It was a beautiful land and because of that beauty it was the sort of land that devoured men. Generations of men who had been born here had given their souls to it, knelt and worshipped it and, when the time came, had gone forth to die for it.

The train rattled in through the outskirts of Derry, forsaking the green fields and high hills for the greystone timidity that characterizes the city's architecture.

He walked out of the station and, wanting to be alone with himself and his thoughts, booked into a nearby hotel. Derry was still what it had always been. He left the hotel and looked around at the familiar city, a shambling industrial slum that had existed as a habitation long before men learned how to make machinery and had then taken a fresh impetus when the machines came along.

Nealis almost walked past Fogerty's before he recognized it as the place where he had taken his first drink paid for with his own money. Fogerty's, where manhood had begun. On impulse, he turned sharply back and as he did so, he cannoned into two men in the uniform of the Royal Ulster Constabulary. Their reactions were incredibly quick. Nealis recognized that much. One policeman pounced on him with a roar of anger, his baton poised to strike as Nealis fell. The other was against the wall of the pub with his right hand already on the butt of his pistol. It seemed to Nealis that they remained in their positions for an age, like some still-life tableau.

'What's the hurry?' the one with the baton said at last. A small crowd had gathered. Archetypal citizens of any Derry street corner. The constable with the gun eyed them warily. Nealis started to get up, slowly. The one with the baton watched him.

'Bastards,' someone in the crowd shouted irrelevantly. The policeman with the gun kept his hand on the butt.

'Sorry,' Nealis said, 'I was not looking.'

'Watch where you're bloody going, then,' said the one with the baton.

'Bastards,' the same voice called out mechanically. Nobody paid much attention to it.

'All right, break it up,' said the one with the baton to the crowd. With a final glare at Nealis, he nodded to his companion, who clipped the flap of his gun holster shut. The two policemen pushed through the thin crowd and walked off towards the Foyle Bridge.

'Did them bastards crack you one?' The question came from an old man whose breath smelled heavily of Guinness. 'The bloody street isn't safe with them bastards about.' Nealis ignored him and brushed the dust from his suit. 'Coppers,' the old man went on in a voice brimming with contempt. He spat on the pavement to emphasize his feeling. 'Cunts, all of them.'

'Forget it,' Nealis said. He wondered if the two RUC men had been involved in the street fighting the previous weekend. For some reason he remembered Cyprus and the universal hatred he had seen in the eyes of little old men like this one. He had been trigger-happy then. Maybe that was how the two policemen felt.

'We'll get the bastards,' the old man persisted. 'You see, we'll . . .'

'Piss off,' Nealis said savagely. He turned and strode angrily away.

He had regained his composure after walking a hundred yards, but the incident nagged at his mind. It was no longer a pleasant walk on a cloudy August Saturday through the streets of his home town. For the first time, he began to notice other pairs of RUC men standing watchfully on the corners. A sign caught his eye, daubed in yellow paint on a grimy wall. 'RUC=SS' it said. It struck Nealis as being odd. There should be so many more likely parallels in the Irish mind, it seemed. Even in a city where slogans were part of the fabric of every wall, this one seemed alien.

By now, the mood of reverie had vanished completely. The atmosphere of tension cloaked him like an overcoat on a hot day. Even the small knots of men who congregated on the corners didn't seem the same. They had always had their troubles, God knew. Unemployment and the attendant miseries of hunger had been their lot for generations, but it seemed to Nealis that they had always managed to retain a certain corporate humour. Now there were different faces. Humourless, suspicious, sullen. Nealis shrugged as he walked. Maybe he had grown up. 'Me Da'' had stood on many a street corner. How did anyone really know what their father had been thinking during all those years? Me Da'—that poor old half-crippled man who had spawned him. In and out of work, tanner cross-doubles on slow horses, determinedly drunk on three pints of Guinness, slipping the boys a penny for a bag of broken biscuits from Tatty's on the corner of Clement Street, complaining about the bullet in his lung. He recalled it now. Me Da' had talked like the old man outside Fogerty's. Me Da' had taken him once to see an Orangeman's parade. Nealis had loved it and shivered with excite-

9

ment at the pipes and drums and fifes and flags and banners, and the colour and the noise. But Me Da' had wept when they got home. It had been the only time he had seen Me Da' weep. Me Da' hadn't taken a drink that day, either. He just wept and banged the kitchen table with his fist. Those bastards, he had said, they had ruined his life and put a bullet in him and kept him out of work so that he hadn't a decent pair of shoes to wear. Mother Kate had told the boys not to heed him and go and play football, but Me Da' had said it was time they knew. Frank had climbed on Me Da's knee and cuddled him but then Frank was the youngest, and there wasn't room on Me Da's knee for another. He had gone to Mother Kate but she was in the kitchen lighting the gas under the tea kettle. She had rubbed his hair and told him to go and play with the boys. When Me Da' died, he had been sorry, but it had been Frank who had lain awake that night and had confided to Michael that one day he would do something about Me Da' and said he would shoot the head Orangeman if he could but he didn't have a gun.

Me Da'. That poor old sod.

An armoured car passed him slowly, toiling along The Diamond, a slow-moving dinosaur amid the nimble traffic. It had 'Police' painted in white along the side. Nealis had never seen a vehicle like it since his Cyprus days long ago. Cyprus again. Was this battlefield like that had been, with every stranger a potential enemy? Uneasily, Nealis continued walking.

Where the Guildhall Square broke up into a maze of tributary roads was the crossroads where Timms Road ran off to the right and Kilgallen Street opened to the left. Nealis stood at the corner for a moment or two, staring down into the narrow canyon of the street where he had been born. At a glance it hadn't changed much.

Two up, two down, a miniscule kitchen and a lav in the yard, repeated fifty times in a long, parade-ground-straight row facing the wall of a factory which had once turned out fine Irish linen and had now long since changed to making plastic or something or other. The factory wall reached sheer to chimney-top height and there wasn't a window in it, so that nothing but brickwork distracted the eyes of the Kilgallen Street residents when they looked out of their windows. But that was something they rarely did, for why look out of the window when the door was always open and it was easier and better to go and stand on the step and watch the world go by?

Kilgallen Street was a poor, miserable, utterly unexceptional line of houses, but in moments of euphoria, Nealis had boasted of it, told stories of it, pitied those who hadn't been handed such a volume of experience, a book of life, just by being born in such a place. It was nothing to do with the romance of being poor. It wasn't the life from which to weave fairy stories. Mutton stew eked out over three days for the Nealises was a tasteless diet and bread and jam for tea was just as monotonous as it sounded.

But there was one significant change in that barren landscape. Where once had stood the green paint and frosted window of Fitzgibbon's Bar now lay a heap of flame-blacked timbers and bricks. The house immediately beyond it, where the Donovans and their ten children had lived, was scorched and scarred with soot, and the windows were missing. Half a dozen children were climbing over the ruins of Fitzgibbon's, scrabbling amongst the debris and calling to each other when they unearthed some new treasure. Two men stood on the pavement, grinning at their antics.

'Find the bloody till, will ye,' one of the men called out.

Nealis stopped, and the two men eyed him, their faces as blank as the factory wall.

'What happened?' Nealis asked, nodding towards the heap of rubble.

The younger of the two men flashed a glance at the other. 'Petrol bomb,' he said.

'When did it happen?'

'The other night.'

'Who did it?' Nealis asked, knowing the answer.

'They came busting down here,' the other man volunteered. 'We was too late to stop them. The bloody place was alight before anyone knew it, and there's wee Jimmy dancing around in his nightshirt trying to put it out with his hands.'

'Who's Jimmy?'

'He owned it,' the younger man said. 'He's in hospital now. They did ten bars that night.'

'Did anyone see?' Nealis stood with the still faint stench of smoke in his nostrils, picturing the sudden burst of flame, the cries, the panic, the anger.

'Who wants to know?' The younger man was plainly suspicious. Perhaps it was his suit, Nealis thought. He looked too much of the city for Kilgallen Street.

'I used to live here,' he said.

The children on the rubble suddenly cried out in excitement. One of them, a bright-eyed lad in Wellington boots and an anorak, was holding up a bottle.

'By Christ, that's full,' said the younger man and picked his way carefully across the black bricks to take it from the boy. Nealis nodded to the older man and walked on. Past the Donovan house, the Stevensons, the Youngers and the others whose names came so easily. Faces, he couldn't remember. They stared at him, acknowledging his passing with the merest tilt of their heads. Door by open door, he pressed on. And then he was on the threshold of his home.

The door, like all the rest, was wide open. The step had been scuffed by a million feet and was worn into a smooth concave. The cheap lino didn't quite reach the step and in between Nealis could see the floorboards. Fifteen years ago was yesterday, or it might have been. He hesitated for a moment, wiping his chin with his right hand—a mannerism as automatic as blinking when Nealis was in deep thought. And then he stepped across the stone and into the hallway. It still smelled of tea and boiled cabbage.

'Ma? There Ma?'

Silence. And then a short, throaty exclamation, a tug on a door handle and there was Mother Kate emerging from

12

the gloom at the end of the passage, a tall, thin figure cloaked in sheer delight.

'Michael!'

Tears already seeping from her eyes, she sped towards him and buried her head in his chest and sobbed with pure joy.

At length, he gently eased the bony frame from him and regarded his mother. She smiled through her tears and wiped her eyes with the end of her apron. She had dark eyes and lashes the colour of mascara and hair that had once been soot black but was now dark grey. In her youth, she had been a handsome woman and even though the years had eroded her features, still her eyes were beautiful. She blinked them and apologized for herself.

'I shouldn't be blabbing to see you,' she said, shaking her head and smiling in gentle self-reproof. 'It's good to see you, Michael. Good to see you after all this time.'

'It's good to be back,' Nealis said.

'Come in the kitchen.' She took his arm and led him down the passage and then, as if to some stranger, added: 'It's in here.'

The thing which struck Nealis first was the incongruity of the television set standing on a cheap metal trolley with wheels in the corner where Me Da' used to sit in his favourite chair. That, and Frank, who sat at the kitchen table.

'Frank,' Mother Kate said, 'it's your brother. Frank, Michael's home, isn't it great?'

'Is it?' Frank said. With scarcely a glance at Nealis, he picked up a spoon and stirred the mug of tea in front of him with slow deliberate movements.

For a second, Mother Kate was perplexed, and the smile faded gradually from her face.

'Frank! What's the matter with you? C'mon, get to your feet and say hello to your brother. Jesus, Mary and Joseph, is this the way to bring him back into this house? What are you thinking of?'

'Hello, Frank,' Nealis said. 'It's grand to see you.'

Frank looked up. His eyes held Nealis's with a trace of

amusement, then flicked rapidly down to his shoes and up again to his face.

'Aye, the conquering hero returns,' he said with heavy sarcasm. 'Back to see how the other half lives, are you?'

Nealis felt the anger rising inside him. 'I already know.'

'What the hell's all this?' Mother Kate looked from one to the other. 'Conquering hero? What kind of talk is that for two brothers? Frank, are you sick or something? What's the matter with you that you can't be civil to your brother Michael?'

Frank drained the mug of tea and stood up. 'I'll be going, Ma. Don't wait up for me.'

With a look of unexpected bitterness, he eyed Nealis once more briefly and strode from the room.

'God forgive him!' Mother Kate said fiercely. 'I'll split his head when he comes in, so I will.'

Nealis grinned. 'I shouldn't try, Ma. He's bigger than you. God knows what's the matter with him, but he'll get over it.'

'I wonder. He's a quair one, is Frank. I worry about him, Michael, honest to God I do. He's in with a pack of funny people.'

'Funny? Didn't seem very funny to me,' Nealis said, sitting down at the table opposite his mother.

'No, not funny, really.' Mother Kate rubbed her hands on her apron as she must have done fifty thousand times and shot a glance at the door. 'You'll be wanting a brew, son. I bet you never had a brew like your old Ma can make since you left Ireland.'

'No,' Nealis grinned again. 'That's the truth. They don't boil up the teapot in England.' He paused. 'What lot is it that Frank's in with, then?'

Mother Kate shrugged. 'I don't know.' With that, she bustled out to the tiny scullery and Nealis heard her lighting the gas and fishing the cups from the sink. On familiar ground again, Mother Kate began to chat about the old times, his old friends, the days that seemed so long ago.

14

Nealis told her about his work and his promotion and she beamed with pride. They talked for half an hour and drank tea and then, after a break in the chit-chat, Nealis asked about the previous weekend and the trouble in the Bogside.

Mother Kate couldn't catch the shutter which came down over her bright eyes for a moment or two, and she looked away from him making busy with the teapot.

'Don't worry your head about it, Michael.'

'But from what I read, it looked bad.'

She shrugged. 'I've seen worse.'

'Have you?'

Mother Kate shook her head, as if to end the conversation where it had begun. 'Have some more tea,' she said.

3

The evening was soft in the way of Irish evenings; thin rain fell gently, to light like a benediction on the land and through it a slow, amber sun sank into the sea beyond the hills. There was an autumnal gentleness about it; a sensual warmth that was somehow tender and feminine. It was in sharp contrast to the strident grey menace of the streets.

Here in this unbeautiful part of the city, Nealis experienced a deep sense of disquiet, as the feeling grew within him that he had little in common with Derry any more. He had come looking for a half-remembered sense of innocence; instead he had found a deep and disgusting brutishness, a barbarism that had little place in the world he now knew.

He turned slowly into a bar and jostled his way past the drinkers who thronged the doorway to make his way to the counter. The customers were thirsty and the barman was kept busy pulling pints of porter. Eventually Nealis caught his eye and ordered a large Jamiesons. As he sipped it he wondered why he had ordered it. In England his usual drink was a half pint of bitter and a Scotch. Normally he did not drink Irish whiskey.

The crowd at the bar were the same crowd he remembered from his adolescence. Small men in blue jeans or shabby, shiny suits, caps pulled on to the side of their heads. Unskilled and unhopeful, their only regular source of cash came in unemployment benefit. Since he had left a new generation had grown up which thought of jobs as something somebody else had. This was a town of high unemployment and it had been so since the war. In the war things had boomed as the river grew rich on shipping and factories had turned over to arms production. Then came peace and poverty.

There were two men standing behind him and he became gradually conscious of them. He turned and looked at them. One of them, a broad-shouldered man with a florid face, returned his stare and said: 'Are you the policeman over from England?'

'Who wants to know?'

'Ah now, take no offence. I'm Bartley Mulholland and I'm a friend of your brother Frank. You have a good resemblance of him.' Mulholland smiled, showing nicotine-capped teeth, in an attempt to make the atmosphere easy.

The two men stood there, waiting to see if he would offer them a drink. He did not, annoyed by the way in which he had been approached. Eventually Mulholland called for two whiskeys.

'This is Pogue Mahone,' he said, indicating the man with him.

Nealis smiled, remembering the Gaelic meaning for Pogue Mahone. Kiss my arse. 'Pogue Mahone,' he said, 'that's a quair name. How did you get that?'

Mulholland grinned at him. 'When you get to know him you'll find out. It's a phrase he's fond of.'

Nealis relaxed. Mulholland's depersonalizing questions had irked him but now he felt the tension go. The man was obviously a social fool. To go around with somebody known as Pogue Mahone he had to be.

'Are you over for long?' Mulholland asked.

'Open ended. I've got a spot of leave, and I may stay a week or so.'

'That's a good job you have, on the police over there, is it?'

'It's a living.'

'Aye, I suppose in England you can look on it as that. Not like our beloved Royal Ulster Constabulary. It's a crusade with them.'

17

'Well, I suppose they operate in a different way.'

'Too right, they do. Political policemen, I suppose, wouldn't be much in your line?'

'I'm not sure what you mean by political policemen.'

Mulholland leaned closer, smiling confidentially. 'Armed gangsters. Fascists. Men who are more concerned with depriving a large section of the population of their liberty than with ensuring their freedom.'

It sounded like a quote from a speech and Nealis got the feeling that it was a speech which Mulholland had made more than once.

Pogue Mahone joined in: 'Fascists is right. Wouldn't they beat the living shit out of a Catholic as soon as look at him? What's that but Fascists?'

Nealis shrugged: 'Oh well, I'm just here for a holiday.'

Mulholland leaned close again. It was a habit which Nealis found increasingly annoying. 'It's a funny place for an English policeman to be having a holiday. At this time.'

Nealis flushed, openly angry now. 'Look mate,' he said, 'let's get it straight shall we? I'm an Irishman serving in the English police force who happens to be in Derry for a holiday because Derry is where he was born and raised. Okay?'

Mulholland grinned again, another flash of nicotined appeasement. 'Now you're taking me up wrong again. I was just saying what came into my head. Take no notice. Sure, as long as you're on holiday enjoy yourself. Just have a complete holiday and forget about your work, that's the best thing.'

He stopped talking for a moment, staring deeply into Nealis's eyes.

'As I say, it's always the best thing when you're on holiday to forget completely about your work.' He patted Nealis on the shoulder. 'Yes, just you forget about it completely and you'll have a nice easy time. Just forget it completely.' There was an unmistakable warning in his voice.

* * *

After he washed and shaved for the second time that day Nealis went down the hotel stairs and into the dining room. A waiter showed him to a small corner table and he sat there reading that evening's copy of the *Belfast Telegraph*. In the old days the newspaper had been known to the city's Catholics as the 'Lying Telly', because it had been regarded as the mouthpiece of extreme Protestantism. Then it had been taken over by the Canadian millionaire publisher, Lord Thomson. There had been some sort of civil action in the courts which he remembered reading about at the time in which somebody had contested Lord Thomson's ownership. But Thomson had won. Since then the *Belfast Telegraph* had been under attack by such figures as the Reverend Ian Paisley. Everything had to be either black or white, Orange or green. Everything, that is, except himself. He was strictly grey.

His reading was interrupted by the waiter who came across to him to say: 'There's a gentleman over there asking if your name is Michael Nealis.'

He looked in the direction the waiter indicated and recognized a man who was waving at him. He got up and crossed the room, hand outstretched.

'George Simmons,' he said, 'Sergeant George Simmons. Well, I'll go to hell. How are you?'

The other man rose. He was stouter than Nealis remembered him and his face had taken on a florid tinge. He wore a well-cut navy blue suit, and there was an air of prosperity about him. Simmons turned to two men who sat eating with him and said: 'This is Michael Nealis. We were in the Army together in Cyprus. William Dynes and Robert Shaw.'

Nealis shook hands with the men and accepted their invitation to join them.

'How have you been, Michael?' Simmons asked.

'Well now, I can't complain. After the Army I joined the police in Liverpool and they've just made me an Inspector. I'm over here on holiday. What about yourself?'

Simmons had been a regular soldier with five years' service to complete his twenty-two years' engagement when Frank had been in Cyprus. Nealis remembered the old admiration he had felt for him as a brave and competent soldier.

'I finished my engagement and came back here and opened up as a builder's merchant with my gratuity. I haven't done bad. I've three shops now and a couple of yards.'

'Well, that makes a change,' Nealis laughed. 'What are you doing here?'

Shaw spoke up. 'Mr Ross Simmons is addressing a meeting outside the Guildhall tonight.'

'Mr Ross Simmons?' Nealis asked. 'Is that you?'

The other man laughed. 'It is. It was always my full name, but I never used it in the Army. Some of the other fellows in the mess would have thought I was apeing the officers.'

George Ross Simmons. The name had been in the newspapers frequently enough. Nealis felt a vague sense of annoyance with himself that he had not connected it with the Army sergeant he had known. But then, how do you make the connection between an Army sergeant and the leader of a para-military force known as the Ulster Volunteer Force?

The Ulster Volunteer Force—UVF—had been resurrected about three years ago. Its members were dedicated to keeping the Six Counties of Northern Ireland under the British flag. They were also fanatical Protestants to whom anything savouring of the word 'Catholic' was anathema. Reputedly they had guns and were prepared to use them in defence of their beliefs. Some said they had already done so.

Nealis took it all in and said: 'Well, you've moved up to General now.'

Simmons smiled easily. 'Oh, I wouldn't say that. That's just newspaper talk. My organization stands for the defence of the legal constitution of Ulster.'

'Defence against what?'

'Defence against the clandestine and undemocratic forces that are trying to seize power.'

'Forgive me, George. I'm not quite with you. Who would they be?'

'Left wingers. Anarchists. Communists. Republicans.'

'What about the Catholics?'

'Now Michael, I didn't bring them into it. We wish to live in peace with our Catholic neighbours.'

Nealis grinned. 'But do you think that they're getting a fair crack of the whip from the government?'

'I do, Michael. This is a democratic country and the Unionist Party is the democratically elected government of this country.'

It would be wise to stop, Nealis thought. Wiser to turn the conversation to small talk, wiser to relive the khaki camaraderie of Cyprus. Instead he said: 'But what about all these stories about the elections being rigged in Derry? What about the allegations that the Catholics don't get a fair deal when it comes to dishing out council houses?'

'Communist propaganda, Michael. In any case you can't treat the Catholics the same as anybody else when it comes to allocating council houses. They breed so much that a Protestant would never get a council house.'

Simmons lit a cigarette and smiled with the air of a man listening to the unsophisticated arguments of a child.

'That may be all very well in England, Michael, but the problem here is different. You see, if you look at the Catholics closely you will understand—they are disloyal to the state.'

Shaw, the more assured of the two men with Simmons, leaned forward and said accusingly: 'You know, you sound like a bloody Papist.'

There was malice in the look Nealis turned upon him: 'I am,' he said.

Shaw got up and spoke to Simmons. 'Mr Simmons, do you hear what that man said?'

Simmons grinned. He was an easy, affable man, a man in control of the situation.

'Don't be worrying, Bob. Michael's all right. He fought for the Crown and that makes him okay with me.'

When the three men left, Nealis watched as they collected

a bowler hat each from the waiter and a silk sash which they draped across their bodies. Embroidered on the sash were the letters UVF.

Nothing changed, Nealis thought. Bigotry was still king and, to be fair, it was not all one-way bigotry. With a slight sense of amazement he remembered the tightening in his stomach, the feeling of suppressed hostility which he had felt towards Shaw and the other man, Dynes. He wondered about his feelings towards Simmons.

In a sense, a very real sense, he owed his life to Simmons. The incident had happened in the line of duty and formed just part of the task which any soldier in similiar circumstances could be expected to carry out. That, though, was merely to rationalize. The real thing was that somebody had been going to kill him and Simmons had shot the would-be assassin instead. Without Simmons he would have been dead in the heat and dust of Cyprus, with maybe a mangy dog pissing on him as one had pissed on his victim. And yet, he wondered, did Simmons' action leave him beholden to Simmons? Or had Simmons already been paid by the three sergeant's stripes on his arm and the pension he received from the Army? Did a man owe a personal debt in such circumstances? He sighed, not knowing.

The day was gone when he left the hotel, but a huge moon, burnished and golden, lit up the night. There is a dignity about the centre of Derry, a dignity that stems from the stolid worthiness of its main square, and as he walked towards it Nealis felt something like the same sense of assurance it engendered in the worthy men who erected it.

There were new things in Derry since he had last visited. Chinese cafés, Wimpy bars. Ahead of him he could hear the distorted sound of speech through an amplifying system as the Simmons rally progressed outside the Guildhall. He walked down towards it and joined a group standing on the edges of the rally. All around watchful constables, lean and fit in their dark green uniforms, kept an eye open for trouble. One man, obviously a member of the Special Branch, took shorthand notes. Simmons' supporters, easily distinguishable by their bowler hats, sashes and white gloves, stood around. Some of the more important ones, nearer the rostrum, carried swords and Bibles. The idea was, he supposed, to defend the Bible with the sword if anyone attacked it. Catholics again, he thought.

Simmons was on the platform now, a dignified figure holding the microphone and speaking. Nealis was surprised at the power of his voice, the hypnotic effect his delivery was having on some of the bystanders.

'We are Christians,' he was saying. 'Our fathers fought and died for Christianity and it is that same Christianity today that is stretched and twisted upon the rack of man's contempt.'

The words came out like a symphony as the big voice rose and fell, paused and blared with great effect.

'For us, loyal to the flag, loyal to the sacred Protestant faith that we have defended against the might of the Devil and the worst attacks of the Anti-Christ, there is no choice today. We have no choice. Our religion is under attack by atheists, Communists, Anarchists and—worst of all—by those who would lead us along the sin-stained path to Rome. And we have no choice. We must arm ourselves and again prepare to defend it.

'His Holiness, that usurper of Christ, the Pope, has his legions prepared to take us over. Oh, they say they are about Civil Rights and votes and all that, but we know.' The voice dropped to a hiss. 'Brethren, we know. We have seen Papish plots before, and we have defeated them. In the great good of the bosom of Christ we have defeated them. And we will defeat them again.

'Let those who sit at our borders, ravening like beasts in their foul lusts, take heed that the Protestants of Northern Ireland are ready to stand and die before they will let the dog-collared carrion of Catholicism lead them into the arms of the Unholy Mother Church.'

Nealis did not see the first stone that was thrown, but he

heard the cry of pain from Simmons as it hit on the cheek. The flow of words dried and suddenly the meeting exploded into mayhem.

The violence was coming from a tight group of men, about thirty strong, wedged into the centre of the crowd. They were hurling bricks and some of them were laying around them with sticks. One of them, primed with ammunition, lit a petrol bomb and threw it onto the speaker's platform, where it shattered. Flames licked hungrily around the feet of those on the platform and, as they tried to stamp them out, two more petrol bombs landed beside them.

Simmons leaped from the platform, microphone in hand and bellowed into it. 'Will those at the back stand still. We dont want these men to escape.'

A heavy squad of bowler-hatted supporters had gathered around him. They too were armed with sticks.

'Please clear a way,' Simmons bawled.

The crowd made an opening at the front and the bowler-hatted men poured into it. There were about a hundred of them and many of them had produced pick-axe handles. As they advanced the men who had thrown the stones made desperate efforts to fight their way back through the crowd, but the crowd locked on them, holding them in. Nealis looked around, his instinct telling him that he should see what the police were doing to help them. But when he looked he saw that the police had turned their backs on the scene and were moving some distance away.

There were shouts and curses as the Ulster Volunteer Force came to grips with the stone-throwers. Nealis heard the sickening crunch as wood cracked into bone and then he lost sight of the detail as the fighting spread.

Hemmed in all around, the men who had thrown the petrol bombs were soundly beaten by both members of the crowd and the UVF. One man came staggering out of the crowd, his hair matted with blood and his left ear almost torn from his body.

He was the first of many. Suddenly the stone-throwers

mind as he walked, Nealis caught himself dwelling on a snatch of a phrase ... *and that I will, to the best of my power, cause the peace to be kept and preserved and prevent all offences against the persons and properties of Her Majesty's subjects....* It was part of the oath he had taken as a policeman, so long ago. Before today, it had all been pretty simple.

Kilgallen Street when he got there was dark and it had begun to drizzle and most of the front doors were shut. It gave a foreboding air to the street and Nealis, for no rational reason, found himself walking quietly, almost furtively, to his home.

Mother Kate was sitting in the kitchen watching television when he opened the door softly and walked in. She jumped from the chair with a little cry and stood with the knuckles of her right hand to her lips as she always did when alarmed.

'It's all right, Ma. It's only me,' Nealis said, above the sound.

'Michael?' Nealis saw her eyes flick over him in half-disbelief and only then remembered the blood on his coat. 'Michael, what in the name of God have you been doing?'

'There was a fight ... in the Square.'

With a muffled cry, Mother Kate scurried across the room to him and threw her arms around her son. She buried her head in his chest and he felt rather than heard her crying.

'It's all right, Ma. It's nothing. I'm not hurt.' That was a lie and it gave him physical pain to say it, since his abdomen ached badly and he could feel the bruises on his ribs. 'It's all right, Ma.' Slowly, Mother Kate withdrew and held Nealis at arm's length. She wasn't crying any longer, but searched his face with eyes that were old but beautiful.

'Sit down, son. I'll get soap and water and tidy you up.'

'Don't worry about—'

'Sit down.'

Nealis sat in the solitary armchair. The television set burbled on while Mother Kate bustled into the kitchen. Returning, she snapped the set off and set a bowl of water on the kitchen table. Firmly, she gripped Nealis's chin and

managed to fight a way through the encircling crowd and, spurred on by blows and buffets, they started trying to escape in a blood-stained stream. As they did so the waiting police, who had already drawn their batons, charged in on them to fell more of them and make arrests.

One of the fleeing men wheeled away and as he drew alongside Nealis a Volunteer stepped in his path to stop him. The Volunteer collapsed as a pick-axe handle smashed his nose to pulp. Throwing the handle away the man fled, and Nealis stared after him.

A streetlamp had shown his face very plainly, and Nealis recognized the man.

It was his brother Frank.

4

Nealis was numbed at first by the sheer oppressive weight of the sudden violence. The sight of Frank added to his confusion and before he could extricate himself, he had been washed into the cursing, kicking, spitting crowd. Animal instincts had reasserted themselves and the contagion gripped Nealis himself. In anger, and self-defence, he lashed out at the faceless creatures around him, fought for breath, feeling briefly the hurt he sustained. White faces, open mouths, formless bodies, punches, kicks, knuckles in yielding flesh and kaleidoscopic, shapeless movement. It all froze for a second as a man with great clots of blood dropping from his nose engulfed him. Nealis went down, the wounded man on top of him. As he hit the roadway, an aimless boot dropped itself into his stomach. For minutes, Nealis was paralysed, unable even to shift the dead weight of the unconscious man sprawled across him. He lay heaving with his knees drawn tight under his chin, no longer aware of the tumult above him. His eyes focused on a brick in the road which seemed at times half an inch from his face, at other times half a mile away. He wanted to lie there for the rest of his life, but suddenly a figure loomed over him, hauled him by the arm from beneath the unknown man and dragged him to his knees. He heard a shout from somewhere up in the sky telling him to run and he heaved himself to his feet and staggered into a trot. He could see better now and began to feel the pain. Ahead of him, uniforms and a white ambulance. He swerved to one side and ran crouched, holding his aching gut. Others overtook and ran on and then a car, stranded

in the roadway, blocked his flight. He rested on the [...] for a second, seeing with renewed clarity the terrifi[...] of its driver and then he forced himself from it and st[...] away from the square.

In a side street, he stopped and turned to look [...] the scene. The Guildhall Square was almost empty, s[...] police and small groups kneeling and standing roun[...] who still lay on the ground. A lorry was moving very[...] towards him with its headlights on, and as it m[...] gathered most of those still standing in the square [...] him. It drew level with him and stopped. Nealis re[...] placards which almost obliterated the bodywork and s[...] festoons of orange and white crepe. George Ross Si[...] jumped from the tailboard to receive the handshak[...] claps of his followers and the truck rolled away. Si[...] turned, leading the little group past the corner where[...] stood. When he saw Nealis, Simmons stopped, then [...] to within a yard of him. 'You were in there,' Simmons[...] rather than questioned. Nealis stared, too tired to [...] coherently.

'Stay clear of it, son,' Simmons said quietly, almost[...] nally. It was the sort of voice Sergeant Simmons ha[...] with soldiers going into danger for the first time. [...] confident, authoritative. 'Stay clear of it,' Simmons rep[...] 'It won't do you any good. Don't mix in this or you'l[...] unstuck.' He nodded at Nealis, turned abruptly and m[...] away. Nealis watched him. Simmons never seemed to [...] He always marched, head high, chest out, arse in, kick[...] toes out, lad, let's see those arms swinging now, keep[...] bloody head up and look proud. Sergeant Simmons [...] changed. Still a good bloke in a tough spot, Nealis reck[...]

But there were more urgent thoughts on his mind, [...] pulled himself away from the relative comfort of the[...] and began to walk away. The sight of Frank in the th[...] the fighting butted through the ache in his head and w[...] came a dozen different, unanswered questions. Amon[...] many impressions and half-thoughts leaping throug[...]

turned his face towards her the way she used to do when he was small and she wanted to comb his hair. In silence, she began to dab and wipe his forehead, his eyes, nose and mouth. From the corner of his eye, Nealis noticed with some surprise that the cloth she was using was turning dark with blood.

'Like the old days,' Nealis said, between the swabs of Dettol. 'When I got into a fight, I mean.' Mother Kate went on grimly wiping, dabbing, rinsing, cleansing. There was no trace of emotion on her face now. Only a set, determined expression. It was some moments before she spoke.

'It's not like the old days, Michael.' She shook her head as she spoke.

'No, it's not.' The bloody violence of the last hour was too strong to deny it.

'Was it Frank that got you into this?'

'No, I was just there.'

Mother Kate dabbed away in silence, towelling his face dry. 'Michael, will you do something for me?'

'Yes, Ma.'

'Will you turn round now, and go home.'

'Home?'

'Aye, home. Will you go, Michael? Will you?'

'What do you mean, Ma? Why should I go home? I've got two weeks here.'

Suddenly, Mother Kate threw the towel onto the table with an impatient gesture and dragged one of the wooden kitchen chairs to her and sat down facing him.

'Will you listen to me, Michael, will ye?' Her voice was harsh and decisive. 'There's going to be bloodshed in this city, do you know that? There's going to be big trouble and you'll be better off out of it. There's going to be a fight, and it's not your fight any more. You'll be better off at your home. Derry is no place for you to be.'

'Not my fight? What do you mean, Ma? Not my fight any more?'

'I mean you left Ireland fifteen years ago. You've forgotten.'

29

'Forgotten what?'

'Your father knew it would come to this,' she went on, ignoring him. 'He knew. Poor old man he was, I know that. But he was right, wasn't he? He always said we'd have to fight in the end, and he was right.'

'Fight?' Nealis felt a surge of anger sweep through him, irrationally. 'Fight? Christ, Ma, all the Irish ever do is fight. Is that all they can think about?'

Mother Kate's eyes flashed sharply. 'Aye, maybe it is. Maybe the Irish have something to fight for—some of them, anyway.'

'Oh, sure,' Nealis said, scathingly. 'Let's all go out and hit the other bloke. It makes us feel better then, doesn't it? Have a good punch-up, that'll solve all the world's problems. Is that what the Irish think? Christ, don't they ever ask themselves what it has ever achieved? That, and all the talk about the old days and the Black and Tans that Me Da' went on about endlessly, and the Orangemen and all that crap? Talking and fighting is all the Irish have ever been good for, and what have they ever achieved? One bloody mess after another and now there's another one coming up. It's the same old story, the same old sickness.'

'Is it?' Mother Kate leaned forward in her chair, more intense, more lucid than Nealis had ever seen her. 'Is it, son? Well, doesn't it ever come home to you that the old sickness can be cured? Did you know that your father was a gifted man?' She paused, memory quenching the anger in her voice. 'Your father was a gifted man, Michael. He could have been someone. When I met him, he was a fine man, full of kind words ... He loved everyone, did your father. He was a leader in nineteen twenty-two, your father was. A man of reason, a man who believed in the good Lord and a man of peace. And what did it get him? A bullet.' She spat out the word. 'A bullet. Your father wanted to reason with the powers that were cutting Ireland in two pieces. He was on his way to try to talk about it, and what did he get? A bullet.' In the silence, Mother Kate caught up the hem of her apron and twisted it around her fingers agitatedly.

'Ever after that, he was nothing.' She went on, her voice quieter. 'Him who had such grand plans for himself and for me and for his country. He was nothing, Michael. Your father begged for work after that. I seen him begging for work when there was no work for those with the wrong name, or the wrong church. We never had enough, Michael. You were our first son and your father wanted everything in the world for you. He wanted high schools and a proper education and all the good things for you, and for Frank when he came along. But we ended in this house and your father drawing his dole from the broo for years. It took a war to put him in regular work and after that, back to the broo again until he died, God bless his soul.' Absently, Mother Kate crossed herself.

Nealis reached out and touched his mother and she caught his hand, holding it gently, like a mother would a small boy who did not understand.

'I ...'

'No, you never knew,' Mother Kate said. 'Your Da' would get drunk and come home to our bed and weep, but you never knew that, son.' She smiled wanly at him. Then, as if suddenly ashamed of her emotion, she stood up and spoke in a calm, level voice.

'I want you to go home, Michael. Forget it all. You've your own life now.'

'Sit down, Ma,' Nealis said. His mother had never, ever spoken to him that way before, and he was in every sense shocked by what he had heard. He watched his mother sit, and was still unsure of what he was going to say.

'You're a wise old bird, aren't you?' he began.

'No, I'm not wise,' Mother Kate replied. 'If I was, I wouldn't be here.'

'But you're right. I never did know. And what I knew—what little I knew—I forgot. Perhaps it was deliberate. It's possible, you know, to go around agreeing with the image of the Irish and forget you're Irish yourself.' He paused. 'But

31

all this I saw tonight in the Square, surely that's not the answer? Is it?'

'Is there a better one?' Mother Kate fished a Woodbine from the pocket of her apron and held another out for Nealis. He accepted it and they lit their cigarettes in silence.

'Frank's in the middle of it, isn't he?'

Mother Kate nodded, and bit her lip as she did so.

'Civil Rights and all that stuff?' Mother Kate nodded again.

'I saw him tonight,' Nealis said.

'Was he hurt?' Mother Kate asked quickly.

Nealis smiled, despite the memory. 'Not him. The other man.'

'He's afraid of you, Michael. You know that?'

'Me?'

'Aye, you. You're his brother, you see, and a policeman. Frank can't understand that and I think he can't make the others see what there is to you. He didn't want you to come here.'

'Once a copper, always a copper?' Nealis smiled to himself. 'He thinks I'll turn him over to the RUC?'

'Maybe that's what he thinks,' Mother Kate said. 'That's why it would be better if you went. Frank'll be in trouble one day. He's like your father, more than you are.'

'Is he?' Nealis said. He stubbed out the butt of his cigarette and rose to his feet. Mother Kate rose too.

'Is he here?'

'No, he'll be back, but not tonight. He never comes here when there's trouble.'

'He thinks about you, then?'

'Aye, he does,' Mother Kate said.

Ten minutes later, Nealis left the house. He had promised his mother he would call the following day.

'You'll take me to chapel?' she had asked. And Nealis had agreed, without thinking about it.

Now, he trudged down Kilgallen Street and headed back to his hotel.

The sour feeling stayed with him through three stiff

whiskies. Maybe it was the hangover from the violence in the Square. Maybe. Perhaps it was more than that. In any event, he felt nervous and uneasy and angry. He had growled at the barmaid behind the cocktail bar in the hotel when she had been slow to take his order and now he burned with an unreasonable desire to pick a quarrel, to uncork the emotion bottled inside him. There was no-one else in the bar to argue with, however, and he took himself to one of the tables in the pink-lit bar and brooded by himself. Go home, Mother Kate had said. Home to what? A lonely room, the CID office and the endless drudgery of work? He knew inside himself that he worked harder than anyone else in the Division only because he had more reason. It was a refuge for all of them, of course. No-one fooled themselves when they were alone with themselves. A detective's life was a miserable one. None had a proper home life if they put in the hours necessary for promotion and those who put in the work found themselves on a treadmill.

You worked hard to get the stripes and then found that you had nothing else in life, so you worked hard to escape the outside world and then reaped the reward of promotion and even harder work and even less home to go back to. Detective Inspector Michael Nealis. He smiled faintly as he finished his third whiskey. By Christ, Detective Inspector, you know it all, don't you? Come on, Inspector, you've got all the bloody answers, you know all about the seedy side of life only you won't admit it to any bastard, will you ... ? You've got promotion, you've blasted off all right, only there's nothing but cinders at the back of you.

Home. He'd left there thirty-six hours ago. It was to have been a sentimental journey like the song said. Nealis got up and walked into the hotel foyer where there was a telephone booth. He asked for his wife's number and waited to be put through. In the mirror in front of him, he studied his face. Thin face, dark hair that curled, blue eyes, high cheekbones, wide mouth, clean-shaven, he sized it all up like a professional studying an Identikit. Nealis, Michael James, aged thirty-four. Of fixed abode? Yes. The number was ringing now.

'Hello?'

It was a bad connection. 'Hello, who's that?'

'Me.' Nealis said.

'Oh, come on, don't play games.' There was an unusual warmth in Betty's voice. 'Who is it?'

Who else should be calling her at eleven o'clock on a Saturday night?

'It's me, your husband, dammit.'

'Oh.' The single vowel was flat and disinterested. Unconcern and disappointment all wrapped up in a single sound.

'What do you want?'

'I just wanted to talk to you.'

'Where are you?' There was a radio playing in the background, something by Frank Sinatra. He recognized that voice, knew it anywhere, recognized the swinging syrup of Nelson Riddle's orchestra behind it. It was Betty's music. Her smoochy music, she used to call it.

'I'm in Derry.'

'Where?'

'Londonderry, at the City Hotel, on holiday.'

'For Christ's sake, isn't that where all the trouble is?'

He felt an abrupt sense of irritation at the mindlessness.

'Not my trouble. My trouble is Liverpool.'

'What do you mean.'

'I mean you. You're my trouble.'

She started to speak, but there was a murmur behind her voice, the deeper tones of a man cutting across her lilting soprano.

'Wait a minute, Mike,' she said.

'What for, is there somebody there?'

'Well, it's a funny time of the night to ring me.'

'Is somebody there?'

'What's it to you?' He guessed that she had been drinking. Gin and Martini probably. It always brought out that particular sort of truculence in her.

'Look, Betty, I want to know.'

managed to fight a way through the encircling crowd and, spurred on by blows and buffets, they started trying to escape in a blood-stained stream. As they did so the waiting police, who had already drawn their batons, charged in on them to fell more of them and make arrests.

One of the fleeing men wheeled away and as he drew alongside Nealis a Volunteer stepped in his path to stop him. The Volunteer collapsed as a pick-axe handle smashed his nose to pulp. Throwing the handle away the man fled, and Nealis stared after him.

A streetlamp had shown his face very plainly, and Nealis recognized the man.

It was his brother Frank.

4

Nealis was numbed at first by the sheer oppressive weight of the sudden violence. The sight of Frank added to his confusion and before he could extricate himself, he had been washed into the cursing, kicking, spitting crowd. Animal instincts had reasserted themselves and the contagion gripped Nealis himself. In anger, and self-defence, he lashed out at the faceless creatures around him, fought for breath, feeling briefly the hurt he sustained. White faces, open mouths, formless bodies, punches, kicks, knuckles in yielding flesh and kaleidoscopic, shapeless movement. It all froze for a second as a man with great clots of blood dropping from his nose engulfed him. Nealis went down, the wounded man on top of him. As he hit the roadway, an aimless boot dropped itself into his stomach. For minutes, Nealis was paralysed, unable even to shift the dead weight of the unconscious man sprawled across him. He lay heaving with his knees drawn tight under his chin, no longer aware of the tumult above him. His eyes focused on a brick in the road which seemed at times half an inch from his face, at other times half a mile away. He wanted to lie there for the rest of his life, but suddenly a figure loomed over him, hauled him by the arm from beneath the unknown man and dragged him to his knees. He heard a shout from somewhere up in the sky telling him to run and he heaved himself to his feet and staggered into a trot. He could see better now and began to feel the pain. Ahead of him, uniforms and a white ambulance. He swerved to one side and ran crouched, holding his aching gut. Others overtook and ran on and then a car, stranded in the roadway, blocked his flight. He rested on the bonnet for a second, seeing with renewed clarity the terrified face of its driver and then he forced himself from it and stumbled away from the square.

In a side street, he stopped and turned to look back at the scene. The Guildhall Square was almost empty, save for police and small groups kneeling and standing round those who still lay on the ground. A lorry was moving very slowly towards him with its headlights on, and as it moved it gathered most of those still standing in the square behind him. It drew level with him and stopped. Nealis read the placards which almost obliterated the bodywork and saw the festoons of orange and white crepe. George Ross Simmons jumped from the tailboard to receive the handshakes and claps of his followers and the truck rolled away. Simmons turned, leading the little group past the corner where Nealis stood. When he saw Nealis, Simmons stopped, then walked to within a yard of him. 'You were in there,' Simmons stated rather than questioned. Nealis stared, too tired to answer coherently.

'Stay clear of it, son,' Simmons said quietly, almost paternally. It was the sort of voice Sergeant Simmons had used with soldiers going into danger for the first time. Quiet, confident, authoritative. 'Stay clear of it,' Simmons repeated. 'It won't do you any good. Don't mix in this or you'll come unstuck.' He nodded at Nealis, turned abruptly and marched away. Nealis watched him. Simmons never seemed to walk. He always marched, head high, chest out, arse in, kick your toes out, lad, let's see those arms swinging now, keep your bloody head up and look proud. Sergeant Simmons hadn't changed. Still a good bloke in a tough spot, Nealis reckoned.

But there were more urgent thoughts on his mind, as he pulled himself away from the relative comfort of the wall and began to walk away. The sight of Frank in the thick of the fighting butted through the ache in his head and with it came a dozen different, unanswered questions. Among the many impressions and half-thoughts leaping through his

27

mind as he walked, Nealis caught himself dwelling on a snatch of a phrase ... *and that I will, to the best of my power, cause the peace to be kept and preserved and prevent all offences against the persons and properties of Her Majesty's subjects....* It was part of the oath he had taken as a policeman, so long ago. Before today, it had all been pretty simple.

Kilgallen Street when he got there was dark and it had begun to drizzle and most of the front doors were shut. It gave a foreboding air to the street and Nealis, for no rational reason, found himself walking quietly, almost furtively, to his home.

Mother Kate was sitting in the kitchen watching television when he opened the door softly and walked in. She jumped from the chair with a little cry and stood with the knuckles of her right hand to her lips as she always did when alarmed.

'It's all right, Ma. It's only me,' Nealis said, above the sound.

'Michael?' Nealis saw her eyes flick over him in half-disbelief and only then remembered the blood on his coat. 'Michael, what in the name of God have you been doing?'

'There was a fight ... in the Square.'

With a muffled cry, Mother Kate scurried across the room to him and threw her arms around her son. She buried her head in his chest and he felt rather than heard her crying.

'It's all right, Ma. It's nothing. I'm not hurt.' That was a lie and it gave him physical pain to say it, since his abdomen ached badly and he could feel the bruises on his ribs. 'It's all right, Ma.' Slowly, Mother Kate withdrew and held Nealis at arm's length. She wasn't crying any longer, but searched his face with eyes that were old but beautiful.

'Sit down, son. I'll get soap and water and tidy you up.'

'Don't worry about—'

'Sit down.'

Nealis sat in the solitary armchair. The television set burbled on while Mother Kate bustled into the kitchen. Returning, she snapped the set off and set a bowl of water on the kitchen table. Firmly, she gripped Nealis's chin and turned his face towards her the way she used to do when he was small and she wanted to comb his hair. In silence, she began to dab and wipe his forehead, his eyes, nose and mouth. From the corner of his eye, Nealis noticed with some surprise that the cloth she was using was turning dark with blood.

'Like the old days,' Nealis said, between the swabs of Dettol. 'When I got into a fight, I mean.' Mother Kate went on grimly wiping, dabbing, rinsing, cleansing. There was no trace of emotion on her face now. Only a set, determined expression. It was some moments before she spoke.

'It's not like the old days, Michael.' She shook her head as she spoke.

'No, it's not.' The bloody violence of the last hour was too strong to deny it.

'Was it Frank that got you into this?'

'No, I was just there.'

Mother Kate dabbed away in silence, towelling his face dry. 'Michael, will you do something for me?'

'Yes, Ma.'

'Will you turn round now, and go home.'

'Home?'

'Aye, home. Will you go, Michael? Will you?'

'What do you mean, Ma? Why should I go home? I've got two weeks here.'

Suddenly, Mother Kate threw the towel onto the table with an impatient gesture and dragged one of the wooden kitchen chairs to her and sat down facing him.

'Will you listen to me, Michael, will ye?' Her voice was harsh and decisive. 'There's going to be bloodshed in this city, do you know that? There's going to be big trouble and you'll be better off out of it. There's going to be a fight, and it's not your fight any more. You'll be better off at your home. Derry is no place for you to be.'

'Not my fight? What do you mean, Ma? Not my fight any more?'

'I mean you left Ireland fifteen years ago. You've forgotten.'

29

'Forgotten what?'

'Your father knew it would come to this,' she went on, ignoring him. 'He knew. Poor old man he was, I know that. But he was right, wasn't he? He always said we'd have to fight in the end, and he was right.'

'Fight?' Nealis felt a surge of anger sweep through him, irrationally. 'Fight? Christ, Ma, all the Irish ever do is fight. Is that all they can think about?'

Mother Kate's eyes flashed sharply. 'Aye, maybe it is. Maybe the Irish have something to fight for—some of them, anyway.'

'Oh, sure,' Nealis said, scathingly. 'Let's all go out and hit the other bloke. It makes us feel better then, doesn't it? Have a good punch-up, that'll solve all the world's problems. Is that what the Irish think? Christ, don't they ever ask themselves what it has ever achieved? That, and all the talk about the old days and the Black and Tans that Me Da' went on about endlessly, and the Orangemen and all that crap? Talking and fighting is all the Irish have ever been good for, and what have they ever achieved? One bloody mess after another and now there's another one coming up. It's the same old story, the same old sickness.'

'Is it?' Mother Kate leaned forward in her chair, more intense, more lucid than Nealis had ever seen her. 'Is it, son? Well, doesn't it ever come home to you that the old sickness can be cured? Did you know that your father was a gifted man?' She paused, memory quenching the anger in her voice. 'Your father was a gifted man, Michael. He could have been someone. When I met him, he was a fine man, full of kind words ... He loved everyone, did your father. He was a leader in nineteen twenty-two, your father was. A man of reason, a man who believed in the good Lord and a man of peace. And what did it get him? A bullet.' She spat out the word. 'A bullet. Your father wanted to reason with the powers that were cutting Ireland in two pieces. He was on his way to try to talk about it, and what did he get? A bullet.' In the silence, Mother Kate caught up the hem of her apron and twisted it around her fingers agitatedly.

'Ever after that, he was nothing.' She went on, her voice quieter. 'Him who had such grand plans for himself and for me and for his country. He was nothing, Michael. Your father begged for work after that. I seen him begging for work when there was no work for those with the wrong name, or the wrong church. We never had enough, Michael. You were our first son and your father wanted everything in the world for you. He wanted high schools and a proper education and all the good things for you, and for Frank when he came along. But we ended in this house and your father drawing his dole from the broo for years. It took a war to put him in regular work and after that, back to the broo again until he died, God bless his soul.' Absently, Mother Kate crossed herself.

Nealis reached out and touched his mother and she caught his hand, holding it gently, like a mother would a small boy who did not understand.

'I . . .'

'No, you never knew,' Mother Kate said. 'Your Da' would get drunk and come home to our bed and weep, but you never knew that, son.' She smiled wanly at him. Then, as if suddenly ashamed of her emotion, she stood up and spoke in a calm, level voice.

'I want you to go home, Michael. Forget it all. You've your own life now.'

'Sit down, Ma,' Nealis said. His mother had never, ever spoken to him that way before, and he was in every sense shocked by what he had heard. He watched his mother sit, and was still unsure of what he was going to say.

'You're a wise old bird, aren't you?' he began.

'No, I'm not wise,' Mother Kate replied. 'If I was, I wouldn't be here.'

'But you're right. I never did know. And what I knew— what little I knew—I forgot. Perhaps it was deliberate. It's possible, you know, to go around agreeing with the image of the Irish and forget you're Irish yourself.' He paused. 'But all this I saw tonight in the Square, surely that's not the answer? Is it?'

'Is there a better one?' Mother Kate fished a Woodbine from the pocket of her apron and held another out for Nealis. He accepted it and they lit their cigarettes in silence.

'Frank's in the middle of it, isn't he?'

Mother Kate nodded, and bit her lip as she did so.

'Civil Rights and all that stuff?' Mother Kate nodded again.

'I saw him tonight,' Nealis said.

'Was he hurt?' Mother Kate asked quickly.

Nealis smiled, despite the memory. 'Not him. The other man.'

'He's afraid of you, Michael. You know that?'

'Me?'

'Aye, you. You're his brother, you see, and a policeman. Frank can't understand that and I think he can't make the others see what there is to you. He didn't want you to come here.'

'Once a copper, always a copper?' Nealis smiled to himself. 'He thinks I'll turn him over to the RUC?'

'Maybe that's what he thinks,' Mother Kate said. 'That's why it would be better if you went. Frank'll be in trouble one day. He's like your father, more than you are.'

'Is he?' Nealis said. He stubbed out the butt of his cigarette and rose to his feet. Mother Kate rose too.

'Is he here?'

'No, he'll be back, but not tonight. He never comes here when there's trouble.'

'He thinks about you, then?'

'Aye, he does,' Mother Kate said.

Ten minutes later, Nealis left the house. He had promised his mother he would call the following day.

'You'll take me to chapel?' she had asked. And Nealis had agreed, without thinking about it.

Now, he trudged down Kilgallen Street and headed back to his hotel.

The sour feeling stayed with him through three stiff

whiskies. Maybe it was the hangover from the violence in the Square. Maybe. Perhaps it was more than that. In any event, he felt nervous and uneasy and angry. He had growled at the barmaid behind the cocktail bar in the hotel when she had been slow to take his order and now he burned with an unreasonable desire to pick a quarrel, to uncork the emotion bottled inside him. There was no-one else in the bar to argue with, however, and he took himself to one of the tables in the pink-lit bar and brooded by himself. Go home, Mother Kate had said. Home to what? A lonely room, the CID office and the endless drudgery of work? He knew inside himself that he worked harder than anyone else in the Division only because he had more reason. It was a refuge for all of them, of course. No-one fooled themselves when they were alone with themselves. A detective's life was a miserable one. None had a proper home life if they put in the hours necessary for promotion and those who put in the work found themselves on a treadmill.

You worked hard to get the stripes and then found that you had nothing else in life, so you worked hard to escape the outside world and then reaped the reward of promotion and even harder work and even less home to go back to. Detective Inspector Michael Nealis. He smiled faintly as he finished his third whiskey. By Christ, Detective Inspector, you know it all, don't you? Come on, Inspector, you've got all the bloody answers, you know all about the seedy side of life only you won't admit it to any bastard, will you ... ? You've got promotion, you've blasted off all right, only there's nothing but cinders at the back of you.

Home. He'd left there thirty-six hours ago. It was to have been a sentimental journey like the song said. Nealis got up and walked into the hotel foyer where there was a telephone booth. He asked for his wife's number and waited to be put through. In the mirror in front of him, he studied his face. Thin face, dark hair that curled, blue eyes, high cheekbones, wide mouth, clean-shaven, he sized it all up like a professional studying an Identikit. Nealis, Michael James, aged thirty-four. Of fixed abode? Yes. The number was ringing now.

'Hello?'

It was a bad connection. 'Hello, who's that?'

'Me.' Nealis said.

'Oh, come on, don't play games.' There was an unusual warmth in Betty's voice. 'Who is it?'

Who else should be calling her at eleven o'clock on a Saturday night?

'It's me, your husband, dammit.'

'Oh.' The single vowel was flat and disinterested. Unconcern and disappointment all wrapped up in a single sound.

'What do you want?'

'I just wanted to talk to you.'

'Where are you?' There was a radio playing in the background, something by Frank Sinatra. He recognized that voice, knew it anywhere, recognized the swinging syrup of Nelson Riddle's orchestra behind it. It was Betty's music. Her smoochy music, she used to call it.

'I'm in Derry.'

'Where?'

'Londonderry, at the City Hotel, on holiday.'

'For Christ's sake, isn't that where all the trouble is?'

He felt an abrupt sense of irritation at the mindlessness.

'Not my trouble. My trouble is Liverpool.'

'What do you mean.'

'I mean you. You're my trouble.'

She started to speak, but there was a murmur behind her voice, the deeper tones of a man cutting across her lilting soprano.

'Wait a minute, Mike,' she said.

'What for, is there somebody there?'

'Well, it's a funny time of the night to ring me.'

'Is somebody there?'

'What's it to you?' He guessed that she had been drinking. Gin and Martini probably. It always brought out that particular sort of truculence in her.

'Look, Betty, I want to know.'

34

There was a pause, then she said in a voice so soft that he could hardly hear it: 'Yes, damn you, there is somebody here.'

There was a click and the phone went dead.

Nealis went back to the bar. He was perfectly sober but overwhelmingly aware that something was swimming in his system that had to be got rid of somehow. He would have given anything to be somewhere else, or maybe someone else.

'I'm sorry, sir. But I'm afraid the bar is closed now.' The girl was smiling apologetically at him, indicating the latticed steel shutter across the counter.

'I live here,' Nealis said. The girl was still smiling. In the shadow of the lattice-work, she appeared young and appealing. 'Come on now, don't be hard to get on with.'

'Well ...' She pouted, and she was looking at him with mocking acquiescence. Nealis knew he was going to get his drink.

'In there, then,' Nealis said, indicating the lounge adjacent to the bar. 'I'll have a brandy in there. Won't you join me?'

'I'm not supposed to,' she said.

'Then it must be good for you. I'll tell the manager you're an old friend. You never know, it might be true.'

She chuckled. 'All right now. I'll go and powder my nose. I'll be back in five minutes.'

When she re-appeared a few minutes later, Nealis had a large brandy and an equally large gin and tonic on the table before them. She sat down and they talked.

She told him about herself. Her name was Maureen. She laughed, and didn't question what he said. As the brandy warmed him, Nealis leant forward and said: 'What are you doing tonight?'

The girl took a sip of her gin and looked at him over the rim of her glass. 'I'm going home. What would I be doing?'

'You could come to my room for a drink,' he said, leaving the suggestion in the air.

'No.' Her answer was flat and unequivocal. 'We're not

35

allowed to visit guests in their rooms. Anyway, I hardly know you.'

'Right, let's get to know each other, then,' Nealis countered. 'What are you doing tomorrow?'

'I'm working.'

'Take the day off.'

'Jobs are scarce in this town,' she said. 'It's not so easy.'

'Oh, come on. You're only young once. Take a chance. Just tell them you're sick.'

'Oh, sure, it's easy for you,' she said. 'But if they found out the real reason, I might lose me job and I couldn't blame them.'

But even as she spoke, Nealis sensed the girl was half inclined to do so, and he pressed on. 'We'll have a good day out.'

She hesitated. 'All right,' she said suddenly. 'I will.'

They discussed the plan for the following day, agreeing where to meet, what to do and where to go. As he outlined it, her enthusiasm grew.

'Be sure you'll be there,' she said, as they finished their drinks.

'You can bet on it,' Nealis said.

The girl smiled softly, putting her hand in his. 'I'm looking forward to it.'

5

On this Sunday morning Maire O'Dwyer, a slim girl in her middle twenties, was on her way to Mass. Her walk was assured, even arrogant, and it contrasted with the withdrawn gait of many of the women around her. They walked huddled into themselves, as though ashamed of their bodies. Something to do with the misogynistic bias St Paul had given to Christianity, she supposed. It was an old Catholic superstition that women were the vehicles of Sin and, as a girl who had spent her formative years in a convent, she had been made well aware of the belief.

'Maire O'Dwyer, do not flaunt yourself when you walk. It is a sin in the eyes of God.'

'It is a woman's role in life to be modest at all times.'

'Girls who sleep at night with their legs apart are committing mortal sin. The posture indicates a dreadful carnal desire.'

Those had been some of the dictates of the good sisters who educated her. Now she considered the sisters unworldly women who, like most other unworldly women, gave too much importance to sex.

Maire O'Dwyer was a modern girl and if she sinned, did so wittingly. Later it caused problems, because in the dark of the confessional she wondered about the sincerity of her repentance. There were great unfilled tracts in her acceptance of the Catholicism into which she had been born, but she had not rejected her religion. She was on her way to Mass to do honour to the outward form and pray that the comfort of faith, total, complete, unquestioning faith, would be restored to her.

That faith had dimmed and, for a while, been totally extinguished seven years before when Maire had arrived, an eager girl of eighteen, in London.

Three weeks later she lost her virginity.

It was after a beer and cider party. She had gone there from the coffee bar in which she worked and a young man who had been playing the flute in the corner said to her: 'Christ, you're lovely.'

Later in his bed-sitter she had allowed him to push her back onto the bed and feel her, but she baulked when he wanted to enter her.

'Christ kid, you're hung up,' he said. 'Just because a bunch of mouldy old nuns said it's wrong doesn't mean a thing. They're wrong. It's beautiful and natural.'

'I can't do it,' she said.

'Listen, you've been hearing a lot of propaganda all your life. That's all it was. Look at the mess the older generation has got the world into. Just look at it and ask yourself if you can give any credence to people who can make such a balls up.'

He fondled her hair. 'You can bet they've been wrong all the time. So if your mother says it's wrong to let your knickers down, then you can bet it's right to let your knickers down. Because she doesn't know. We don't live in the same world any more.'

'I can't,' she said, 'it's a sin.'

'Please,' he said, 'please, please, please. I need you. I'm dying with love for you.'

After it was over she felt drained and hollow. In fulfilling herself as a woman she had betrayed herself as a Catholic. She was still thinking about that when, three days later, she moved in with the boy, whose name was John.

In the months that followed Maire's sense of guilt slowly diminished, but it snapped back when she went to the doctor one day and found she was pregnant. John did not take off, as she thought he might. Instead he stayed with her in the bed-sitter, comforting her and telling her not to worry.

'But I do worry, John. How can I not worry?'

'It'll be all right, baby. It'll be all right.'

One night he came home with a tall African medical student. 'This is Olu,' he said, 'he's going to help us.'

Olu had a bag of surgical equipment with him for the abortion and he started laying it out on the table.

'No,' Maire said, 'no, I can't do that. It's murder.'

'But what else can we do, baby? What the hell can we do?'

The baby was born three days before Christmas in a nursing home for unmarried mothers in Notting Hill Gate. As soon as it entered the world a motherly nurse wrapped it in a shawl and took it away.

'It's better that you don't have any contact with it, dear,' she said, and that was the way it was. No contact, no easing of the maternal instinct that rushed through Maire like a tide in full flood. They took her milk away from her with a suction machine, and told her they had found a couple to take the baby. Then, after ten days, they let her go.

John came and fetched her and they rode in silence back to the bed-sitter. He had changed the wallpaper, brightening the room with a plain cream-coloured paper that held the light. It was nice. It was very nice.

'You've made the room nice,' she said.

'I wanted it bright for you.'

'Yes, it is nice and bright. Thank you.'

She sat on the edge of the bed, her coat collar still pulled up against the December winds.

'John, can you give me five pounds?'

'Five pounds. I think so. I think I've got five pounds.'

'I'm going home, you see, John.'

'Home? But why? We'll be all right.'

'We won't be all right, John. I've just given my baby away. I could have kept it if we had been all right. We can't be all right, John. Not now, not anymore.'

'You mean if I'd married you?'

'Yes, John. I mean that.'

'Well, yes, but I explained.'

39

'I know you did, and I'm not blaming you. I'm blaming myself, but I've lost my baby and now I need five pounds.'

'But you don't have to go. We'll be all right. I'll be careful.'

'Give me the five pounds, John.'

They went by train up to St Albans where the great trunk road, Watling Street, starts its run towards Liverpool. John stood with her while she flagged cars and lorries. Eventually one stopped and she climbed in. John stood there, blowing into his hands and stamping his feet as the lorry pulled slowly away and disappeared into the night.

* * *

Nealis had long since given up religion, but he felt duty bound to attend Mass with his mother. They sat on the left of the church opposite the Lady altar while on the central altar the priest celebrated the church's most ancient mystery.

'*Kyrie Eleison, Christe Eleison,*' the Greek words came back to him as he sat there, thinking of the time he had spent in this church, serving Mass as an altar boy. A shaft of sunlight pierced the stained-glass window on his left and he watched the motes of dust shivering in its beams. They were transient and unrested, as unstable as his own belief.

Up on the altar the priest had reached the central moment of the Mass, when the bread and wine are made into the Body and Blood of Jesus Christ. Somebody had once told him that this Catholic tradition had grown from the cannibal belief that if you eat a man's flesh you take on his courage. He regretted that anthropologists and other such people had found these explanations; it would be so much more simple and dignified to merely believe.

The communicants were thronging around the rails and the priest, an old man with stooped shoulders, was making his way slowly among them giving them the sacrament. *Lord, I am not worthy that thou shouldst enter under my roof. Say but the word, and my soul shall be healed.*

The old words, the half-forgotten ritual came back to him. It was twelve years since he had taken communion and now, seeing the dedication and gentle acceptance all round him, he felt a sense of loss at having cut himself so firmly adrift.

There was no cure for Catholicism, he thought. You could treat the symptoms, make them go away, but they would always come back. Being a Catholic was something that nothing could alter. A man could stop practising, stop going to church and curse at priests. It did not alter anything. A sinner he might be, or a heretic or even an atheist. Nothing altered. Deep inside he knew he was still a Catholic.

Mother Kate was praying in a low, sibilant whisper. He looked at the frail figure, her black coat dusty with age, and the old hands, veined blue and parchment yellow, holding the beads. He hoped that there was something beyond to give her a return on a life of struggle, for she had had sod-all this side of the veil.

At the end of Mass they waited till the crowds thinned in the aisles before going out. He took two shillings out of his pocket when he saw a man with a collecting box standing at the gate, but put it back when he saw the collection was for the Knights of St Columbus. He did not like the Knights. Years ago he had written them off as a crowd of pious pissheads, drunk Saturday night in their clubroom and eager about their parochial duties on a Sunday morning. There was not, he thought, much to choose between them and the Orange Lodge.

Outside the gate a slim girl with red-brown hair came forward and greeted his mother.

'Hello, Maire,' Mother Kate said. 'Michael, this is Maire O'Dwyer. She teaches at St. Kevin's. This is my other son, Michael.'

The girl gripped his hand boldly, like a man, and looked at him directly as she shook it. She had cornflower-blue eyes, he noted, and a high-boned delicate face with a trace of wistfulness about the mouth.

'Glad to meet you, Maire,' he said.

'A pleasure,' she smiled.

For a while they stood talking and then on Mother Kate's

41

prompting they began to walk home. 'Maire only lives a couple of streets from us,' she said.

'What do you think of this trouble that's going on?' Maire asked him.

'I suppose it had to come,' he said, 'but it's a pity.'

'It is a pity, but I think it's the only way.'

Maire was a member of the Civil Rights movement and had been since she had been at a teachers' training college in Belfast. She had been on several of the marches and was scathing in her judgements on the authorities.

'Everybody has the right to protest,' she said, 'but when we try it here they send their thugs to beat us up.'

'Well,' said Nealis, smiling, 'a policeman's lot is not a happy one.'

It was he who first saw the armoured car as they turned into the street. It was standing outside his mother's house and four policemen stood on the pavement beside it. As Nealis walked up to the house one of the policemen stopped him.

'Do you live here?'

'My mother does. Why? What's the matter?'

'We want to come in and search. Open up.'

'Search? What for?'

'You know what for.'

Nealis's policeman's instinct made him wary. His mother was at the door, opening it and looking fearfully over her shoulder at the policemen. Each of them carried a pistol at his belt and one carried a submachine-gun.

'Look,' Nealis said, blocking the door, 'you'll have to show me your warrant if you want to search here.'

One of the policemen, a burly man with the red face of a countryman, came forward. 'Warrant, you say? We need no warrant to search this fucking kip. Get out of the way.'

He pushed Nealis hard in the chest, sending him reeling into the hall. The four policemen came in, one staying beside the door.

The big policeman, an inspector, looked at Nealis: 'Who are you?'

'What's it to you?'

The big man came forward, raising the blackthorn stick he carried. 'Look, I'll advise you to be civil. Otherwise I will leave your head open.'

The pent-up anger nearly burst out of Nealis, but some instinct of self-preservation warned him to be cautious. The thought crossed his mind that it would seriously upset his superiors if he were arrested for obstructing the police.

'I am Michael Nealis,' he said. 'Why?'

'Have you a brother Frank?'

'I have.'

'Where is he?'

'I don't know.'

The inspector nodded and two of the policemen left the room and went upstairs.

'You're a bloody liar, Nealis.'

Nealis did not say anything. He glanced around the room and saw the shocked face on Mother Kate, the look of cynical detachment on Maire.

'I said you were a bloody liar.' The big man moved forward and pushed his face hard up against Nealis's. He recognized the technique. Interrogation by intimidation. He was not impressed. He had seen the same thing carried off by experts.

Keeping his voice low so that only the big man could hear him he said: 'Listen, mister, if you don't stop crowding me I am going to have you. Maybe not here, maybe not now. But sometime, sometime soon.' He kept a smile on his face while he said it and glanced to check that the two women had not caught the gist of what he had been saying. They had not.

The inspector's hand clenched the stick. 'I've warned you to be quiet,' he said. 'Now take heed, or I'll have you in. And then we'll see.' He broke off into a huge laugh. 'Oh Jesus yes. Then we'll see about what you're saying.'

He went to the foot of the stairs and bawled: 'Is he up there?'

'We don't see him, sir.'

'Turn the kip over. Turn it right over. Make sure he's not hiding anywhere now.'

From upstairs came a thunderous crash as the bed was upturned, followed by another crash which mystified Nealis.

He leapt forward and took the stairs two at a time. At the top he looked around. A chest of drawers was lying on its side, the drawers pulled out and scattered over one of the rooms. In the other a wardrobe had been upturned, a table thrown on its side and bed and bedding lay scattered on the floor.

The inspector had followed him up. 'Go easy now, boy,' he said. 'We're only carrying out our duty.'

'What do you want?'

'We want your brother. It's a very serious charge. He's a swift man at beating people up, is he not? Well, we'll get him —and then we'll see.' He smiled, enjoying himself: 'We'll take you along with him maybe. You have a pugnacious type of face and you're not very polite.'

'I'll report the damage you've done here,' Nealis said.

'Report away, boy. It's only our duty we're doing.'

The big man went down the stairs with Nealis following At the bottom he called for his two constables to come down. 'Well,' he said 'he isn't here, but we'll get him. Have no fear of that. If you see him tell him it might be better for him to come to us. We might feel more kindly towards him if he saved us the bother of looking for him. Tell him to ask for Inspector Kiernan. Come on, boys,' he said to the constables. They trooped out through the door to where a small crowd had gathered.

The two women had gone into the back room, Maire to comfort Mother Kate who was sobbing. As he reached the door Kiernan looked at the altar to the Sacred Heart which Mother Kate had built there. It had stood there as long as Nealis could remember, a shrine at which he remembered

44

saying his nightly prayers.

Kiernan closed the door. 'That's a nice wee ornament,' he said, pointing at it with his stick. There was a statue of Christ, a bleeding heart pierced by thorns showing plainly on his chest. Before it a small red glass held a wax nightlight which burned slowly. 'A nice wee ornament,' Kiernan repeated.

Nealis knew what he was going to do. He moved forward to stop him, but it was too late. The stick flashed and the statue and glass fell to the floor. The glass shattered and the severed head rolled slowly away from Christ. The nightlight, which had landed upside down, went out.

'You bastard,' Nealis said.

The big man smiled and lunged with his stick. Its hard metal point caught Nealis high in the stomach under the rib cage. As it made contact Kiernan thrust upwards and a sharp pain tore through Nealis. He collapsed, breathless in a chair, his lungs pumping for air while beads of sweat stood out on his forehead.

There was a grin on Kiernan's face as he bent down and stroked Nealis's head. 'Remember now, be civil. That's the ticket. Be civil.'

Nealis could not speak. He just sat there, rasping for air, while he watched Kiernan go through the door.

6

The whole pack had moved into the City Hotel in the time it took Nealis to shower, change his shirt for a sweater, smoke a cigarette and walk down from his room. He recognized them instantly as the Press. It took no kind of mental agility to do so, for the noise and the chatter stemmed from a nucleus of men crowding into the bar, littering the carpet in the foyer with photographic equipment. The telephone booth was surrounded, the receptionist was attempting to deal with a flood of different requests and only the television film crews seemed to have any luggage. They had come, Nealis guessed, on the mid-day train from Belfast. Like vultures in the desert, they had homed on the carcase. Nealis was standing at the edge of the mêlée sifting through the faces when a heavy hand banged on his shoulder.

'Hello, skipper. How's it going?' Jimmy Hadlee, Liverpool-based reporter for one of the London national papers, thrust out a meaty fist and shook Nealis vigorously by the hand, grinning amiably but, as always, regarding Nealis through heavy-framed glasses with eyes which seemed to penetrate the brain. Good old Jimmy. A bloody nuisance if ever there was one.

'Hello, Jimmy.' And then he added a lie. 'Good to see you.'
It was usually, but not here, not today.

'The pleasure's mine,' Hadlee said. 'By the way, I heard you made it to D.I. Congratulations. I take it they've sent you here to put things right?'

'You're joking, of course,' Nealis said, looking at his watch.

'Maybe. But you know, it would be a good move. Takes a

46

Mick to know a Mick, eh?' Hadlee laughed easily.

'Nothing like that, Jimmy. I'm on leave. Visiting the old home town, things like that, you know.'

'Being a bit tight-lipped, Inspector?'

'No. Honest as always.'

Hadlee laughed again. 'Come and have a drink. Fill me in a bit. I've never been to this bloody town before. Where's the action?'

'In the bar,' Nealis said. 'Sorry Jimmy, I can't stop.'

'OK, OK. You are staying here, aren't you? I'll see you later.' Hadlee paused. 'Saw your missus yesterday.' To Nealis it seemed there was a sharp edge of calculation in Hadlee's remark. A touch of the needle, perhaps? Hadlee knew a lot of people, a lot of things.

'Yes?' He looked at his watch again. It was a little after two and she had said two o'clock sharp. 'I've got to go now, Jimmy. See you later. You can buy me a drink then.'

He walked out of the hotel and onto the front steps. She had said she would pick him up in her car, but he didn't know what car she drove and so stood uncertainly on the step, uneasily aware of Hadlee's eyes watching him from the foyer. He had been looking forward to the afternoon ever since Maire had accepted his suggestion, but now he was ruffled and edgy for some reason he could not accurately define. Then he saw her. She was standing on the pavement by the open door of a small red Mini with her right arm half-raised to signal him.

Walking towards her, he noticed for the first time that the sun had broken through the mid-day cloud. It was shining on her hair and picked out a soft glow of red around the well-groomed curls. She was dressed in a dark green anorak over a white sweater and an orange skirt. She, too, had changed for the occasion. He helped her into the car and climbed into the passenger seat.

'Well, where shall we go?' she said as they drove north past the bus garage and the RUC barracks.

'Anywhere you like.'

'You want to walk?'

'Sure.'

'Well, then, I know where we can leave the car and climb a couple of hills. It's away over towards the border. Will that do you?' She smiled over to him as she finished and he nodded, saying that would be fine. Nealis relaxed in his seat watching the buildings of the town fade and give way to the particular green of the Irish countryside beyond the docks and the Naval jetties on the River Foyle. But his appreciation of the view was only an excuse to look at her. He would have picked her out as Irish from a thousand yards. The high cheekbones, the tiny nose, the blue eyes, the pale skin, the vivacity, the loveliness.

'What are you looking at?'

'You.' She flushed very slightly and shrugged her shoulders in a kind of happy embarrassment.

They said no more for a couple of miles, until Nealis pulled out his cigarettes and offered her one. She asked if he would light one for her and he did so, feeling an intense pleasure in doing it.

'Will you be staying in Derry for long?' she asked as she took the cigarette.

'A couple of weeks, probably. It depends.'

'What does it depend on?'

The directness of her question threw him off balance for a moment. What did it depend on? Events? Mother Kate? Frank? His wife? This girl? Or just on him?

'Oh, on a lot of things, I suppose. Anyway, I'm due back two weeks tomorrow.'

'You're a policeman, aren't you?'

'Yes.'

'And you live in Liverpool and you've just got promoted to ... what is it, now? ... Detective Inspector.'

'Right first time.' Nealis smiled. 'You seem to know a lot.'

'Oh, it's your mother. She never stops talking about you. I think she's very, very proud of you. Talks all the time about how well you're doing.'

48

'It must be very boring,' Nealis remarked. 'But she never told me about you. Have you known Mother Kate for long?'

'Well, you know, everyone in Bogside knows Mother Kate. She's a fine woman. I think she's very wise. She doesn't know that, of course, but she always talks good sense about things, about you, and ... oh, well.'

'And what?'

'Well, about your brother. She worries about Frank.'

'Do you worry about him, too?'

'A little.'

'Are you fond of Frank?'

'I like him. He's a friend, like lots of other friends.' Maire flashed a quick glance from the road to the man sitting at her side. He was staring intently out of the nearside window. Sensitive as ever to the feelings of other people, she was aware that their conversation had taken a wrong turning and that it was up to her to bring it back on course. She had been surprised at herself earlier in the day as he had walked her back to her home from Mother Kate's, accepting his invitation to spend the afternoon with him. She had heard a lot about him from Mother Kate, but, as always, the picture built of words had not fitted the flesh. Michael Nealis was not at all the rather chilly dedicated professional who had emerged from his mother's account of his career. There was something warm and humorous about him. It was in his eyes. There was a formidable strength of character there, too, but over all else a sadness about him. Perhaps that was why she had agreed to his suggestion to walk in the country, just to find out what it was that went on behind those eyes.

'We're nearly there, now,' she said to break the silence. 'Just up that road. We'll park there and climb the hill, shall we? You can see the Loch from here, and the lighthouse.'

'Sounds ideal. Right away from it all. There'll be no people, I hope.'

'No people. I promise.'

She stopped the car at the foot of the hill, pulling it off the road to park on the heather, and they began the gentle walk uphill to the flat peak.

At the top, they stood to survey the scene. Below them the shiny water of Loch Foyle flowed emptily to the sea, meeting it at the twin headlands a couple of miles away. Behind them, more hills swooped and rose in green undulation up to and beyond the border and all around there was silence. The sun was shining quite fiercely and the only breeze was a warm, slow movement of air. Maire slipped off her anorak and sat on the silky grass. Nealis joined her.

'Ireland's a lovely place,' she said, as they both looked out across the Loch. 'I haven't travelled as much as you, but I doubt if you could find a nicer place on this earth.'

'Me? Travelled? Well, Cyprus, Germany, a holiday in Italy and two weeks in Spain, if you call that travelling. But I agree with you, this little island is as beautiful a place as there is. Which makes it all more of a pity that the natives are so damned complicated. They all ought to be travel-poster peasants and ride about in traps and live in white-painted cottages like the Americans think we do.'

'You think the natives are complicated, do you? Are you complicated?'

Nealis laughed without humour. 'I'm more complicated than the entire population. But what I meant was all this that's happening right now. I mean, what the hell's going to be the outcome of all this street fighting?'

'Justice, perhaps. Perhaps this street fighting is the only way for people to get what they are entitled to.'

'Oh, come on, you're talking like you're reading from a text book. All that's happening is that Protestants and Catholics are fighting each other with the RUC joining in for good measure. Do you seriously believe it will achieve anything?'

'I don't like to see it any more than you do,' she said, 'but there's a reason to fight, and while that reason exists people will be prepared to fight. And thank God they are.'

Nealis sighed. 'If you think that's the solution then you're wrong. And what's more, you may be deluding a lot of people who are much less intelligent than you.' Maire was staring at him with an expression tinged with contempt and Nealis regretted what he had said. 'Look, Maire, I'm sorry for that...'

'I'm not,' she retorted angrily. 'You say what you think. You have a nice holiday and then go back to Liverpool and your policemen and leave us here to do what we think is right. But I'll tell you this. What's happening here is that thousands of ordinary people are finding their voices at long, long last and are beginning to speak up for themselves. My God, all they want is justice.'

When she had finished, Maire abruptly turned her face from him and sat gazing at the ground. Her shoulders were trembling. Nealis fished for a cigarette and lit one in silence.

'Do you want a cigarette?'

'No.'

'Well, for God's sake don't just sit there,' Nealis exploded with sudden inexplicable anger. 'I thought we came out for a pleasant afternoon, not for a political discussion.'

'If you remember, you invited me,' she flared. 'But I've had enough. I'm going.'

'Back to Frank?'

She moved to hit him and moved fast, but not quite fast enough. Nealis caught her arm and forced it behind her back. She struggled and punched with her other fist, but he encircled her body with his free arm and pulled her close to him. She stood quite still for a second or two, then kicked hard at his shin, bringing her knee up. Nealis bent to avoid it and she slipped half free as he stumbled, and lost his grip. She made no attempt to run away, but walked calmly back to where her anorak lay on the ground. She picked it up and brushed it while Nealis stood ten paces away watching her. From where he stood, he could see the tears dribbling down her cheeks, despite her effort to control them.

'I'm sorry, Maire,' he said, moving close to her. 'Truly, I'm sorry.' She turned from him again and stood brushing the straw from her coat. 'It doesn't matter,' she said. She walked away down the slope and Nealis followed. At the roadway, she unlocked her car, slid into the driver's seat and unlocked the passenger door briskly and without glancing at him. Nealis opened the door and bent to look inside. Maire was in the process of starting the motor.

'Look,' he said. 'I've told you I'm sorry for losing my temper with you, and I am. But if you are going to ignore me, I'm damned if I am going to ride back to Derry in silence.'

'Walk then,' she said fiercely. Before Nealis could reply, she let in the clutch, U-turned and moved swiftly away. Nealis watched the car speed down the road and disappear round a bend. He started to walk.

He discovered her half a mile farther along the road. She had pulled onto the grass and was sitting in the car with her head on her arms, crying.

Quietly, he opened the nearside door and slipped into the seat. She didn't move until he reached out with a tentative hand and touched her arm. Then she looked up at him, red eyes, shiny, tear-damp cheeks, her eyelashes spilling more in small trickles and looking unbelievably beautiful. They didn't speak, but moved slowly towards each other in total silence. Nealis shivered slightly, involuntarily, as he caught the whiff of her perfume and felt the warmth of her near him. Her eyes, which had been questioning his, closed, and his lips brushed her salty cheek and then found her mouth in a warm, liquid, agonizing-sweet kiss. Her arms slipped quietly around his shoulders and her fingers rested gently on the hair at the nape of his neck, still soundlessly. In that chaste embrace they remained motionless for minutes. There was no more, no need of more at that moment. Nealis wanted her, more of her, all of her, but that would happen, if it was going to happen, at some other time.

At last, an age later, Maire opened her eyes and looked at him. He was frowning. It had been a long time since she had wanted to kiss a man—just to kiss him, not as a prelude, but as a complete act, a pure coition. They had not yet spoken, but she knew—against all reason, contrary to any logic, in defiance of any rational thought—she knew she loved him and that they would become lovers.

Nealis reached out and stroked her hair, and she inclined her head to brush his wrist with her cheek. Her skin was soft against him and he touched her face with his fingertips, stroking softly until she caught his hand in hers and held it tight.

They sat in the car for another hour, talking about themselves. She told him about the convent and London and her life since then and listened to him tell of a thousand things about himself she wanted to know but which did not matter in the least. Then they drove for a while to the end of Loch Foyle and sat again looking out to the flat sea and the white lighthouse with its timeless, pulsing light. After a long silence, Nealis said: 'Tell me about Frank.'

'What about him?'

'All about him. You know him better than I do. I left Derry fifteen years ago and the Nealises are not good correspondents. Frank's my brother and I hardly know a thing about him except that he's better than me at football and packs a wicked left hook. Oh, yes, and he snores.'

'I didn't know that.'

'Didn't you?'

'No.'

Nealis nodded. 'He's mixed up in all this business, isn't he?'

'Yes.'

'How deep is he in, Maire? He wasn't in that fight last night just by accident. And the police didn't come looking for him in Kilgallen Street just by chance. They know him, don't they?'

'They know all of us, Michael. I don't know that much about Frank and the people he moves about the town with, but I do know that he is absolutely sincere in his beliefs.'

'And what are they?'

'Much the same as mine. Perhaps more so. Frank's been on

53

the receiving end of the injustice. In and out of work and that sort of thing. It's small wonder he's bitter, like so many others.'

'And he resents me for getting out, I suppose.'

'Perhaps he does. But I think he's jealous of you. Not for what you've got, but for what you are. He admires you, Michael, in some kind of way.'

'Even though I'm a copper?'

'You're his brother.'

'Do you know where he is? He must be staying well out of sight somewhere with the boys in green looking for him.'

'I know fine where he is,' Maire hesitated for a fraction of a second. 'He's at my home.' She saw Nealis stiffen and the slight narrowing of his eyes. 'Don't be angry again, Michael. There's nothing, but my house is as good as any for him to stay while there's trouble.'

Nealis nodded. 'All right. But I don't like it. They can easily knock you off as well for aid and comfort or accessory or something. I think it would be a good idea if we headed back to town. I want a word with my brother.'

They delayed for a few minutes more. She asked Nealis to drive, saying she wanted to watch him without killing them both by driving off the road.

It was dusk when they left the lighthouse and Nealis had to switch on the lights as they drove towards the city and it was some time before he became aware of the faint orange glow in the sky over the rooftops.

'Something's on fire,' he said. 'Looks as if it's...'

'Oh, no!' Maire was staring intently through the windscreen, sitting stiffly on the edge of the seat.

'What is it?'

'Frank! He said tonight. He was saying something about defending Bogside tonight, as if he knew.'

'Oh, Christ.' Nealis rammed the Mini into top gear and accelerated into the city. There were thickening crowds on the streets as they neared the centre and a traffic jam built up a few hundred yards from the RUC barracks and Nealis

54

could see a police armoured car blocking the road.

'We'll go on foot to the hotel,' he said, swinging the car across the main road and into a side street. 'You'll stay in the hotel, do you hear.'

'And where are you off to?'

'If there's big trouble, I'm not sitting on my backside with Mother Kate in the middle of it.'

'I'm coming too.'

'We'll see.' Out of the car, Nealis grabbed Maire's arm and pushed her at a run back to the main street and through the crowds heading towards the city centre. A posse of RUC were making desultory attempts to stem the flow but Nealis pushed by and reached the hotel. On the steps, he collided with Jimmy Hadlee and a photographer.

'What the hell ... oh, hi there, Inspector. Shouldn't you be going the other way?'

'Stuff the gags, Jim. What goes on up there?' Nealis jerked his thumb over his shoulder in the direction of the city walls and Bogside.

'Christ, I can't keep up with the tribal idiosyncrasies of the Irish, but all bloody hell goes on, Mike.' Hadlee's face was, for once, grim. He rarely addressed Nealis by his forename and then only when perfectly serious. 'The Ulster Volunteers bombed a pub, they say, and some silly bastard tossed a hand-grenade at a church in retaliation.'

'Jesus! Anyone dead?'

'Not yet. The Bogsiders are busy barricading themselves in. There's a hell of a lot of petrol flowing around the streets and most of it is alight, but they're only using stones just now for weapons.'

Nealis turned to Maire, who still held his hand. 'You stay here. In the hotel. I'm coming up there.'

'Don't be bloody daft, Mike,' Hadlee cut in. 'The place is stiff with cops. They don't need you.'

'My mother lives up there,' Nealis said. 'I'm going.'

'That's different. I'll come with you, if you like. I've just come down to file my early piece and I know where the action is and where it isn't. It'll be better than blundering through all the shit on your own.'

'Thanks,' Nealis said. 'Maire, you stay here in the hotel. I'll be back.'

'I'm coming with you, Michael. I live up there, too.'

Nealis nodded. They were wasting time. He gripped Maire's hand tightly and led her across the street towards the city walls, with Hadlee slightly ahead of them both. They hardly spoke a word as they followed Hadlee who kept up a fast pace towards the glow of the fires and the now audible noise of the battle.

The sound of half a city engaged in civil warfare is in the beginning just a noise—a low throbbing, indistinct growl. As it draws nearer, the ears can detect individual sounds over the whole. The shout of a man. The scream of a woman. The pizzicato tinkle of glass shattering. A sudden chorus of voices shocked into a higher pitch than the rest. The throbbing grows louder, the individual sounds more shrill until they come from all directions, robbing the ear of selectivity. At last it is overburdened and the senses are swamped by the encompassing roar and the world becomes a raucous, monstrous, mind-bending cacophony that stuns the brain.

The further they progressed, the more pungent became the stench of smoke and brighter the glow of fires. Nealis had no idea where Hadlee was leading them, but managed to catch the reporter as the three of them slowed to pick their way over a tangle of fire hoses somewhere near the Guildhall.

'Where are we making for?' Nealis bellowed the words into Hadlee's ear. Hadlee pointed ahead and yelled. Nealis caught the words 'bird's eye view'. Holding tight onto Maire's arm he followed.

Nealis felt his heart skip a jump as he suddenly recognized where he was. They were making for the top of the city wall which overlooks Bogside. Against the glare of the fires, he could see crowds pressed against the ramparts of the walls. Regardless of Hadlee now, he dragged Maire with him, plunging through the fringe of the mob to one certain part of the ramparts and when he reached it, charged straight ahead, deaf to the protests of others and almost oblivious of Maire.

He reached the stone parapet and looked down. He felt the adrenalin in his system flood through him at the shock.

Kilgallen Street was alight from end to end.

7

It had started a few hours before when some youths had come
down from the Orange enclave of The Diamond district to
taunt their neighbours in the Catholic enclave of Bogside.
There were twenty of them, young men determined on a
night's relief from the boredom of a Northern Irish Sunday.
They faced up to the Bogside and unfurled some banners,
their faces taut with excitement. One of them began to beat
a lambeg drum and some girls came up to watch. They were
young, nubile girls and the young men began to strut and
crow, striking attitudes of masterful aggression. The young
girls looked at them and felt curiously excited.

From the dark canyons of their streets the Bogsiders
watched for a while in silence, but as the lambegs beat louder
and the taunts came more freely they began to feel angry
and ashamed that this should be happening to them. It was
Kevin Corceran, a baker's lad by day and a dreamer by night,
who brought matters to a head. As hundreds of eyes watched
from the darkening shadows he walked up the centre of the
street, picked up a stone and hurled it at the man who was
playing the lambeg. For a moment he was trapped there,
alone in the centre of the stage, the central character in a
great drama. The stone left his hand and flew in a high trajectory towards the Protestant group. There was a cry from
one of the girls as it hit her. Other figures joined Kevin in the
centre of the street. He was half aware of them throwing
stones at the offending group. He bent mechanically to collect
more ammunition, feeling angry at the Protestant bitch who
had got in the way of his stone.

Within thirty minutes the huge turbulence that had been heaving just below the city's life came boiling to the surface as men and women set out on an orgy of hate and destruction. News of the skirmish spread quickly through the Bogside and up the hill to The Diamond and as it spread the call to battle was clearly heard. Men brushed aside their protesting wives and went out into the streets with sticks and cudgels and, occasionally, guns.

The invading Protestants surged into the narrow defile of Kilgallen Street, jostling the police who had managed to spread themselves in a thin ribbon between the two opposing forces, and leaving behind a devastated area of shattered windows and houses afire. Under the force of the attack the Catholics fell back, fighting with stick and stone for every yard they retreated. As they gave way before the advancing crowd they ripped up flagstones to use as missiles and tore down telegraph poles to blockade the street. Somebody found a supply of milk bottles and others found petrol and these were rushed to the retreating Bogsiders. The ranks opened to allow men through to hurl petrol bombs at the attackers. Spluttering through the air like small, lethal meteorites they flew in a fiery trajectory, casting quaking shadows over the street.

Still down Kilgallen Street they came, and as they did so pockets of Protestants began fanning out into the side streets.

Bartley Mulholland, watching all this from a distance of about a hundred yards, was a self-satisfied man. He was with Pogue Mahone and a third man. The third man, known to the natives of Bogside merely as Larry the Yank, had appeared in their midst about a month before. There were rumours that he was an anarchist, a Communist agent, a front man for the Irish in America who poured regular amounts of money each year into the old country. He was surveying the scene now, with Mulholland, and he too was looking pleased.

'They've had about enough now,' he said.

'Oh, I don't know.'

'Leave it much longer and they're going to break through.

Every goddam building in sight is going to be burned down. They're going to break through any minute now.'

By now the police had dropped any pretence of neutrality. They were no longer acting as a buffer between the invaders and the invaded; instead they were spearheading the Protestant attack.

Mulholland said: 'You might be right.'

'I am right, Bartley. If they get through now they'll mop up. They'll really kick the bejasus out of this place. There won't be anything left to fight about.'

'Okay,' Mulholland said. He nodded at Pogue Mahone.

'You know what to do, Pogue?'

'I do, rightly.'

'All right, get it rolling.'

Pogue settled his cap more firmly on his head and hurried away. He passed the sign on the wall which announced *Free Derry* and turned left down a street where the overhead lights had all been extinguished. At the bottom of the street a large two-decker bus stood hard against the kerb. The driver and conductor were standing beside it, arguing with a group of men who surrounded them. Pogue walked up to the driver: 'We are taking this bus for use by the Citizens' Defence Association,' he said.

'Jesus man, what are you going to do with it?'

'None of your business.'

'But it's my bus. What am I going to tell them back at the depot?'

'Tell them to kiss my arse,' Pogue said. He gestured to one of the bystanders who climbed into the driver's seat. He settled himself and poked his head out of the window. Pogue looked up at him.

'Christ man, you make a fine bus driver.'

'Aye, I might ask the 'broo to get me on down at the depot some time.'

'Bartley says you're to go up Fahan Street. They're moving over in that direction. Get up as far as you can and watch. We'll be clearing them back. As soon as you see us move them back move it in.'

'Right you are.'

'You other fellows come with me,' Pogue said. The men, about eight or nine of them, turned and followed him.

Bartley Mulholland was still standing in the same spot when Pogue returned with the men. He nodded and put a thumb up to Mulholland, then led the men into a house.

'Better get them moving,' Larry the Yank said. 'If the other crowd over-run the bus the crap'll hit the fan. Better tell them to get a move on.'

Mulholland nodded and went inside the house. 'I want you to hurry up, lads. The bus will already be in Fahan Street. I hope to Christ he hasn't moved up too far. You know the plan, so away you go.'

The men trooped out of the house carrying rifles. The rifles had been made in Czechoslovakia and they had been obtained by the American. They were streamlined, modern rapid-fire weapons and the men who carried them knew only their theory. None of them had yet fired one.

They moved rapidly through the streets, the lights of the huge Creggan housing estate shining behind them, and made their way around the backs of the houses in Fahan Street. There they silently entered various houses and positioned themselves in front upstairs windows.

As they watched, they saw Bartley Mulholland and Larry the Yank making their way quickly up the street. They stopped and moved into the shadow of a doorway. Further up the street a tight group of men, each of them carrying several petrol bombs, had been making their way to the front of the Bogsiders. Bartley looked out of the shadows, assessing the situation before blowing a whistle.

The men with the petrol bombs lined up solidly side by side and, with a concerted precision, began lobbing the ignited bombs at the Protestants. It was the heaviest attack the Protestants had suffered and their line wavered and then broke as they tried to get back out of range of the missiles. As they did so the men in the windows opened fire. They were on single shot and they were firing selectively. About half a dozen bullets tore the air above the ranks of retreating Protestants. None of them found a home, but the shrill whine that they made carried a sufficiently grave message. As the Catholics stood still, cheering, both police and Protestants fell back up Fahan Street, pursued by petrol bombs and occasional bullets. As they did so the confiscated bus lumbered after them, not getting close enough to obscure the line of fire from the men in the windows. At the top of the street the bus pulled roughly across the road, leaving only a yard or two on either side for attackers to come through.

The petrol bomb throwers came quickly behind it and raced upstairs to smash out the windows and hurl more bombs at the attacking horde, which now stood, beaten and baffled, under the arch of Derry Walls that leads to the Apprentice Boys' house.

Bartley Mulholland walked up with Larry the Yank. 'Well,' he said, 'the fight's over.'

Larry winked. 'Don't you believe it, baby. This is just the storm before the storm.'

* * *

Nealis came down the steep hill clutching Maire's hand and hurrying. There were knots of excited people all around, talking and gesticulating as they re-lived the events of the past few hours. As he entered Kilgallen Street he saw that the street was blocked by fire tenders and littered with hose pipes. There were no police around, but firemen were working ceaselessly, playing streams of water on burning buildings.

Flames soared into the night, reddening the face of the sky and making the sound of distant thunder as the hungry fire ravened through the walls, roof and ceilings of the old houses. Here and there men who had been injured lay on the ground, moaning softly as gently weeping women knelt to comfort them. A policeman's cap lay in the gutter and as Nealis passed it a small, eager-eyed boy darted forward to claim it. He put it on and walked away whistling.

Nealis pushed his way through the smoke and the noise and the confusion until a fire officer stopped him. 'Don't go any nearer now. It's dangerous.'

'But that's my mother's house.'

'Take it easy. We are doing our best.'

At Nealis's shoulder Maire started sobbing.

'Is she in there?' Nealis asked.

Flames were belching through the roof, the whole house was a coruscating shell of flame.

'I don't know.' The fireman turned away, too busy to be bothered, too realistic to be bothered. If there had been anybody in there they would have suffocated long before the flames got them. There was no sense in being bothered. He moved away to direct a group of firemen who were playing their hoses through a gaping hole in the roof.

Nealis stood there looking, feeling pain. Fuck them. His mother. A woman, a good woman, a kind woman. The bastards. Gone? Dead? The fucking bastards, the dirty lousy bastards. Mother Kate gone? By Christ, by Jesus, by Christ....

A woman came up to him. 'Are you looking for your mother, son?'

'What?' He turned, wondering who she was, what she wanted.

'I said are you looking for your mother?'

'My mother?'

Maire said: 'Yes, yes. Where is she? Do you know what happened to her?'

'She got out,' the woman said. 'I know she got out.'

'Got out?' Nealis looked at her. 'Where? Where is she?'

'Ah sure I didn't see where she went. All them ones fighting. I didn't see. But she got out. I saw her get out all right.'

'What happened?'

'Them ones from The Fountain and The Diamond came down throwing petrol bombs into the houses. My house is burned out, too. We are all lucky. My husband and my boys were out on the street fighting them and I was out, but I've nowhere to lay my head.'

The passion rose in the woman's voice. 'Not a bloody roof to lay my head under. Thirty years we were in that wee house, me and my man. And the children. All born and raised there.' She sat down on the pavement and began to rock backwards and forwards as she wept.

A small crowd had gathered around them. One of them, a man with ginger hair, said to Nealis: 'Why don't you go and look at the headquarters? There's a lot of people there.'

'Come on,' Maire said.

The headquarters had been established in a house in Westland Street. A group of men were gathered outside and as Nealis approached they walked off in pairs.

'Vigilantes,' Maire said. 'We've no police here, so they keep order.'

The control room for the headquarters was in a room off the hall.

There were several members of the Citizens' Defence Association working there, tabulating the property damage on a wall chart and working up the deployment of vigilantes on another wall chart. Bartley Mulholland and Larry the Yank sat in a corner, smoking.

A man sitting at a desk looked up as Nealis came in.

'I'm looking for news of my mother,' Nealis said. 'She was burned out of Kilgallen Street.'

'Name?' the man said.

'Nealis, Katherine Nealis.'

The man wrote it down. 'We haven't heard anything yet, but sit yourself down for a minute. Some of the vigilantes may know something.'

Nealis sat down, Maire alongside him.

'Hello boy,' Mulholland said.

Nealis nodded at him. Larry the Yank blew out smoke and remained impassive.

'Well, what do you think of that lot?' Mulholland asked.

'My mother's house has gone,' Nealis replied. 'Christ

knows where she is.'

'Ah Jesus, poor Mrs Nealis. A lovely woman,' Mulholland said. 'But wait now, sure nothing may have happened to her at all.'

'Maybe. They say she got out of it.'

'Ah well, that's something. Only hope now that the police haven't lifted her.. That'd be a bad go.'

'No,' Nealis said, 'she wouldn't be lifted. She wouldn't be doing anything to be lifted for.'

'These are queer times. You never know. You never know who'd be doing what when the likes of them brave buckos come down to burn women and children in their beds at night.'

A man came in carrying a telephone. He opened a window and thrust a length of cable through.

'You'll be right in a minute,' he said. 'I'll just get one of the manholes up outside and plug you straight in.'

Nealis looked at the man at the desk. 'Is the Post Office still working?'

'Well now, yes, and no. That man's our own post office. We need a phone in here to keep in touch with the vigilantes and he's just rigging one for us. We can't be cut off if we are going to patrol the place properly.'

After ten minutes the man came back. 'You should be right now,' he said. 'Here's your number.' He handed a slip of paper to the desk-man, who copied it onto a large piece of white cardboard and stuck it up on the wall.

Two men were sitting drinking tea and resting. The desk-man handed one of them the slip of paper. 'Fergie, take a race round and tell all the vigilantes I want a check call from each of them every fifteen minutes. Tell them to make the first call as soon as you give them the number.'

Fergie got up and went out, picking up a beef sandwich from a plate on the way. Mulholland rose and crossed the room to speak to the man at the desk.

'There's going to be more of this, Rory,' Mulholland said to him.

Rory looked up. 'You're right, Bartley.'

'It's the only bloody way we'll get it sorted out,' Mulholland said.

'Ah no, now we've made some progress in the past year.'

'Progress me bollocks,' Mulholland said.

'Well, we've got some concessions coming. The English government isn't going to let this pack get away with it for much longer. They're already threatening them.'

'Now listen to me,' Mulholland leaned forward in a characteristic stance. 'There's only one solution for the troubles of Northern Ireland. Only one solution and that's blood. Until there's a bit of bloodshed then nobody's going to take much notice. Do you know that, Rory, to cleanse ourselves we'll be needing a whole river of blood.'

'Now I wouldn't go as far as that. Maybe this is the last of it.'

'Last of it my arse. They'll be at it again on Thursday when the Apprentice Boys have their parade.'

The Apprentice Boys, most luminous heroes of the Orange Order, had closed the gates of Derry against an attacking Catholic army and kept it safe for Protestantism. Every year on August 12 the members of the Apprentice Boys order march around the walls of Derry to celebrate that famous three-centuries-old victory.

'No no, Bartley. They'll ban that parade. They won't let the Apprentice Boys walk.'

'You bet your bloody life they will. If they don't they'll have the whole Orange Order at their throats—and it's the Orange Order that runs this government.'

'Surely to Christ, though, even this crowd has more sense than to let them march when things are like this.'

'No sense at all. Or maybe too much sense. It might just suit their book to see the Catholic working class knocked back into line by the bully boys of the Orange Lodge.'

The telephone rang and Rory looked at it in surprise.

'God almighty,' he said, 'the bloody thing works.' He picked it up. 'Yes, hello.' He listened for a while, then said:

'There's a man here looking for a woman called Katherine Nealis. She was burned out in Kilgallen Street.' A pause. 'Well, see if you can find anything out.' He put the phone down and looked at Nealis.

'He's going to ask around. He says most of our people are dispersing. The other crowd have all gone home but the peelers are hanging around waiting to have another crack if they get the chance. Well, we're ready for them.'

'Imagine the bastards, coming down to burn poor old women and innocent children in their beds,' Mulholland said.

Larry the Yank spoke. 'You'll have to watch for a sneak attack.'

'We're ready for them,' Rory said again.

Nealis suddenly felt he wanted a cigarette. When he reached to get it he was surprised to find he was holding Maire's hand. He had been holding it for a long time without knowing. When he took it away she smiled at him, her blue eyes full of warmth. He lit the cigarette and took her hand again, squeezing it gently.

The telephone rang and Rory pounced on it. When he had finished, Rory said: 'Well, we think we've found her, Mr Nealis. A woman was taken from Kilgallen Street to the Knights of Malta hospital station. I'd try there if I were you.'

The Knights of Malta, a group of voluntary doctors and mainly male nurses, had set up an emergency hospital behind Waterloo Street, facing the city walls. Nealis and Maire hurried there.

Several men were lying around in beds, most of them with their heads swathed in bandages. Through another door there were women. Nealis stopped as he went through the doorway and looked around. Mother Kate was lying in a corner bed. She looked peaceful and old.

'What's the matter with her?'

'She got trapped by a falling beam, we believe,' the man said. 'It broke her ribs and we think one of them may have punctured a lung.' It had been a long night and he was not in the mood for wrapping things up. He took Nealis by the arm and started ushering him out. 'Come back tomorrow. We'll know better then. Tomorrow.'

'Can I see her now?'

'We've given her sedatives,' the man said, remembering the huge dose of morphine the doctor had ordered for the woman.

'So she's sleeping?'

'She's sleeping. Come back tomorrow.'

The man tightened his grip and pushed more firmly, propelling Nealis through the door and out into the night. Then he went back inside to stand looking at a small boy who lay twisting and moaning in bed. He was a very small boy and he had freckles and he was to die of multiple burns before the day dawned.

8

In that chilly morning, a strange stillness gripped Bogside.
The rays of the sun, as if fearful of what they might reveal,
groped tentatively through the smoky sky and gradually
turned shadows into people and diminished the glow of the
fires that still crackled here and there. Everyone still on the
streets moved quietly. It was as if the evidence of their eyes
robbed them of their voice and everyone seemed to speak in
whispers and walk on tiptoe. At the corner of Glenna Street,
where Maire O'Dwyer lived, clumps of men and women
stood mute, staring towards the ruin of two shops gutted and
looted during the night, their wares spilled and trampled into
the muddy sidewalks. Working silently, a flurry of women
served tea from a makeshift counter outside the corner
house. They took no payment. In another place at another
time, it might have been called the blitz spirit. Nealis, sipping
tea, wondered idly, professionally, if they had stolen the
ingredients from one of the shops, and then found himself
smiling at the mechanical workings of his brain. He didn't
really care. He was too grateful for the hot tea and too tired
to worry. The entire world had gone mad the previous night:
perhaps it was more rewarding to contemplate the unselfish-
ness of the women than to question the means.

People were sitting, dazed and abject, around the street,
occupying chairs and old horse-hair sofas that had been
dragged from the burning houses. The poor possessions of a
poor people littered the pavements. Maire sat down on one
of the chairs, a deep armchair with a rexine cover. She
reached up to touch Nealis on the arm.

'What are you puzzling at?' she asked. She looked exhausted, but still managed to smile at him. He shrugged without answering. 'Better get some sleep,' he said, and when she nodded, helped her to her feet. No-one took any notice of them as they trudged down Glenna Street to her home. She opened the front door and walked slowly down the passage. Nealis hesitated.

'Come on, come in,' Maire said, turning to him and holding out her hand. Then, as if reading his mind, added: 'There's no-one else here.' Her home was identical to Mother Kate's, but there was a difference in Maire's home. There were bookshelves in the front room with books on them, and the decoration there and in the kitchen had been carried out with an eye for colour. There were the remains of a meal on the kitchen table and in the middle of the dishes, an alarm clock. Maire picked it up and wound it automatically. The hands stood at a quarter to six.

'Time you were in bed,' Nealis said. She smiled and yawned, and then the smile vanished from her lips.

'It was terrible last night,' she said. 'I almost began to wish ... Innocent people ought not to get hurt, but they almost always do. Your poor mother. Will she be all right?'

'I don't know. She's in the best place, that's all.' Nealis walked up behind Maire and put his arms around her. 'But there's nothing you can do about it now. Or me, for that matter. The best thing you can do is to get to your bed and sleep a little and not worry.'

She turned in his arms and buried her head in his chest. She said something but her voice was muffled. Then she moved away from him, still holding his hand, leading him to the door in the corner of the kitchen which opened onto the stairs. He followed her up the stairs to a room at the back of the house. It was small with only a bed and a dressing table in it. It had been recently decorated in blue and white and there were two or three prints of modern paintings on the walls. Maire pulled back the covers of her bed and sat down, pulling off her anorak. Sleepily, she kicked off her shoes and slid her legs under the sheets and lay back on the pillow.

'Here,' she said softly, patting the space in the narrow bed beside her. Nealis slipped off his jacket and shoes and lay beside her, cradling her head in his left arm. He kissed her once, gently, and she sighed and put her arm across his body and fell asleep.

Looking at her drowsily, Nealis felt a kind of tenderness which pricked his eyes and brought him close to tears. It was absurd. Absurd that he should be lying there with her like this, only to sleep; the warmth of her body enfolded him, comforting him, and as she slept he nuzzled the softness of her cheek, breathing gently. Nealis felt sleep stealing over him. Poor Mother Kate, he thought. He turned in the bed to face Maire. She smelled sweet and her breasts pushed against him filling him a with a longing that transcended sex or the quick, sudden cravings of passion.

When Nealis awoke it was, as always, suddenly and fully alert. The voices in the room below registered with him the moment they had begun. Now he lay listening, trying to place them. The police? Maire had said they knew where she lived. For just a moment the realization struck him. He was a policeman. Was this how people reacted when he came into a house? He tried to move away from Maire, but she woke the instant he did so.

'What is it?' she asked. Her eyes were confused and a little frightened.

'Someone downstairs,' he whispered. 'Stay here and be quiet.'

'Don't go.'

'I'll be back. Stay here.' Nealis slid from the bed, pulled on his shoes, gathered his jacket and moved silently to the top of the stairs. Then he relaxed. His brother's voice was unmistakable.

There were two others in the kitchen with Frank. Mulholland and the American. They had been speaking about the barricades but stopped abruptly as he came down the stairs and turned their heads towards him. Frank was the first to speak. 'You? What are you doing here?' Nealis saw his eyes flick upwards to the stairs for a brief moment.

'I've just got here,' Nealis said, not knowing why he lied.

'You get around,' Frank said.

Nealis smiled. 'And I always seem to find you there.'

While they spoke, Mulholland slipped a cigarette to his lips and lit it. Bloody liar, he thought. Just got here? Just got off the nest, more likely. Was that why he lied? Or was Frank's brother, the policeman, playing some game?

'Sorry to burst in,' Mulholland said. 'We came to keep Frank company, you know.'

'Sure,' Frank said. 'You know Bartley Mulholland. This other fellow's Larry—'

'He knows,' the American said quickly.

'What's the hurry?' Mulholland moved deliberately across the room and sat on a chair by the table. 'We've all had a busy night.' He looked slowly at the ceiling and back to Nealis. 'Perhaps we should rest a wee while.'

'Rest all you want,' Nealis said. 'Frank, have you been to the hospital?'

'Hospital? What hospital?'

'Didn't you know Mother Kate's in there? She's been hurt.'

Frank whipped round. 'What, me Ma. Hurt? What are you on about, hurt?'

'She was in the house when it all started. You didn't know about it?'

'No, I didn't know. Where is she?'

'In the Knights of Malta. She's unconscious now. There's nothing much to be done until she comes to. I'll phone them.'

Frank glanced at him and threw his cigarette into the kitchen fireplace with a quick, angry gesture. Nealis watched him and felt something like contempt.

'You didn't know about it, eh, Frank? Have you seen the house, Frank? There's fuck-all left of it. And have you seen the rest of Kilgallen Street? Or have you been too busy playing the boy hero up on the barricades to bother about that?'

'That's a bloody lie!' Frank roared. 'I got me Ma out of the house long before the trouble began. Would I leave her there when I knew damned well that the house was going to get it?'

'You knew?'

'Of course I did: Jesus Christ, wake up, man. You think all of this happened last night by bloody accident? Don't you know they knew fine where I lived and that was one of the first places they would go for when the fighting really got started?'

'How did you know that?'

'Look, the RUC were there at the house this morning, weren't they? You were there.'

'So?'

'So if they were poking around, it was a sure thing the other bastards knew too, isn't it? Why do you think me Ma's house was the first to get it, for God's sake? They were there first.'

'Who went for it, Frank?'

'The Ross bloody Simmons mob,' Frank yelled, 'that's who.'

'How do you know? How do you know it was his lot?'

'I know, and I'll tell you something else. One of these days I'm going to take the head right off his bastarding shoulders, so I will.'

Nealis felt a sudden flash of anger. It had been building up in him when he first arrived in this city where the talk was all of killing and maiming. 'Don't be a prick,' he said.

'I'm no prick. You're the prick.'

'I'm your brother.'

'And you're a policeman. A lousy, rotten, cock-sucking copper.'

Nealis leaned forward, jabbing his forefinger to within an inch of his brother's face. 'Don't say that, Frank. Don't say that to me.'

Behind them Mulholland was grinning. 'For Christ's sake

boys, for Christ's sake be easy. Be easy, will you. It's not right for two men, two brothers, to be killing each other.'

Frank was standing there, looking at Nealis with a deep and implacable hostility. The silence went on for a long time, then Frank pointed at him.

'Listen mate, you're going to have to make up your bloody mind. There's no room in this city for half-arsed English coppers to sit on fences. Whatever you are you carry the name of Nealis, and that is an honoured name in this town. If you have any manhood, any balls about you, decide where you are.' He moved closer to Nealis, lowering his voice. 'I'll tell you where I am. I was out there last night with a rifle. I was shooting at that scum from up the hill, and while this goes on you'll find me behind a rifle. Where will you be? Where will you be, brother?'

He turned and started to leave: 'I'm going to see me Ma.' Larry stood there without taking his eyes from Nealis.

Mulholland spoke. 'You're surprised, eh, Nealis? You think this is all a Saturday night row with beer bottles, do you?' He advanced to stand squarely in front of Nealis. 'Well, I'm telling you it's not. It's terrorism and bloody murder, that's what it is. They couldn't get Frank, so they got his mother. That's what it's all about, friend.'

Nealis felt the anger in him pouring out as he spoke. 'Well, if you're so bloody smart, why in the name of Christ do you leave old ladies to fight your battles? My mother's lying in hospital right now, friend'—he spat out the word distastefully—'because she was there when it happened and you were someplace else, no doubt with a glass of whiskey in your paw, telling the rest of the world how to put itself in order. Jesus Christ, you make me sick.'

'Do I?' Mulholland spoke calmly. 'Then before you throw up, perhaps you had better know some of the facts of the case, Inspector.' Without thinking, Nealis thrust forward and gripped Mulholland by his tie and yanked him upward. 'Don't play funny games with me, Jack. For the purposes of this matter, I'm not an Inspector or even a copper. I'm the man whose mother is lying between life and death on your account!' He released the other man, who had remained effortlessly cool, and pulled a cigarette from the packet on the table.

'I'm sorry about your mother,' Mulholland said. 'I didn't know she was in any danger—and nor did Frank. But it happened and there's no-one can be blamed for that. It makes you damned wild, doesn't it?'

'Of course it does, you bloody fool. Wouldn't anyone be wild?'

'We're wasting time.' Larry spoke for the first time. 'Let's get the hell out of here, there's things to do.'

'I'm coming,' Mulholland said. 'But I wanted our man here to understand a few of the facts of life.' He addressed Nealis again. 'I don't think you understand them yet, but if you're going to stay in this part of the world for long, it might pay you to open your eyes and take a look around you and see what's happening—what's really happening. But before you do, I'll give you a wee clue. There's a lot of ordinary folk here—people like your mother, you might say —who are suddenly doing what needs to be done out there on the streets and at the barricades. You may not like me and you may think that me and others like me are making them do it, but I don't have a magic wand. I couldn't make them do it—they're fighting because they want to fight, because they're at last sick to fucking death of their lives and they want to tell that to the world. You think about that.'

When he had finished, Mulholland walked out of the house, followed by the morose American. For a while, Nealis didn't move from the chair into which he had sunk. He lit another cigarette and stared through the swirl of smoke at the dirty dishes on the table. He had his back to the stairs and was unaware of Maire entering the room. She approached him and slipped his jacket from the back of the chair and put it round his shoulders. Nealis glanced at her almost absently.

'I'll make some tea,' Maire said. 'Are you hungry?'

75

'I want to get out of this place,' Nealis said suddenly. 'I don't belong to this lousy place any more. Do I?' He had continued to stare at the table as he spoke. Maire was getting cups out of the kitchen cupboard, and said nothing.

'Did you hear what I said?' Nealis asked.

'Yes.'

'So?'

'So what, Michael?' She brought two cups and two saucers and placed them on the table, clearing a space among the other crockery.

'So what?' Nealis laughed without humour. 'So I'm up to my armpits. Up to my bloody neck.'

Maire took a teapot from the cupboard and walked slowly into the scullery. Her face was pale and she had difficulty in focussing on the gas ring when she lit it and put the kettle on the flame. When after a few minutes the tea was made, she returned to the kitchen. Nealis was still sitting. She poured out two cups of tea and put one in front of him and sat down opposite him.

'I'm sorry,' he said at last. 'I'm feeling sorry for myself.'

'If you are going to go, it would be better if you went now.' Maire stirred her tea determinedly as she spoke. She did not look up. Nealis reached across the table when she had finished and pulled her chin up in the palm of his hand.

'If I were to go now,' he said, 'I'd regret it for the rest of my life.'

'You could be making a mistake,' she said. 'Frank was right you know—oh, I was listening, I heard. If you stay you'll have to decide.'

Nealis shook his head: 'Maybe. Maybe you do decide these things. Or maybe the decision is taken for you the moment you are born.'

'That could be right,' Maire said quietly.

'Do you know what it is?' Nealis said. 'This bloody country reaches out and drags you into itself. Like an old whore she is hungry for men, and when she gets them she drains them of their manhood. The Irish as a race are a nation of eunuchs

76

and that's what it's all about. The more they try to prove they're men the more they become conscious that they've been gelded, and the more they realize that the more they try to prove they are men. Eunuchs! They've been gelded by the church and the state, their balls chopped off by King Billy, robbed of their potency by the blessed works of St Patrick. God blast this lousy, stinking country.'

Maire reached forward and touched his head.

'Michael, it's your country.'

'It's a heap of dung.'

'But your country, Michael.'

'Christ help me, Maire. Christ help us all. Ireland my country.'

9

Nealis was away for nearly an hour. He walked through the Bogside, looking at the debris of the previous night's action, on his way to the emergency hospital. A doctor there refused to let him in.

'She's under drugs and wouldn't know you. She couldn't even speak if she did know and it's wiser if you stay out. It'll be a couple of days yet before we'll be able to tell, one way or the other.'

Nealis argued for a while, but the doctor was adamant.

When he returned to Maire he looked pale and the lines on his face which had so easily creased into a smile were set in an expression of withdrawal. He sat at the table chain-smoking while Maire busied herself about the kitchen. He hardly spoke, and Maire did not question him. When she had finished she said: 'I'm going down to the school. Some of the children are being looked after there. I may be able to help.'

Nealis rose from the table. 'Sure. I'll take a walk down to the hotel.'

'Oh, all right. When will you be back?'

'What? Oh yes. I don't know. Soon.'

She watched him stub out his cigarette and put his jacket on. She realized then that she knew almost nothing about him and that all the things she had taken for granted and all the feeling they had generated in her might be invalid. She wanted badly to ask him not to go, but could not bring herself to say it.

They walked down the street together, to where they would

take different directions. At the corner they stopped. Nealis kissed her hair and held her hands tightly for a moment.

'I'll be back soon,' he murmured. And then he walked away, up the hill out of Bogside towards The Diamond, the centrepoint of the old walled city of Londonderry. She watched him go. He strode athletically, one arm swinging and the other thrust in the pocket of his trousers. Then he turned a corner and disappeared.

Nealis was as conscious as Maire had been that the gentle flow of their relationship had been disrupted and felt there was nothing he could do to repair it.

There were too many other things. His depression was all to do with the things, the events and the people he was walking away from. He needed to get away, if only for an hour, from the fetid atmosphere of Bogside. It all seemed suddenly so oppressive. He walked into The Diamond and stood for a minute or two watching the movement of people across and around the square. There were flags flying from many of the buildings and bunting in similar red, white and blue. A banner reading *God Save Our Queen* had been stretched across one of the streets leading into the square and dotted here and there were Orange Lodge banners—an orgasm of patriotism, potent with its own special magic and meaning.

Nealis turned to his left to walk down the hill to the city centre. There was a bar just down the street and the sight of it roused his thirst. It was crowded inside and thick with Guinness-flavoured talk of the night before. Nealis took his whiskey and walked to the end of the bar counter, noticing with some surprise his unkempt, unshaven face looking back at him from the mirror.

He was interrupted by a man who stood alongside him, a big sweaty man who clutched a pint glass of Guinness in his left hand. 'What's it like out, now?'

Nealis looked at him, assessing him and wondering whether the man could be talking about the weather. As the man took a huge pull at his pint Nealis decided that he was not.

79

'Pretty quiet,' he said.

'I never seen you here before. Are you a Derry man?'

'I am.'

'Were you down there last night, then? By God, that was a fight.'

'It was that.' Nealis was conscious of a feeling of being surrounded, aware of the latent hostility around him.

The man said: 'We'll eat the place when Wee Jimmy gets here. We'll settle the Bogside once and for all.'

Nealis drank some whiskey, thinking. 'Right.'

'Did you ever shoot a gun?' the man said.

'I did. I was a soldier,' Nealis said.

'Ah well, Wee Jimmy's the man you want to see.'

Just then the door at the back of the bar flew open. Framed in the doorway was the man they evidently all knew as Wee Jimmy. He had an acute sense of the theatre, for he stood on the threshold of the bar without speaking until the first gasp of surprise had ebbed and there was total silence.

'Right, me boys,' he said in a thunderous voice which belied his small frame. 'We've got the stuff in here. There's guns for them that can handle them. Step forward all those who's man enough to carry a gun for Ulster and who'll use it against the Papists when the time comes.'

There was a murmur of approval around the bar and after a moment of hesitation one man stepped forward. Wee Jimmy jerked his thumb over his shoulder and the man walked past into the back room. He was followed by another, and then more.

'We want men who can handle a gun,' Wee Jimmy bellowed. 'You lads who've been in the Army step up here and take a gun. There's a prize for the one who puts a shot up the Pope's arse.' The joke convulsed the bar and Wee Jimmy surveyed his merry men with his hands on hips.

'You'll be taking one, will you?' the sweaty man persisted. Nealis paid for his drinks and sank the second one in a single swallow.

'Maybe I will,' he said, but pushed past his companion

and made for the front door. He had his hand on the latch when Wee Jimmy's voice filled the room once more.

'Hold it!' For a second, Nealis paused. 'You there at the door!' Nealis turned. Men had withdrawn to each side of the bar, leaving an open channel between Nealis and Wee Jimmy, who had the sweaty man by his side. Slowly, eking out the effect, Wee Jimmy advanced until he stood three paces from Nealis.

'Who are you? What are you doing here?'

'Ask Ross Simmons.' It was all Nealis could think of to say, but the effect was enough. Wee Jimmy's composure was shattered. He turned for help to the sweaty man, but he had dived into his glass for another draught. Nobody spoke as Nealis lifted the latch. His last glimpse of Wee Jimmy was the sight of his face, a picture of perplexity framed in the closing door.

Back at the City Hotel ten minutes later, Nealis ran a shower and stood soaking under the refreshing stream of wet warmth. He stood naked while he shaved, then dressed in fresh clothes and began packing his gear into his single travelling grip. It occurred to him that he had not asked Maire about the coming night.

But that was just another uncertainty amid all the other unresolved problems. Anyway, there was no point in paying for a hotel room he was unlikely to use. He picked up his watch from the dressing table. It had been smashed during Sunday night and the hands had stopped at twenty to three —about the time he had been searching for Mother Kate. He threw the watch into the waste bin, picked up his case and left.

He left the case by the reception desk, asking the receptionist to make up his bill.

'Where are all the scribes?' he asked, as she did her sums.

'Who?'

'The Press. Where are they all?'

The girl sighed and raised her eyes to heaven in the manner of someone seeking help which was never likely to come.

'That lot,' she said, 'they're the end. They've all run off to a Press thing at the police barracks.'

Nealis nodded. 'I'll have a last beer before I go. I'll settle with you on the way out.' He was halfway to the bar, when the girl called him.

'Mr Nealis. I nearly forgot. There's a telegram for you.' Nealis puzzled, regained the desk and took the flimsy yellow envelope from her.

'It came this morning,' the receptionist said. 'Hope it's not bad news.'

Funny how people always said that, Nealis thought. Funnier how telegrams nearly always were. He retraced his steps and entered the bar with the cable still unopened. He'd need another drink before he read it, and he stuffed it into the pocket of his windcheater. Maureen was behind the bar and was bearing down on him before he even remembered she would be there.

'You're a cool bastard,' she opened. Nealis felt mildly surprised at her command of language.

'That's not nice,' he said. He had no wish to tangle with the girl any more, but at least with her it would be a short, simple argument if argument it was going to be. At least there'd be none of the polemics. 'Let me have a small Scotch—with no ice.'

'I saw you yesterday,' she went on, ignoring his order. 'Off in the car with some other girl. You've got a bloody nerve, you have. You couldn't care less about me, could you?'

'Look, Maureen, let's both forget it, shall we—and give me my Scotch.'

'Forget it?' she flared. 'Why should I? I could lose my job over you.'

'Oh, for God's sake grow up,' Nealis said with sudden savagery, remembering the telegram still unread in his pocket. 'If you're not going to serve me, I'll go somewhere else.' Maureen snatched a glass from the shelf and jabbed it viciously under the dispenser. She brought it over to him and threw the whiskey into his face.

'Bastard!' she growled. She stood looking at him wide-eyed as he shook the burning liquid from his face. She was clearly so horrified at what she had done that Nealis began to laugh. Seeing this, Maureen smiled, hesitantly at first, then laughed with him.

'You're a little bitch,' he said.

'I know,' she said simply. 'I'm sorry. It's just that I liked you.'

'You've a fine way of showing it.'

'Look, let me get your drink. I'll put that other one down to spillage.'

'Thanks. That'd be nice.'

She brought him the drink. 'Are you leaving?'

'Yes, 'fraid so.' He pulled the telegram from his pocket and stared at it.

'Hope it's not bad news,' Maureen said.

'You're the second person to say that,' Nealis said. 'Let's hope you're right.' He tore open the envelope and pulled out the white telegram form.

'*Imperative you return immediately,*' it read. '*Divorce proceeding. Betty.*'

It had been telephoned from the house. Typical that he should be paying for the means of bringing the message.

'It's not good?' Maureen inquired.

'It's not good.' Nealis climbed off the bar stool. 'Thanks for the drink, love. I'll see you.'

'See you,' echoed Maureen sadly.

When he had paid the bill, Nealis asked for a piece of hotel note-paper and an envelope, took them across to a table in the foyer and sat down. The neat paper sheet mocked him as he struggled to find the words he needed. How could he say he was going, that he wouldn't be back that night, without writing a book to explain to her? So much had crowded into his life in a few hours. Maire, Frank, Mother Kate. The image of his mother stopped the flow of his tangled thoughts for a moment. It was a hell of a time to be leaving the old lady like that, and Nealis felt a quick pang of guilt. But it was erased by the need to go and clear up one mess before facing the next. He could hardly explain it to himself, but maybe Maire would understand.

He had not thought of Betty or of home or of his job or anything that used to be important to him, not since Saturday night. Christ, she'd wasted no time since that bitter phone call. Betty wasn't the girl to let the bitterness drift away with sleep. And now it had come to it—what was there to say in a brief note? Goodbye, it's been fun, but I've got to get back to sort my life out and see what bits I can pick up, and while I'm about it, find out if it's going to affect everything I've worked and slaved for all these years? No. It didn't mean anything to anyone else in the world that he had flogged away at his job all God's hours to get somewhere and to be someone instead of just another Mick.

What the hell. It's your problem, boy. Keep it brief. There might be a time for explanations, but not now.

Nealis took the pen from the rack on the desk and wrote.

Maire. Or was it *Mary?* Never mind. *I'm sorry—but I had to leave. It had been my intention to return* ... sounds like a police report ... *but there are things, important things, I have to straighten out. It means going back to Liverpool tonight. There's no point in my trying to explain to you. I'll do that when the time comes but* ... the words were running away with him by now ... *I can't leave here without telling you that being with you has been the greatest joy of my life. Believe that, Maire.*

He signed the note and put it in the envelope, addressed it and handed it to the receptionist for posting. Then he picked up his bag, called a taxi and was driven to the station over in Waterside.

At Belfast Airport he booked on an areoplane to Liverpool. 'Single or return?' asked the man on the other side of the ticket desk.

'Single,' Nealis said, too confused to think how or when he would return.

10

In the corner of a wharf in Belfast a small group of Scotsmen were standing, clapping their hands together and singing. They were part of the Glasgow contingent of Apprentice Boys who had sailed over to take part in the parade and as they sang they were joined by other men who had travelled from Apprentice Boys' clubs in Liverpool.

Some of the men lurched around a little, for it had been a convivial night's crossing and, occasionally, a whiskey bottle had passed among them. They were happily and slowly getting drunk. It was not long past dawn, but the men's voices rose in the still air, a column of sound piercing the surrounding quietness.

> Have you seen the Holy Pope,
> And have you seen his daughter,
> Pissing in the holy pot
> And calling it holy water.

The two groups from Liverpool and Glasgow were each several hundred strong. As they came off the ship the bandsmen carried their instruments and stacked them neatly on the side of the wharf from where a lorry would carry them to the train for Derry.

The bandsmen were already dressed for the parade. They wore Scottish clothes, kilts and white gaiters and small black forage caps. At first glance they might have been mistaken for one of the Scottish regiments of the British Army. Along with the drums and the fifes they had brought silken banners carrying pictures of the original twelve apprentice boys. It was an honour to carry the banners and young men competed for the privilege.

The officers were moving around, supervising the preparations for the move to the station. Apart from the bandsmen most of the men were dressed in a casual mixture of lounge suits and sports clothes, but the officers wore dark suits and bowler hats. Around their necks they wore the silken collarettes of their particular club.

The group who had been singing began a chant:

We'll tighten up the rope, and we'll hang the bloody Pope,
And we'll never let them cross the Boyne water.

A docker who had been looking on with a wryly amused face turned to his mate and said: 'Them Glasgow boys are the ones. They're the ones who'll sort out the Papishes in Derry.'

His mate nodded: 'Aye, any bother from the Papishes and them Glasgow ones will kick the living shit out of them.'

* * *

In Lurgan, Armagh, Portadown, Dungannon and countless other towns and villages throughout Northern Ireland preparations were being made on this morning for the procession in Derry. Each town had its own clubs, named after the original twelve apprentice boys, and in some of the bigger towns there were twelve clubs.

So the fervent army gathered in the towns and villages—field, farm and factory forgotten, as they prepared to make their annual pilgrimage.

* * *

Mid-morning in Derry and the vast, exalted throngs of Apprentice Boys had invested the city with all the trappings of their fervour. Everywhere there were banners, drums, fifes. The drummers laid down a hard, insistent beat that spread galvanically through the waiting crowds. It was customary for the men with the lambeg drums to show their fervour by beating them with their bare knuckles until the blood poured, but the time for that was not yet. Now they just stood there, the massive drums thrusting out from their chests while they beat them with their rattan canes. The sounds clashed and merged in the morning air as the bands of various clubs played differing tunes. Some of them were flute bands and some of them were pipe bands. Children, faces sticky with sweets and lollipops, wandered near them and women, faces flushed and eager, looked approvingly at their men. Near together the skirl of the pipes tended to drown the sweetness of the fifes, but it did not matter to anyone there. The whole, shapeless mass of sound was a paean to the traditions of the old city, a vast shout of jubilation that had about it the echo of a conquering army exulting over a vanquished city.

There were police out in force this day, but they were mainly concentrated in the Guildhall Square and at the main entrance to the Bogside. From behind half-completed or half-demolished barricades the Bogsiders looked out truculently. They had heard the music and they had recognized the note of a conquering army. Into the city had come thousands of Apprentice Boys and as they prepared to parade around the walls the colours of their banners mixed and mingled, startling as a kaleidoscope under the hard white light. If they were affirming their own beliefs they were also challenging the beliefs of others.

Eventually the parade started. They went up on to the walls, shambling along behind the shrieking arrogance of the pipes, lumbering and amorphous. As they went along the walls they looked down and saw the upturned faces of the Bogsiders. Somebody threw a penny down to them and others joined in. A hail of pennies showered down and a woman, peering over one of the turrets of the wall, said: 'Look at them down there. Look at them asking for it.'

There were some more of the sort of incantations which

the Scotsmen had been singing on the wharf at Belfast that morning, but at this stage the hostility was purely vocal. As the Protestants sang their songs the Catholics countered with hymns.

It was three o'clock in the afternoon when the parade came marching past Waterloo Place. This, people had been saying for weeks, was where the trouble would happen. A sullen, hissing crowd of Catholics had gathered here and as the Apprentice Boys approached backs were consciously straightened and heads lifted. The men with the bands found a new spring in their step and the pipes blared more loudly than before.

There was a heavy concentration of police here. They had built barricades and they stood behind them wearing riot helmets and carrying shields and batons. Most of them had piles of stones at their feet. An army of journalists and television cameramen watched them, but they did not move.

On the line of march the Apprentice Boys had broken into this most potent hymn:

> We'll fight but not surrender,
> We'll come when duty calls,
> With heart and hand and sword and shield,
> We'll guard old Derry walls.

On the other side of the road the Catholics took up the vocal challenge. Words floated through the air and were drowned as both sides tried to out-sing the other.

> Faith of our fathers living still in spite of dungeon, fire and sword.

The police had batons and shields, the Catholics sticks and petrol bombs.

The first fusillade of stones went sailing across from the Bogside, raining down on the ranks of the police and the Apprentice Boys. The march stopped and men began to push

88

in towards the Bogside. More stones came over and there were roars of anger and hate as the Apprentice Boys moved irresistibly forward, driving the police before them. More stones from the Bogside, cut heads and minor bruises. Then some of the Protestants found stones and started throwing them.

The television cameramen sighed, picked up their cameras and moved in for their pictures.

11

This was a city stripped for action; an angry city in which the grumbling discontent had gone on too long. It was on this day that the Bogside changed from a festering slum, dwarfed by the walls of the city, into being a state of mind. It was a confused and bloody state of mind—a siege mentality. For the Bogsiders the enemy was at the gate, and his admission could only be followed by a fearful wave of looting, arson and rape. They came tumbling out of their little houses to repel him.

It was a throwback to the days of the tribal hordes who had ravaged the country in the long-dead days of the Celtic twilight, and it should not have been happening in the twentieth century. But as the Apprentice Boys, their banners and their martial clangour infusing the air with a confident menace, came pouring into Waterloo Square, old memories stirred and revived.

They looked like an invading horde and in response the primeval urge to guard home, wife and family passed among the men of the Bogside and drew them onto the streets to battle away.

In Waterloo Place a strange situation had developed. The police, after a mild initial onslaught, were now standing their ground, apparently content merely to guard themselves against the hail of missiles. Although most of them had small piles of stones at their feet they were not returning the fire. Behind them the thronging Apprentice Boys kept up a continual jostling as they tried to move the police forward, but the police were adamant. They were not going to attack.

The hail of stones came on in unabating intensity, but the police stood their ground and watched impassively as some of their colleagues were injured and carried off to hospital.

Off to their left, along the unlovely stretch of Waterloo Street, the word had been passed for houses to be evacuated. Straggling groups of women and children, each of them clutching small bundles of possessions, scuttled along the street to dig themselves deeper into the Bogside, like animals making for their lair.

Men who had suddenly taken on the official role of stewards pointed the way for them. Behind the lines the tactical centre of Free Derry was fully operational, dealing with the rash of new and unexpected problems that had arisen now that the fight was finally on. Bartley Mulholland saw the women go from the spot where he stood hurling stones, making a furious pace for those around him to follow. He let the stone he had in his hand go and watched to see if it had found a mark, then turned and walked after the women.

Derry on this day was a cosmopolitan place. For some days small groups of outsiders had been arriving in the city. Many of them were students from Europe, but there were Englishmen and Americans, some of them black Americans, too. Of those he had seen Mulholland placed most value on the French students. They had been at the barricades in Paris when the coalition between the students and workers almost tumbled President de Gaulle from office. What Bogside needed was men who knew about barricades and street fighting techniques.

At this moment they were working in the streets, directing the efforts of the men who were putting up barricades. Flagstones were being torn from the ground, telegraph poles pulled down and wooden rafters and other heavy pieces of timber forced into position. Mulholland grinned, thinking that French intellect and Irish brawn made a great combination.

A man wearing a construction worker's yellow helmet passed him. The man was running up the middle of the road pushing a wheelbarrow full of milk bottles. Further down the road another man was swinging at a petrol pump with a pick-axe. As he did so another was already attaching a sign to a small shop. The sign said 'Munitions factory' and men were already going in and out of it carrying jerricans. A guard who stood outside was holding a small transistor radio to his ear. As Mulholland passed he grinned: 'We're on the air, Bartley.'

'Good work. That's good work.'

The man said nothing, concentrating on his radio. He was listening to Radio Free Derry, the station that had been set up to service the Bogsiders. It was being operated from a house on the way to Creggan and Irish nationalist songs were interspersed with news flashes and exclamatory talks.

Mulholland walked around the Bogside, seeing the panic, the anger and the determination upon the people's faces. He felt a deep satisfaction.

A group of Bogsiders had been sent to Sackville Street to attack the parade on another front. This had not been one of the obvious trouble spots, so there were no television cameras and no reporters. Instead there was just savagery. There was a pitched battle going on between the police, reinforced by civilians, and the Bogsiders. Both sides were throwing stones and at several points along the line hand-to-hand battles were going on. Cudgels, batons and axe handles flashed in the waning sunlight and men slid to the ground, blood pumping out of their heads. As Mulholland watched, the first petrol bomb appeared. It was thrown by a Bogsider and it landed in the middle of the police. Another followed and burst against a policeman's chest. Flames licked up around his body, searing his face and he let out a soundless scream as he put up his hands to protect his eyes. There must have been detergent in the petrol. With detergent the petrol sticks better and the flames burn more deeply. Somebody caught the policeman by the legs and hurled him to the ground. Then they rolled him on to his stomach, dragging him on the road, trying to put out the flames. Another man came through the crowd with a bucket of water. They rolled the policeman over again and he threw the water over him. The flame quivered and died, but then picked up again farther down his body.

Back at Waterloo Place the one-way battle was still going on. The police looked drawn, nervous, but they were not attacking. The battle had been raging for two hours now and there were fewer policemen than there had been and suddenly their resolution cracked. One of them bent down and picked up a stone.

'Give it to the Fenian bastards, boys,' he shouted.

He threw the stone and it hit one of the Bogsiders. The policemen lost weariness as they realized that the time of waiting was over. They had had enough, and the promise of action rejuvenated them. Now it was a two-way barrage of stones and the Bogsiders, caught without protection, wilted and drew back slightly until fear stopped them. Over to the left a group of men started to use the petrol bombs which had been held in reserve for a police attack. The police turned to deal with this new menace and as they did so the stone-throwers moved up on their flank and pelted them with large chunks of concrete.

Pogue Mahone was among them and Mulholland gestured to him. He came across, looking hot and dusty. 'Jesus, Bartley, we're giving it to them.'

'You are that, Pogue.'

'I got one of them. Split his head from arsehole to breakfast time.'

'Good on you, man. Now look, it's time we altered tactics a bit. We've got them baffled, now's the time to really get stuck in.'

'Jesus, I think we are stuck in.'

'Pogue, pass the word for the boys to fall back. Tell them to get behind the first barricade. Get them back.'

He watched while Pogue went back among the stone-throwers, passing the word among them. The stone throwing went on, but little by little the Bogsiders retreated to a position behind the first barricade. As they filed round the sides some men got on top of the barricade to make sure that there was no loss of fire power.

Beyond the barricade a crowd of women waited with flasks of tea and coffee and sandwiches. Some of the men took them but others, their stomachs knotted with excitement, refused. The women entreated them until they took a sandwich. Mulholland, watching them, thought that no matter what, women still retain their deep, commonplace sense of what is important.

Up at the front, by the barricade, a young man with flowing hair and a wild black beard said to Pogue Mahone: 'The flics. They have had enough.'

Pogue did not know what flics were, but he guessed the man's meaning. 'The dirty bastards,' he said. Then to the police: 'Come on you dirty bastards. You can kiss my arse. Come on.'

Behind him other men took up the chant, adding their own insults until the waves of vilification swept over the waiting police, inflaming their anger until only a slender thread of discipline held them in place. The thread broke as night fell. With a massive roar the policemen charged forward, beating on their riot shields with their batons so that the sound resembled the noise of distant cannons. They took the first barricade easily but then, with their impetus spent, they were a target for the stones and petrol bombs of the Bogsiders. These came in torrents and for a while the police were forced on to the defensive. Even so, the crowds of civilians behind them pushed forward and suddenly the police were in control of William Street and several little streets leading off it.

It was time for the police to re-group, and as the Bogsiders retreated along Rossville Street the police stopped. Strategically the advance had meant nothing, for they had not yet entered the Bogside and to do so they would have to push into Rossville Street. Behind the police the civilians were surging forward. Trapped between them and the Bogsiders, the police turned on the Protestants and tried to push them back, but in vain.

Propelled by the weight behind them the police started to advance down Rossville Street and as they did so the Bogsiders came forward to meet them.

The two forces came together in a tangle of hate and a scream of pain. There were the axe handles, the batons and cudgels again. And this time, gunfire. One of the Bogsiders dropped to his knees, clutching at his face as a bullet went through his mouth, another spun round in the act of throwing a stone as he was shot in the shoulder.

Tough and determined, the police now cut a swathe through the Bogsiders. There was no shouting or chanting. Instead men reserved all their energies for attacking the enemy. Remorselessly the Bogsiders were driven back down half the length of Rossville Street by a precise, efficient foe that batoned and bludgeoned with deadly indiscrimination.

Behind the police the civilians were running riot. The sounds of battle were punctuated by the sharp crack of glass as windows in both houses and shops were smashed in by the advancing horde.

Beaten and battered by the ferocity of the police onslaught, the Bogsiders scampered behind a barricade where reinforcements awaited them with a plentiful supply of stones and petrol bombs. As they retreated the police came heavily behind them, batoning stragglers into the ground. At the barricade they were met by a hail of stones which momentarily took the edge off their attack.

A squad of petrol bombers moved forward and began to lob their missiles over the barricades into the closely-packed police ranks. There were cheers as several policemen caught fire, and as the police milled about in confusion, the Bogsiders leapt back over the barricades to attack them.

This time it was the police who retreated. Some of them were wounded and some had lost the protective headgear and shields they had been carrying. Ruthlessly, the Bogsiders smashed into them. One man was wielding a piece of jagged pavement stone. Working with a machine-like precision he smashed it into the faces of the policemen. The collective violence was too much for the police vanguard. They turned and started trying to make their way back to safety through their own ranks and as panic spread among them the whole force turned and rushed for the safety of the area outside Bogside.

Jubilation spread among the Bogsiders as the police fled, but there was little time for jubilation among the serious-faced group of men who hurried to repair barricades at the top of Rossville Street.

It was a moment of intense joy for Mulholland. He had been one of those attacked some months previously when a squad of drunken RUC men had stormed into the Bogside in the early hours of the morning to beat up anyone they could find. They had smashed in front doors and beaten people as they lay in bed, and there had been little reason for it save the support which Bogside gave to the Civil Rights movement.

It was something which the Bogside had neither forgotten nor forgiven. Now, this was their revenge.

Mulholland walked down the street and turned into a bar. Inside there were a group of men who had been in the fighting. Among them was Larry the Yank and a couple of French students. Mulholland joined them and called for a drink.

'It's going well,' he said.

'Yeah.' The American was laconic.

'Believe me, boy, we've got the bastards on the run now. They're on the run this time.'

Larry frowned. 'That could be a mistake. You don't want anything too decisive—on our side anyway.'

Mulholland grinned: 'Don't worry, boy. They'll be back, but there's no harm in savouring the taste of victory between times.'

'Yeah, okay. But don't forget we've got to get on with it.'

Mulholland nodded: 'I know. I have it firmly in mind. The next thing is to get out of the Bogside and start a few shenanigans in their territory. Christ knows, they've done enough here.'

The battling went on throughout the evening and into the early morning. Occasionally the police would make a charge along Rossville Street, but each time the waiting Bogsiders managed to force them back. The name 'Free Derry' took on a concrete meaning for the men behind the barricades, for whatever else it was it was certainly free of policemen.

After midnight one of the vigilante patrols reported unusual activity in the area of Little James Street. A crowd of men had massed on the border of the street and they were taunting the police. The word spread around Bogside, and soon many more people had arrived.

The police by this time were weary—weary but vengeful. The Bogsiders had the stimulus of achievement to keep them awake. It was a night on which nobody wanted to go to bed and it was not long before the taunting had turned to stone-throwing. Suddenly, like water pouring through a breached dam, the Bogsiders had fought their way into Little James Street, driving the police before them. As they went some threw petrol bombs into shops and houses until the street was ablaze. Elated by the ease with which they had entered the street, the Bogsiders thrust on. A few hundred yards away lay the commercial heart of the city, but as they pushed forward the police ranks opened and a new factor intervened.

It was more policemen, but now they were wearing gas masks and in their hands they carried gas grenade launchers. The horde stopped, mutely amazed by this new phenomenon, and as they did so the police fired their first salvo of CS gas.

It ripped into the crowd, choking, blinding, stealing their breath and searing their lungs. The Bogsiders turned and ran. As they did so the wind caught the gas and sent it drifting in slow pursuit.

'Christ,' Mulholland gasped, 'Christ almighty, they've really done it.'

Larry the Yank was with him. He had a wet handkerchief

97

wrapped around his face. He looked around to where the television handlights were starting to come on. He nodded to the television crews as they turned their cameras on the scene.

'That does it,' he said. 'Come on, Bartley, we can go take a sleep.'

12

The taxi had pulled away from Speke Airport and was moving swiftly through the red brick outskirts of Liverpool before Nealis realized he was still sitting with his overnight bag on his lap, his fingers tight around the carrying straps and that his stomach muscles were aching from sitting on the edge of the seat. He forced himself back onto the seat cushions and let the bag down to the floor. His hand went unconsciously to the packet of cigarettes in his pocket and he noticed there were only eight left. Twelve since buying his ticket and his throat was sore, but he lit another one anyway. He felt a kind of dread at the thought of meeting her again. There would only be more acrimony, more verbal teeth and claws with which to lacerate each other. It had been like that for a long time but he couldn't remember how long ago it had started. Maybe it hadn't even started, just developed, a cancer which had gradually gnawed away the flesh of their relationship until it was reduced to the bone, to the reality of a ghastly mistake.

He stared from the window without really seeing anything. His mind was filled with a million thoughts, but he couldn't put them in any kind of order: they merely constituted a dull ache at the back of his eyes.

The lights were on in the lounge when the taxi dropped him outside the house and he thought he saw the merest flicker of the curtains. There was a heavy scent of roses and halfway up the short path, he stopped to inhale the perfume. He had planted the roses himself in a rare moment of green-fingered domesticity but had never been there to appreciate them.

99

She opened the door within seconds of his ring and stood elegantly poised, wearing a black catsuit with her black hair pulled tightly back into a pony tail in the way he had always preferred it. She regarded him without expression for some seconds, then turned and walked down the carpeted hall, leaving him to walk in and close the door. He followed her into the lounge. It was still the same, if a little more tidy than when he had lived there. Black leather furniture, coffee tables, flowers in rough pottery vases. He had sweated to pay for them all. And drinks on a trolley. He still paid for them.

'You're late,' she began. 'I thought you might have come last night. You got my telegram?'

'Yes. I got it this morning.'

'Drink?' She had walked to the trolley and now stood with a half-bottle of gin over two glasses. He nodded and she poured two small gin-and-tonics. She handed him one, took the other and sat down.

'You still live well,' he observed, raising his glass and drinking.

'You think so?'

It was the beginning, but he wasn't ready for it yet and he sidestepped the argument with a shrug and a change of course.

'How have you been?' he asked.

'As well as can be expected, I suppose. It hasn't been fun.'

'No, I suppose not.'

'You got my telegram?'

'You already asked me. Yes, I got it.' He fished it from his pocket and dropped it on the coffee table. 'It doesn't say much.'

'I should have thought it said everything,' she replied. 'I told you I want a divorce. You can't say much more than that about a marriage, can you?'

'Perhaps not. Although I think I could write a book about it.'

'It would make pretty crummy reading.' She stared at the floor in the silence which followed, while Nealis sat down on a straight-backed chair by the window.

'I shouldn't think you were surprised, were you?' she asked.

'No, not surprised, just ... oh, well.' He drank from his glass and let the tonic wash over his teeth and prickle his tongue. 'It's a miserable business, isn't it?'

'It's been a miserable business for me, Michael. It has been for years, and I'm not prepared to go on being tied to you. I know you've always avoided the idea, but you'd better brace up. It's finished and I want a divorce. I don't care how we do it, either. I just want it—and soon.'

'All right, all right. It's finished. You don't have to start getting bitter again.'

'Bitter?' She flared, and Nealis knew he had said the wrong thing, made the same tactless mistake as ever. 'Bitter? My God, Michael, don't you think I have enough to be bitter about? You don't have any idea, do you? I used to sit alone in this house waiting for you to come home and you'd turn up in the middle of the night and then expect me to leap all over you because you were the wonder boy of the force. I wanted a marriage, Michael, not a bit part in bloody Z Cars.'

'You knew what I was when you married me,' Nealis retorted. 'You knew all about it and you know as well as I do now that the reason I flogged myself to death was to get promotion so that there'd be plenty more money and the reason I wanted more money was to give you a good home and all the things you wanted in it. My God, Betty, if we're going to rake up all the old ground, let's get our facts straight. You're a copper's wife—*were* a copper's wife if you like. You thought that was fine, didn't you, until you realized there was more to it than free tickets to the pictures?'

'My mistake was in thinking there was more to you,' she said savagely. 'When I married you, I believed all you told me, about the life we could have and how marvellous it was for you to have a woman behind you. But you didn't need a woman, you needed a housemaid!'

'I did not,' Nealis said quietly. 'I can't tell you what I wanted, but I knew I hadn't got it within a few months of marrying you, Betty. Oh, I'm not blaming you for that. It's just that we had different ideas about what a marriage should be. I guess I wanted someone who would take account of all the faults I have and still ... well, love me. Does that sound foolish? If it does, then I'm foolish.' He shrugged and went across to the trolley and poured himself another drink.

'We've said it all, many times,' Betty said. 'And it doesn't make the slightest difference, does it? Look, you're you and I'm me, and the truth of the matter is that we should have run a mile from each other when we first met, instead of doing what we did.'

'So now we get a divorce.'

'So now we get a divorce.'

'Bloody marvellous.'

'Yes,' she said crisply. 'As a matter of fact, I think it will be.'

'I didn't mean it like that.'

'However you meant it, you're right. It will be bloody marvellous. At least there'll be an end to all this. And perhaps there'll be an end to living alone. I've lived alone, to all intents and purposes, ever since we were married. Seven years of waiting for you and watching television. Good God, there must be something better in life than that.'

'I didn't get the impression you were alone the other night when I phoned,' Nealis said. 'Or was that the television repair man I heard?'

'Funny,' she said sarcastically. 'Very funny. It just so happens that I've grown tired of playing the hermit. I waited for you for years. I used to worry about you and cry on my pillow until I realized you didn't give a damn about anything except your rotten job.'

'That's not true.'

'Isn't it? Well it seemed like it to me, and that makes it true. Anyway, I'm not waiting any longer. I want a divorce and that's it.'

'So you'll rush off and marry some other poor Joe? Well, by God, I wish him luck, because he's going to need it. Christ knows, I tried with you, Betty. I tried hard to give you all the things you consider vital to life. You wanted the best, so I worked my guts out trying to give them to you. But that wasn't enough, was it? You wanted status. And that's where our particular little story starts and ends, doesn't it? You wanted to be a lady of leisure and I'm only a copper. That used to stick in your throat when you had to say it, didn't it? All right, go ahead, we'll have a divorce and you can start all over again. The only thing that won't change is you. You'll still be what you always were, Betty, a spoiled, self-indulgent brat!'

'Oh, go and play your violin somewhere else. What makes you think you're so wonderful?'

'It's for sure you don't,' Nealis said. 'But look, all this is pointless, isn't it? We've made a bloody mess and all we're doing is tramping about in the mess and picking up bits to throw at each other. It's done, it's finished. Let's leave it like that and get on with the business. I take it you'll be going for cruelty or something. There isn't much else.'

'I'm told that will do.'

'And then you'll be off to the altar in a flash, eh? Who's the bridegroom?'

'It doesn't matter.'

'No. All that matters is that I was cruel to you, right?'

'I suppose so.'

'Do you love this other fellow?'

'Yes.'

'Slept with him, have you?'

'Stop playing detective, Michael. It's nothing to do with you any more.'

Nealis smiled wryly. 'Yes, I guess that about sums it all up.' He paused. 'I'd like another drink. May I? Will you join me?'

'Why not?'

He poured two more glasses of gin. 'I wasn't playing the

103

detective, you know. Just curious. Do you mind if I ask you something?'

'Go ahead.'

'Did you ever sleep with anyone else—while we were together, I mean?'

'Once,' Betty said. She sat looking at the glow of the electric fire, without moving. Nealis knew now that it was utterly and completely over. He had asked her the question simply to satisfy himself that he had been right. He had known she had. It had been during the Straker murder case. There had been no reason for him to suspect her and she had never given him the slightest reason to think she had done it. But he had known, and it had changed him. He had loved her until then, even amid the furious arguments, but the betrayal had taken something out of him which he had never been able to replace with all the work and the study that he had crammed into the breach.

But she had never admitted it. Until now. And in a curious retrospective way, it hurt him more. He realized, as he looked at his wife, that it had all been a colossal, monumental waste.

'I'm away, then,' he said at last.

'Yes.'

Nealis walked to the door and opened it, walked out and slammed it behind him. Opposite the house he saw a car parked, with sidelights on. In the faint glow of the dashboard light, he could see someone sitting alone at the wheel. He walked past, to the corner of the road and then he heard the car door slam softly. He looked back towards the house. Betty had drawn the curtains back slightly and was standing in the window. A few seconds later, the front door opened. Nealis turned away and walked on. For her, at least, the new life had begun.

* * *

The following morning, Nealis awoke with a familiar feeling of doom. Indecisively, he clambered from his single bed and lit the first cigarette of the day and put the kettle on the little gas cooker and waited for it to boil. The cup of black instant coffee tasted terrible, but he drank it, more as an excuse to kill time while he tried, and failed, to make his brain throw up the right answers to countless questions. Eventually, he washed and shaved, dressed and walked out of the room.

He walked into the city, deliberately avoiding the old haunts, the professional places and familiar faces, wanting only to be alone and anonymous. He found a pub down by the docks and stayed there until closing time, moving on to a nearby drinking club. He had raided the place frequently years ago, but it had survived and prospered. They knew him in there and accepted him without malice and, more important, without question.

Slowly, as the empty day spun out, Nealis's mind became anaesthetized. There were drinks and glasses and barmen and mirrors and bogs and men and women, all in a hazy kaleidoscope. By seven in the evening the sleazy nightlife of the port of Liverpool began to brace itself for another round of tawdry excitement, and Nealis was sitting in a club where the music beat at his brains. The thoughts he had tried all day to put away from him finally would not be dismissed. Nealis hauled himself to his feet and reeled out of the club into the street. He fancied he could smell the salt in the air. He knew he wasn't far from the docks. His face was sweating and he felt hot and cold, but he broke into a trot until he came to the yellow sodium lights of a familiar main street and turned towards the dock entrance. He caught a glimpse of a clock, already illuminated in the dusk. The hands pointed to eight-twenty-five. There was time enough for the night boat.

Ten minutes later he walked onto the Irish ferry and turned to lean on the guard rail, panting and slightly dizzy, but at the same time bursting with a kind of unfocussed triumph.

He remained there, staring at the great gloomy edifice of Liverpool while the ship eased herself gradually from her berth and began to vibrate.

The last wire holding her to the dockside was thrown off and the ship moved free.

*   *   *

Nealis arrived back to a Derry that was choking and red-eyed from CS gas. On the first night of the fighting the city had gained the distinction of being the first spot in the British Isles to have chemical gas used against the civilian population. The gas had drifted over Bogside in a thick cloud, indiscriminately attacking the children who lay abed and the warriors who manned the barricades. Vinegar-soaked handkerchiefs were put into widespread use, but they gave little relief. Bernadette Devlin, whom some saw as a reincarnation of Joan of Arc and others as the personification of evil, appealed from the barricades to the Southern Irish government for gas masks, but they were not forthcoming.

The main road into the Bogside was thick with police, tired men who had been besieging an unrelenting and merciless foe for a night and a day now. They were unshaven and without sleep, their uniforms stained and torn, their movements jerky and unco-ordinated. Nealis filtered around them and detoured through the wandering crowds before making his approach from the peaceful end of Bogside. He was stopped at a barricade as he made his way towards the bottom of Westland Street.

There were half a dozen vigilantes around the barricade. One of them, a tall man who carried a cudgel in his right hand asked: 'Who are you?'

'Nealis, Michael Nealis.'

'Oh yes, have you a brother?'

'Frank, that's my brother. And a mother. Kathleen Nealis. She's in the Knights of Malta hospital.'

The man looked in a small red book which he produced. 'Where have you been?'

'I had to go up to Belfast.' Nealis did not feel inclined to go into explanations.

'Have you come back to help? We need men.' The questioner turned a searching gaze on him. 'There's a lot of work to be done in here. Maybe some fighting. Are you able for that?'

'I want to see my mother. She's hurt. I want to see how she is.'

'Aye, that's natural. You'd want to do that. But then? There are a lot of mothers in Bogside. A lot of mothers and women and weans. If you come in here you have to think about everybody.'

'Can I come in?' Nealis said.

The man moved back from the path, unblocking the narrow entry past the barricade. As Nealis stepped through the man nodded at one of the vigilantes.

'You go with him,' he said.

'It's all right. I'll be okay.'

'No doubt, brother. But he goes with you.'

The vigilante fell into step alongside Nealis and they went swinging through the shambles of streets up to where the Knights of Malta had their hospital. At the hospital a doctor, a worried man with grey hair and cigarette ash mantling his waistcoat, told Nealis that there had been no change in Mother Kate's condition. She was still critical, he said.

'Critical?' Nealis felt the flood of adrenalin through his system. 'What do you mean, critical? Let me see her, for Christ's sake.'

'Look, I'm sorry,' the doctor said. 'But it won't do any good. She's unconscious.' He turned to go, but Nealis grabbed his arm. 'Will she be all right?'

The doctor pursed his lips. 'We'll know better when she comes to. Honestly, lad, there's nothing anyone can do just now. Come back if you like, later.'

Nealis nodded, helplessly. He'd come back. Meantime, there was Maire.

From the hospital Nealis, still with his escort, walked down through the tangle of streets to Maire's house. He stood outside it for a time, looking at the door, unconscious of the man who stood at his side ringing the bell.

There was a long wait and then Maire opened the door. She was wearing a long, blue candlewick dressing-gown and she looked tired. She stood staring at him for a moment, puzzled. Then she said: 'You came back?'

He half-smiled, unsure of himself: 'I came back.'

Her eyes took in the vigilante. 'With an escort?'

The atmosphere was easier now. Maire turned to the man. 'Sure you don't have to escort him, Festy. He's all right.'

'Big Doonican said I was to come with him, Miss Dwyer.'

'Ah that Big Doonican, suspicious of everybody ... Well, here we are now. Come in, Michael.' She glanced at the vigilante. 'Do you want to come in too, Festy?' There was a slight hint of derision in her voice.

Festy looked about him, awkwardness in every movement. 'Ah Miss Dwyer, I don't know. I don't know ... if he's a friend of yours, well, that's good enough. That's good enough for me. I'll tell Big Doonican.' He turned and shuffled off.

Inside the door it was dark. The light from the living room threw out a shaft of illumination, but it did not quite reach into the area behind the door and it was dark and secret there. Nealis put his arms around Maire and pushed her up against the wall. The scent from her hair crept into his nostrils and her body moulded against him, warm and gentle.

'Maire,' he said. His fingers swept across her head, caressing the soft hair and bending her head back until he could see her lips, red and ripe and trembling slightly. Her eyes were wide as she looked at him, calm and waiting. As he bent to kiss her she strained against him, communicating with every fibre of her body.

It ended with the kiss and she took his hand and led him into the living room. The television set was flickering in the corner with the sound turned down and a coal fire burned in the grate. She sat on the settee and when he sat beside her she pulled her feet up and nestled against him.

'I'm glad you came back,' she said.

'Do you know why I came back?'

She raised her head from his shoulder and smiled into his face. 'No. Tell me.'

He kissed her again.

For a time they just sat there in silence, unwilling to let anything break the mood they had found, but eventually he asked her: 'How's it been?'

She shrugged: 'As you see. Just as you see. Everybody's doing what they can. I'm doing what I can too.'

'You too? What are you doing?'

She smiled. 'Well now, Mr Nealis, it's meself that's after driving one o' dem ambulance things.' As she said it she mimicked a thick southern Irish dialect.

He was surprised: 'What, up to the Knights of Malta?'

She grinned at him, crinkling her nose, making herself deliberately girlish. 'Ah no, Mr Nealis. Out thonder, down over the border to where the fine white praties grow.' She grew more serious. 'It's something they've got organized to get the men out. Some of them are too bad to be treated by the Knights—they just haven't got the facilities—and if we handed them over to the civil hospitals in Derry, God knows what would happen to them. So we smuggle them out by the back roads and over the border to Dundalk. There's a hospital there where they'll be looked after. Here they'd end up in a prison hospital—or the mortuary.'

'That's a bloody dangerous game. What about the border patrols? Jesus Christ woman, that's a bloody dangerous game.'

She smiled at him again. 'Well Mr Nealis, I'm a bloody dangerous woman. Give me a kiss.'

After a moment she said: 'I wanted to take your mother out, but they wouldn't let her be moved. Poor woman, Michael. She's very sick.'

'I know,' he said.

'Some of the men are talking about getting a safe conduct so that the women and children can be sent up to the city hospital for treatment, but there's a lot against it.'

'You don't think anybody'd harm women and children, do you?' he said. 'No, Christ, these men at the hospital—they're

109

doctors. They've taken an oath to protect life. No, surely ... they're doctors.'

'Well,' she said, 'even that is not enough. Do you think we're going to hand over men who need a few stitches, need them because some RUC thug opened their heads with a baton ... do you think we're going to let the hospitals even have the chance of turning them in?'

'No,' he said, 'I suppose not.'

Maire turned up the sound on the television set when the news came on. For once the opening pictures did not show street fighting. Instead it showed a film of a military convoy on the move while the news reader announced: 'The Southern Irish government are tonight moving military units up to the border with Northern Ireland. The units are to set up field hospitals and emergency housing centres for refugees from the fighting in Northern Ireland, it was announced in Dublin.

'All reservists in the Irish Army have been called up and all leave has been cancelled. At the same time, the Southern Irish government has offered to put its troops into the embattled Bogside area of Londonderry in a peace-keeping role.

'It is believed that the Irish representative at the United Nations in New York is to raise the question of Northern Ireland before the Security Council and call for an intervention by United Nations troops.

'In the Bogside and in other centres throughout Northern Ireland fighting went on today as ...'

The picture changed, showing Bogsiders hurling petrol bombs from the high flats which had become the central part of their defensive system.

Maire rose and switched the television set off. She looked puzzled. 'Does that mean they're going to invade, do you think?'

Nealis shrugged: 'God knows. They'd be fools if they do.'

'But they must mean something?'

'Maybe.' Nealis turned it over in his mind, trying to make sense of it. He knew there were only eight and a half thousand men in the Irish Army. There were as many B-Specials in Ulster as that. Exactly as many. Add the RUC to the B-Specials and the Irish Army was outnumbered, even if some of its troops had not already been committed in Cyprus.

In any case, did they have the guts for a quick, pre-emptive strike? A headlong rush across the border with tanks—if they had any—and artillery might give them Derry, Belfast and a few other key towns before any effective opposition could be organized. The southern Irish were notoriously mad —but were they mad enough for this?

Then too, if they invaded Northern Ireland they invaded British sovereign territory and that would bring the British Army into the game. As a former soldier of the British Crown, Nealis had a well-developed respect for the Crown's Army. It would be an unequal contest in which the Irish Army would be crushed with a dreadful certainty.

'Maybe they're just doing what they say—setting up hospitals and refugee camps,' he said.

Maire's eyes were shining with excitement. 'But if they came in wouldn't that force the United Nations' hand? There'd be a dispute between two member nations—England and Ireland—and they'd have to send security forces in to keep the peace.'

'It could be that,' he said, 'but the Irish Army will have to be prepared for a hell of a defeat if that's what they want to do. I've been in the British Army, and I'm telling you the lads from the South wouldn't stand a chance against them.'

She looked ready to argue, but bit back the temptation. 'Well now, aren't you the great little Jingo?'

'Balls,' he said smiling. 'I'm just telling you.'

After a while Maire announced that she had to go out to the headquarters. Nealis walked with her. At the headquarters a man gave him a document identifying him as a person authorized to be in the Bogside area. The document was signed on behalf of the Derry Citizens' Defence Committee.

Maire, who had been chatting with a group of men and women drinking tea in a room behind the office, came back.

'It looks as though I'm going to find out about those Free State units,' she said.

'Oh, how?'

'I've got an ambulance drive to do tonight.'

'Where to?'

'We're not sure yet, but we believe the nearest field hospital has been set up at Buncrana.' Buncrana is a small seaside town, about eight miles away and across the border from Derry.

'Is it a proper ambulance?'

'No. It's a Ford Transit belonging to one of the local shoe-makers. If you put mattresses inside you can carry four lying down passengers. If they can sit you'll get a lot more in.'

'Fine, but what about the border patrols?'

'The way I go you don't see any border guards.'

Nealis turned away from her and walked over to the man at the desk. 'Are you still looking for men?' he asked.

'Indeed we are,' the man said.

'Put me down as an ambulance driver, then.'

'Are you a good driver?'

'I'm a very good driver.'

'Okay, but I'm not sure when we'll have a run for you.'

'That's all right, I've got my run. I'll go with Maire and give her a hand.'

The man looked up and grinned. 'Jesus, that's not a bad idea. If I was a few years younger I'd do the same myself.'

13

Nealis pulled the truck onto the grass verge beside the narrow road just on the crest of the hill. He felt for the light switch in the unfamiliar dashboard layout and doused the side-lights. In the total silence of the starlit night, he could hear the breathing of the four people in the back. He listened for a moment more and concluded they must be asleep, then slipped from the cab and stretched himself, standing in the roadway.

'Michael?' Maire's voice was a whisper, but even at that level, he could detect the element of alarm.

'It's all right,' he whispered back through the open sliding door of the driving cab. 'Everything's all right.'

In truth, he was dying for a piss and his eyes ached and he felt abominably tired. It must be almost three, he thought, as he relieved himself at the roadside, and the fact of not having been to bed for thirty-six hours was making driving at night an unwelcome strain. When he returned to the cab, Maire was sitting in the passenger seat. 'Where are we?' she asked softly.

'God knows,' Nealis said. 'Whoever marked this bloody map must have been as drunk as a fiddler's bitch.' In the darkness, he heard Maire giggle. 'Take a look at this,' he went on, fishing for the map and torch beneath the seat. 'Half the time the route goes across fields.'

He spread out the map and lit the torch. She leaned across to him and her hair brushed his cheek. 'We're somewhere about here. We left this village—Buncraig—about three miles back and I think we're on this road which joins the main road about two miles from the border. I think we ought to press on this way. don't you?'

'What about the police? They're watching the main roads.'

'Are they there all the time?'

'I was never stopped,' Maire said. 'But I stuck to the back roads. One of the others was stopped last night, they say, and all the people in it were arrested and driven back to Derry.'

'Hmmm. Well, let's take the risk. How are the patients?'

'Asleep.'

'OK, we'll get moving.' Nealis started the truck and pulled onto the road. There were four wounded men in the back. Three had burns and another a gunshot wound in the leg. Any policeman in the world would ask a hell of a lot of questions of anyone driving that kind of cargo in the middle of the night. And with the B-Specials it might not stop at questions.

Nealis rubbed his eyes as he drove, keeping his speed well down until the junction with the main road. Once on the highway, he turned left and stabbed his foot down on the accelerator. The truck surged forward, its headlights gobbling up the twinkling cats-eyes in its blunt snout. As it cruised Nealis felt himself nodding, having to make an enormous effort of will to keep his eyes open and the wheels of the vehicle astride the centre line.

They had travelled for some miles when Nealis saw the border post. At the same time, he felt Maire's hand tighten on his arm. He braked as smoothly as he could to avoid disturbing the injured men in the back and stopped about five hundred yards from the border. There were floodlights rigged up over the road and he could clearly see half a dozen B-Specials armed with rifles tumbling out of the tiny customs building and stringing across the road to await the truck. There was a car parked at the side of the road and as he pulled up, Nealis saw the rear lights of the car dim briefly. He guessed the driver had started the engine.

The policemen remained motionless, staring down the road

at the truck. The car had not yet moved.

Nealis watched. Stopping the truck had compounded the mistake of taking the main road, he knew that. If he had been on that border patrol, *he* would have been suspicious.

'What are we going to do?' Maire whispered.

'Get the hell out of it,' Nealis said quickly. He rammed the gearstick into first and hauled the wheel round. One of the men in the back let out a muffled cry of pain as Nealis executed a tight three-point turn. Completing it, Nealis saw the police car at the border post making a similar manœuvre. As he accelerated, he could see its headlights flashing. He calculated he had half a mile start on the pursuing car. Not much on an open main road. 'Watch out for a turning,' he said, but Maire had already climbed into the back of the truck where one of the injured men was now moaning in agony. The headlights in the driving mirror vanished as he pulled round a curve. Nealis strained his eyes, leaning forward over the steering wheel, searching for a turn-off along the straight section of the road but he could find nothing before the headlights behind him emerged from the bend and lit up the driving cab in their reflection. There was another, tighter bend in the road and Nealis took it flat out, feeling the truck lurch dangerously to the nearside when he forced it across the highway to take the corner.

'What the bloody hell you think you're doing?' A man had hauled himself to the back of the passenger seat and was tugging at Nealis's shoulder.

'Fuck off!' Nealis roared. The truck was on an even keel and once more the headlights of the police car had vanished. From the corner of his eye, Nealis saw a signpost flash by at the roadside. He swore again. He had almost missed it. The other man had broken his concentration, and now there was hardly time for thinking. The break in the grass verge to his left was barely fifty yards away.

'Hold on!' As he yelled the warning, Nealis stamped on the brakes, swung right and then hard left to send the truck careering into the left-hand turning. The road was heavily wooded on either side. Nealis glimpsed a track leading into the trees to the right. He jabbed his hand at the light switch and thankfully hit it first time, driving blindly into the track, using the handbrake to bring the vehicle to a slithering halt in the mud, and cutting the engine simultaneously. At the same moment, the ball of light from the police car headlights drifted past the trees on the main road.

From the back of the truck, Nealis could hear moaning and cursing. The man who had been beside him now lay motionless. Nealis leaned across and shook him. He stirred and sat up.

'You're a bloody lunatic!' he rasped, nursing a bandaged arm. 'We'll all be at the fucking graveyard before we get to hospital.'

'I think jail is the top of the betting right now,' Nealis said. 'That was a police car chasing us. If they'd have found you lot, you'd have been inside before your feet touched the ground. Now shut up and let's get out of this place or they'll be back.' He leaned over the back of the driving seat. 'How you doing, Maire? All in one piece?'

'More or less,' Maire said in the darkness. 'This man is in pain, though.'

Nealis did not reply. He listened for a moment for the sound of the police car returning, but there was only silence. Dumb cops? He smiled to himself. It had been exciting, exhilarating, to be on the other side of the line for a while and he felt buoyant, careless, almost intoxicated.

But there was still the journey to complete. He backed carefully out of the track and onto the road. Heading away from the main road, he navigated by instinct, using lights only when absolutely necessary until he felt it safe to stop and study the map. It was little help. 'Anyone know where we are?' he asked in the general direction of the rear.

'I do.' The man beside him spoke for the first time since they had left the wood.

Nealis looked across at him. 'Well, why the hell didn't you say so? I've been buggering about for half an hour trying to find the road to the border, haven't I?'

'You never asked.'

It was so absurd, Nealis began to laugh and then the other man chuckled. 'Sure, it's no joke really,' the other man said at last. 'Here's me with my arm in a sling and three others back there who's no more than walking wounded. Let's get across the border and get me fixed up. I've to get back to Derry to knock shit out of a few more bloody Protestants yet. But you're doing fine. Keep down this road and I'll tell you when to turn.'

While Nealis followed his directions, the other man broke into an old rebel song. It was picked up by the others in the back and Nealis heard Maire's voice joining in. It was one of the songs Me Da' used to sing when he came home on a Friday night and the sound of it took Nealis back across the years of his manhood to those old days. And to Mother Kate, and the smile on his face faded. We'll fight for freedom, the song said, but it wasn't a maudlin melody any more. The fighting was a fact and the blood was real.

They crossed the border by a series of tiny roads and were in the Free State before Nealis realized it. Soon, they came to Dundalk where the signposts pointed the way to the Irish Army first-aid post. Nealis stopped the truck in front of a floodlit marquee and was greeted by an Irish Army Medical Corps captain who briskly supervised the unloading of the injured men and saw them into the tent. Nealis sat down on the running board of the truck and waited for Maire, who had accompanied the men into the treatment centre.

'Cuppa tay?' Nealis looked up to see a soldier grinning cheerfully down at him with a steaming tin mug in his hand. Funny how old-fashioned they looked in the outmoded peaked caps, Nealis thought. He took the mug and pulled a packet of cigarettes from the pocket of his windcheater. The soldier accepted one, and sat down on the running board alongside Nealis.

'How's things over there?' he asked, taking a light from Nealis.

'Pretty bloody.'

'Aye,' the soldier said.

They smoked in silence for a moment.

'You know what we ought to do?' the soldier said suddenly. 'We ought to go in there and sort that place out. We ought to just go in and sort that bloody place out, so we should.'

'You think so?'

'I'd give my arse for the chance. We all thought it was going to happen yesterday with us mobilized and moving up here. We stopped, but we should have kept right on. We'd have been in Derry now and then, by Jesus, we'd have sorted that place out.' The soldier pitched the butt of the cigarette to the ground. 'Going back to Derry, are you?'

'Yes,' said Nealis.

'Well, here's something to take back with you.' He reached into the pocket of his tunic, looked round swiftly, then pushed a heavy round metal object into Nealis's hand. He was up and gone before Nealis could speak. He looked down at the thing in his hand. It was a grenade. Simple men with simple solutions? Nealis stood up and walked beyond the glare of the floodlights and threw the grenade, still with the safety pin intact, into the bushes.

*　　*　　*

On the following two nights, Nealis and Maire made the same journey from Derry to the border, returning in the morning to rest and then prepare for the next trip. Nealis welcomed the para-military order of his life in those days. It excused the need for interpretative thinking and he was merely content to be doing something active and to be with Maire.

Each day, the flow of casualties grew. Maire's house had been turned into a clearing station on the second day of the ambulance runs and she threw herself into the work of organizing, nursing, feeding and transportation, seemingly without rest. Nealis tried in vain to make her sleep more but she would not hear of it, saying she was perfectly capable of staying awake for a week if she had to. Convent training, she said. Meanwhile, outside their part of the world, the battle for Bogside erupted daily, and there was still the week-end to come. The morale of the Bogsiders was extraordinarily high and in the fraternal atmosphere of siege, Bogside became a kind of kibbutz. Radio Free Derry had a listening concentration the BBC would envy, and people avidly read stencilled broadsheets bringing news from the front line a bare five hundred yards away.

* * *

In the early evening of the third day, Nealis found Mulholland waiting for him when he drove the truck to Maire's door to pick up the casualties for that night's run. The big Irishman, unshaven and red-eyed though he was, greeted Nealis as lustily as ever.

'Bejasus, it's good to see you working for your keep,' he roared. 'I heard you been having a bit of fun with some of your friends, eh?' Nealis smiled.

'Aye, you're doing well by us poor freedom fighters.' Mulholland paused, studying Nealis's face closely before continuing. 'But perhaps you'd like a wee change of scenery tonight, eh?'

'What are you getting at?'

'Well now,' Mulholland said. 'There's a small job needs doing tonight. On your way back from the border, that is. A friend of mine and a few bits of his gear.'

'What—'

'It's just a small detour,' Mulholland went on quickly. 'There's a farm near the border, owned by a fella name of McGuinness. This pal of mine, he's waiting there, you know. I said I'd pick him up tonight. Save his poor old feet, you know. You can go on the ambulance run and deliver the patients, come back across the border and slip into McGuinness's farm, pick up me pal and bring him back. Will you do it?'

'I suppose so. Who is this friend of yours?'

'Oh, you'll not know him. Name of Gibson. Look, come in the house and bring your map.'

They went into the house and Nealis spread out the map of the Six Counties while Mulholland pored over it and then marked a cross on the Derry-Donegal border. 'That'll be your place now. Can you be there at three?'

'Sure,' Nealis said. 'You mentioned some gear this man has with him. What kind of gear is it?'

Mulholland shrugged. 'Just some luggage you know. He's come a long way and he'll be staying a bit.'

Nealis nodded.

'I'll get a message to him. Tell him to wait for you about three tomorrow morning. Bring him to the headquarters. I'll be there to greet you with a drop of something. OK?'

He left Nealis looking at the map. Nealis could feel the distant ring of warning bells in his head, the same uneasy feeling as always when he spoke to Mulholland, but he shrugged it off when Maire came into the room to discuss the journey and the cargo. She looked pale and her movements were fractionally slower than usual.

'Why don't you skip tonight's run?' Nealis said gently. 'I'll manage on my own. There's no need for you to come. You'll kill yourself at this pace.'

'I want to come,' Maire said. She took his hand in hers and kissed his fingers quickly. 'It's the only time we have alone together, the journey back.'

'We won't even have that tonight,' Nealis said. 'I told Mulholland I'd pick up one of his chums at a farm near the border.'

'Oh. Well, never mind, but I still want to be with you.'

They loaded the truck and moved away from the house shortly before midnight. By one o'clock, using now familiar roads, they had crossed the border.

An hour later, Nealis and Maire drove back alone across the border but instead of driving east to Derry, turned north towards the cross on the map. Once, Nealis pulled up and leaned from the truck to look back in the direction from which they had come.

'What's the matter?' Maire asked.

'I thought I saw headlights behind me. A long way behind, though.'

'The police?'

'God knows. I suppose there must be other people about besides us and the police. Anyway,' he went on, smiling, 'there's no law yet saying you can't take a pretty girl out for a drive.'

He kissed her longingly, not wanting to stop. But at the back of his mind, the uneasy feeling he had had when speaking to Mulholland kept banging away at him, and he released her.

'Let's get this thing over with,' he said. Another check revealed no light or sound, and he switched on the motor and drove on. They came to a village and Nealis slowed while Maire studied the map. She directed him to a lane turning off the road and from there to a gateway. There, they saw a weather-roughened sign with the name 'McGuinness' just discernible in peeling paint.

'This is the place,' Nealis said. 'Let's pick up our friend and get off home.'

He drove slowly up the rough path, past a Dutch barn, into a yard and stopped in front of a single-storey stone house. There was no sign of life. Nealis, still conscious of his uneasiness, turned the truck around so that it faced the path and the gateway. Then, cautioning Maire to remain in the vehicle, he dropped lightly to the ground and walked to the front door. He knocked softly, waited and then knocked again. From behind the door, he caught the first sound. Someone was on the other side of the door.

'Who's there?' The voice was suspicious.

'I've come from Derry,' Nealis began. 'Mulholland.'

The door opened slowly, but it was dark inside and it was several seconds before Nealis recognized the shape of the gun barrel. The twin muzzles of a shotgun.

'Come inside. Shut the door behind you,' said the voice at

121

the other end of the gun. Nealis did so. Another few seconds, and then a match struck suddenly and Nealis saw a giant of a man holding a shotgun. The match travelled a yard or two and Nealis heard the rattle of an oil lamp followed by the spreading glow of light as the wick ignited. The giant watched him, one fist gripping the gun.

'Are you McGuinness?' Nealis asked.

The other man ignored the question. 'You've got about five minutes to leave this house. I didn't bargain for this. Take your friend and get out.'

'What didn't you bargain for?'

'Him.' McGuinness picked up the lamp with a sweep of his arm and held it up. In the corner of the room, hunched in an armchair, was another man. His face shone starkly white and he was holding his gut with both hands. Even at a distance of ten feet, Nealis could clearly see the blood on the man's hands.

'What happened to him?'

'It doesn't matter, but he can't stay here. You pick him up and load him and his gear on your lorry and leave, d'you hear?'

'I can't move him,' Nealis protested. 'He's badly hurt. Look at him.'

'I know damned well he's badly hurt. The people who brought him here said they'd run into the police and this one here got a bullet in the belly.'

'But you can't—'

'I'd do a lot of things,' McGuinness cut in. 'But I'll not have a dead man on me hands and a load of guns, too.'

'Guns?'

'Aye, guns.'

Nealis knew now why he had been worried all that night. This was what the ringing bells in his head had been about. Wanted men and gun-running, this was really dangerous stuff. But there was little enough time for polemics. McGuinness was still holding the gun and Nealis could think of no sufficient reason for arguing with him.

122

'There's a girl outside in the truck,' he said. He did not want Maire to make a sudden appearance just in case McGuinness was that nervous. 'I'd better get her to help me with him.'

McGuinness savoured the thought before replying. 'You do that, but don't get in the thing. I'm not letting you leave me with this lot.' Nealis walked slowly to the door, with McGuinness following. He was acutely conscious of him at the back of him as he approached the truck and spoke to Maire through the passenger door.

'We've got another patient. Come and help—and don't stop to ask questions.'

Maire said nothing. She climbed down from the seat and followed Nealis back into the house under the careful eye of the big farmer. Nealis indicated the man in the armchair.

'Take a look at him, Maire. He looks pretty bad from here.' Maire moved swiftly, bending to her knees and gently moving the man's hands from his stomach, speaking soothing words as she did so. The man was young—no more than twenty, Nealis guessed.

'He's very seriously wounded, Michael,' Maire said over her shoulder. 'He ought to be in hospital this minute. It will be mad to move him.'

'Take him!' McGuinness towered over the three of them, the shotgun held at his hip. 'I'm sorry enough for the poor bastard, but he'll not die here. Take him, d'you hear me!'

'Go and pile up the mattresses, Maire. I'll bring him.' Nealis's voice was sharp, in command. He strode across to the chair and picked up the man, who groaned and convulsed in Nealis's arms, then passed into unconsciousness. Maire had already left the house. McGuinness watched as Nealis carried the wounded man out and eased him into the back of the truck, where Maire carefully covered him with blankets.

'Right. Now the guns,' McGuinness said.

Back in the house, McGuinness showed him two travelling trunks on the floor of the kitchen. The lid of one was open. Inside were a couple of dozen automatic carbines and boxes of ammunition. McGuinness indicated the door.

Nealis closed the lid of the trunk and began dragging it across the floor. McGuinness lifted the other in his arms, hoisted it to his shoulder and picked up the shotgun again.

They were halfway across the yard, between the house and the truck, when they both saw the headlights. A car had pulled up at the gateway down the path. McGuinness had stopped dead, but now he sprang forward and threw the trunk into the back of the truck.

'The bloody police!' he cried. 'Get the hell out of here!' He dashed back to Nealis, picked up the second trunk and threw that into the back of the truck, slamming the door, muffling a yelp of pain from inside. 'Get out—now!' he whispered hoarsely. 'If you come back, I'll blow the heads off the lot of you. Get out and keep going. Your bloody IRA man will get us all hung.' While he spoke, he propelled Nealis to the cab of the truck and pushed him up into the driver's seat. He kept his grip on Nealis's arm for a second.

'Go—and good luck to you.' With that, he strode back to the house. Before he reached the door, Nealis started the motor and headed for the path. There was nobody at the gate. Nealis turned right and drove towards the village. Then he heard shouts from the road behind. Ahead, picked out in a truck's lights, he saw three or four policemen emerge from the trees, holding rifles. One stepped into the road with his arms upraised. Sweating with fear, Nealis instinctively trod on the accelerator, gripping the wheel with all his strength. The truck leapt forward. The policeman in the road made a wild dive for the trees, and then the first shot exploded.

Others followed. Nealis heard something hit the back of the truck, echoing like a drum through the steel bodywork. He was level with the police now. One man was calmly sighting his rifle, turning as the truck roared down the lane. The glass on the sliding door shattered and the door slid backward on its runners and then two more bangs resounded through the truck. The road junction bore down on them. Nealis braked, swore as he made a clumsy gear change. Another rattle of gunfire echoed from the road. A bullet screeched along the side of the truck and whanged away into the night, but Nealis had made the turn now, out of the line of fire. The road ahead was empty. Someone must have answered his prayers. He felt sick with terror and he drove madly, heedless of direction and not daring even to look back.

He yelled over his shoulder to Maire, but dared not slow down yet. There had been no reply and Nealis tried to reach behind him and steer the speeding vehicle with one hand but he almost lost control as a tight bend took him by surprise. Only after some ten minutes more did Nealis slow down to a halt. He fumbled for the torch and began to climb over the seats to the back of the truck. Maire was there, cradling the wounded man on her lap. In the torchlight, it was a sickening sight. Maire was covered with blood. There was a cut on her head and the blood had trickled down her face and where she had tried to wipe it out of her eyes, there were dark red smears across her cheeks, diluted by tears.

The wounded man was curled up like a fœtus. Maire looked up into the torchlight, but she did not move. 'Are you all right?' Nealis asked uselessly. 'Your head, it's ...'

'He's dying, Michael.' Maire's face, disfigured with blood, was a portrait of misery. 'He's dying,' she repeated. 'He's only a boy.' He clambered across the mattress and one of the packing cases to reach her.

'Maire,' he whispered, cradling her. 'You're trembling like a leaf. Are you all right?'

'I'll be fine,' she said. 'We'd better go ... it'll be light.'

Nealis remained close to her for a few brief moments, then climbed back to the driving seat. His watch read nearly four-thirty. It would be light in less than an hour.

* * *

They arrived back in the Bogside shortly after dawn. By the time Nealis stopped the truck, Mulholland himself was standing on the pavement. He had a hip flask in his hand and he raised it in salute.

'Here y'are, me buck—'

'Stuff it,' Nealis said savagely. 'You'd better take a look at your pal first.' He sprang from the truck and pulled Mulholland round to the back doors and opened them.

Maire, still cradling the boy in her lap, turned to look at them. Nealis felt his gut turn a somersault, knowing what she was about to say.

'He's dead.'

Mulholland's gaze swept over the truck. There were bullet holes in the back doors and both sides.

'Rough was it?'

'Yes,' Nealis said. 'Get your pal out of there.' He hauled himself into the truck and went to Maire. Gently, easily, he moved the corpse from her and lifted her to her feet, supporting her with his arm. On the roadway, she clung to him, sobbing, while three men brought out the body.

Nealis turned to walk Maire away from the scene.

'You brought the gear, I see,' Mulholland said.

'Yes. I brought the gear.'

14

The fighting had been going on for fifty hours and the bright air carried the smell of blood. Both sides were punch drunk and whipped, like boxers who had stayed on their feet through long punishing rounds. Their muscles jerked in tiredness and pain spread through them. It was time for somebody to throw the towel in, but there was nobody to do it.

Then the soldiers came. British infantrymen, who had been whiling away their time cleaning their boots and standing stiff on parade, were suddenly given live ammunition and told to protect the peace. The long green convoys of military lorries snaked their way across the face of the divided land and a khaki line spread itself between the contending factions. The Royal Ulster Constabulary was put under the orders of the Army commander and within hours the situation began to change.

In the Bogside the soldiers were welcomed, for the Bogsiders saw them as protectors, and they were welcomed in the Falls Road. But among the loyalists there was discontent. Many of them saw the move as a sell-out to the Catholics and there were some sporadic attempts to break through the military lines to get at the Fenians. The troops held firm, a breakwater whose only purpose was to keep two raging torrents from merging into a more destructive concourse.

In Derry and Belfast the barricades remained in place and the Catholics refused to allow either police or military into their enclaves. As a gesture of retaliation the Protestants put up their own barricades. Behind the Catholic ramparts life went on as before. The people organized their own vigilante patrols and the secret ambulance service continued to ferry out the sick and the maimed for treatment in the Free State. The tension started to relax, and as it relaxed old, forgotten laws of hospitality began to reassert themselves.

It was the women who first remembered about hospitality. They saw the soldiers standing on the dark street corners, young, puzzled-looking men, and so they offered them cups of tea. Some of the soldiers were black, and one woman, her mind on her schooldays when she had collected pennies for the African missions to save the black babies, asked one of them: 'Tell me, son, are you a Catholic or a Protestant yourself?'

The soldier looked around the rubble-scarred face of the Bogside and grinned: 'Ma'am, with the colour skin I got, I already got enough trouble.'

So peace broke out, slowly and uneasily, a peace with an uncertain future.

*　　*　　*

On the morning after the soldiers arrived Nealis got Mother Kate out of Bogside and into a proper hospital. It had taken a trip to the Army headquarters and an interview with an officer to get the necessary pass to move her out. In the event the Army provided the ambulance that carried Mother Kate over the Foyle Bridge and up the hill to the city hospital. She was still unconscious and Nealis rode in the back of the ambulance with her, looking sadly down at the straggling dark hair and feeling embarrassed by the unrelenting gaze of the medical orderly who travelled with them.

The medical orderly looked at Nealis because he did not want to look at the old woman on the stretcher. She was so still that the orderly thought that she was either dead, or due to die at any minute. The orderly had only been in the Army for six months and he had never seen a dead person. Sometime, he thought, he would have to see one, but he did not want his first experience to involve an old woman, an old woman civilian who had no right to be in the back of a military ambulance that was properly for the use of wounded heroes. There was an obscenity about sick old age, and he turned his eyes away from it and on to Nealis.

At the hospital it was all calm order and efficiency. They took Mother Kate from the ambulance and wheeled her into one of the wards. They did not speak to Nealis, save to direct him to an admissions clerk who wanted particulars.

She was to be X-rayed before the doctors could say anything about her condition. Eventually, Nealis left her, an old woman lying painlessly unknowing in the stiff, white bed.

* * *

As each day went by Maire looked increasingly frail. The lustre was dying in her eyes and the spring disappeared from her step. The strain was beginning to show and he wondered how long she would be able to continue the ambulance runs before cracking up. It was beginning to tell on him too, but he had more stamina. The indications with him were a tendency to bad temper and the cigarettes which he smoked incessantly.

Eventually he decided to do something about it. He waited until Maire came down from the room in which she had been sleeping and led her into the kitchen. There were casualties in the living room waiting to be taken south.

'Maire, it's time you had a break,' he said. 'You're killing yourself.'

She smiled. The smile was tight and polite, a smile without warmth.

'I mean it.'

She turned her eyes upon him, large eyes that had grown larger in the past few days. 'It can't be done,' she said. 'There's so much...'

'It can be done. It's got to be done, and I'm going to see to it.'

He thrust his way out of the house and pushed urgently up the hill to the Derry Citizens' headquarters. There were the usual bunch of vigilantes, orderlies, message passers and strategists gathered inside. The man sitting at the desk was

129

called Connery. He was a lean man with calm eyes. Nealis thought his eyes were calm because he did not understand what was going on.

Connery was shuffling papers, signing dockets and dealing with the typewritten paraphernalia of bureaucracy that had sprung into being to keep Free Derry running. Strange, thought Nealis, after the revolutionaries come the clerks. Given time the clerks take over and then it's time for the revolutionaries to have another go. All wars, all battles and all dissent are ultimately caused by the paper pushers. Connery looked up at him.

'How are things on the ambulance run roster?' Nealis asked.

Connery drew yet another piece of paper towards him and studied it. 'Let's see now. You're due for a run tonight. You and O'Dwyer.'

Nealis took out a cigarette, lit it and then remembered to offer one to Connery. 'I was wondering. Can you replace us on a couple of runs?'

Connery looked at the sheet again. 'Yes, I suppose so. You've been working hard. But it's finding someone else. Let's see now.' He looked at the sheet again and ran his finger down it.

'If you can replace us on the run tonight. Just tonight. It'll give the girl a chance to rest. She's about had it.'

'Wait a minute now.' Connery got up and went into the back room. After a few minutes he came back with a man Nealis recognized as Big Doonican, the man who had challenged him at the barricade.

'The big feller here will do it,' Connery said.

Doonican grinned at Nealis. 'It'll be a grand change to get out of here,' he said. 'It's getting to be a bit claustrophobic you know.'

'It is that,' Nealis said.

Nealis returned to Glenna Street, prepared to override any argument from Maire. 'Pack a few things in a bag,' he told her.

'What?'

'Pack a bag. We're getting out of here, at least for today. We'll be back tomorrow.'

'What have you been up to? What is all this?'

'I've got somebody else to do the run for us tonight. We're going to have a rest. Everybody's entitled to a rest.'

'But look . . .' she said.

There was harshness in his voice as he took her elbow and propelled her towards the stairs. 'Don't bloody argue. We're going. We move out in half an hour. Now get ready.'

When she returned she had brushed her hair back into a pony-tail. Her face was made up, but the shadows still showed beneath the make-up on her eyes. 'I'm ready,' she said. She was smiling despite her tiredness.

They packed the bags into the boot of Maire's Mini and Nealis took the driving seat. He eased the car into first gear and slid away. A group of children were playing football in the street, scrambling with the ball among the rubble and debris. The children had happy, dirty faces and the happiness was reflected in the faces of their parents.

Battle had been joined, and in not losing the Bogsiders had won. Guerillas always win when they do not lose, and conventional forces always lose when they do not win. That was the way it was and it did not need a Clausewitz to define the strategy of civil explosion.

At the barricade on the way out they were stopped and searched. Soldiers looked in the boot and raised the bonnet, looking for weapons. One of them knelt and peered beneath the car before they were waved on.

Nealis headed the car up past the Guildhall and along the quay and on to the bridge over the River Foyle. There were barbed-wire entanglements here and again the car was stopped. Across the bridge, Nealis turned the car right, following the line of the river south through Ballymagorry and on towards Strabane. The soldiers were in Strabane too, standing a good-humoured guard, their rifles slung across their shoulders.

At Strabane they crossed back over the river and into Lifford. Maire had been dozing in the passenger seat, but as they went over the bridge she opened her eyes and asked: 'Where are we going?'

'We're through the county of Tyrone and we're now in the county of Donegal,' he said. 'You've been asleep.'

She brushed a tendril of hair back from her forehead. 'I know. God bless me, smell that air.'

Nealis breathed in. The air was pure and fresh, a change from the acrid, fume-filled atmosphere of Derry. 'It's good,' he said.

They drove on for a while in silence, Maire looking out at the green countryside flashing past the window. There were stone walls here, walls built with back-breaking effort to enclose the country and contain its goodness within the limits a man could work.

'Have you ever been to Sligo?' Nealis asked.

'No, but I know all about it. That's Yeats country down there.'

'Do you know Yeats?'

'A little ... I like his poetry.'

He laughed. 'You're a jewel of a woman. Beautiful, appealing and you like Yeats. Bet you can't cook, though.'

'I can so.'

'Great stuff. You and a plate of mutton broth and a verse of Yeats—what more could a man want?'

'Michael, are you mocking me?' Her tone was schoolmistress-severe.

'Mock you, me love? Mock you? Sure, and wouldn't I rather be after swimming through a river of alligataties and fighting a duel to the death with a wild rhinoceros and buck leppin' in me bare feet to the top of the Himalayas before I'd do the likes o' dat?'

'Oh, you're mad.' Her voice was pleased, like that of a little girl.

He grinned and winked at her.

'You know,' she said, 'I could never work out what Yeats was all about.'

'Tenderness,' he said.

He geared down to take a sharp right-hand bend in the road and pulled up as a flock of sheep came whirling around the car.

'Look at the fluffy little bastards,' he said, laughing.

'Tenderness?'

'Oh yes, tenderness. He was full of it. It had to get out some way, so when he had nothing to be tender about he would make something up.'

'You make him sound a little bit...' She reached for the right word. 'Phoney.'

'No, he wasn't phoney. He was a man whose powers and imagination never came to terms with modern life. He needed a refuge, a magic castle. So he built himself one through his poetry. Maybe that's what we should all do.'

She looked at him softly. 'This is something new.'

'New?'

'I haven't seen this side of you before.'

'Ah, you see, you're making the mistake everybody makes all the time. A man is not composed of sides. A man is the total of what's inside him, his life, his experience, the things that shape and mould him.'

'But poetry? Yeats?'

'Well, I like him. I always have. Maybe it doesn't go with a copper's size nine boots. In fact, from a professional point of view, it's probably a defect in my character.'

'Go on,' she said, 'about Yeats.' She felt warm and secure beside him.

'What's there to tell? He was a great man, that's all. A man who can make your soul weep.'

'He has that effect on you?'

'Yes. And I'm old enough not to be ashamed of it.'

She looked at him softly. 'Michael, you need never be ashamed of anything with me.' Her hand reached up and touched his face.

'Do you know *The Lake Isle of Innisfree?*' Nealis went on. 'He changed reality into a dream in that poem. The lake isle is just a clump of mud with a bit of privet on it and a few patches of coarse grass. It sticks up out of the water, a dirty knobble that you wouldn't spare a second glance for, but that's not how Yeats saw it. For him it was an enchanted island, full of peace and birdsong, with beauty moving everywhere. That's how he wrote it. More and more I'm becoming convinced that any dream is better than any reality.'

They were down through Bundoran now, running through the sparse, rocky country of Leitrim, all flat and inhospitable, on their way through the Dartry Mountains towards the squat, elephantine peak of Benbulben.

'I know the poem,' Maire said.

'Say it.'

'No, Michael. Please ... you say it for me.'

He glanced at her, 'I'm not sure I remember it word perfect, but I'll try.

'I will arise and go now, and go to Innisfree,
And a small cabin build there, of clay and wattles made:
Nine bean-rows will I have there, a hive for the honey-bee,
And live alone in the bee-loud glade...'

Nealis paused before the last verse and Maire said: 'Michael, why are you a policeman?'

He grinned. 'Men become policemen because they cannot be poets. Last verse coming up.

'I shall arise and go now, for always night and day,
I hear lake waters lapping with low sounds by the shore;
When I stand on the roadway or on the pavements grey
I hear it in the deep heart's core.'

She was leaning back in the seat, head back and eyes closed, listening. When he had finished she leaned forward and kissed him on the side of the face.

'Thank you, Michael,' she said.

* * *

Sligo is an old town in an old county, but it has never been rich and only recently has it begun to get spoiled. Nealis drove across the narrow bridge spanning the bottleneck where Lough Gill spills into the Atlantic Ocean. He gestured at the streets crowded with tourists: 'They've made a shrine out of this place. Looking for the Holy Grail. Or maybe they think the Playboy of the Western World will come along the street and hand them a chapter of holy writ.'

'I think people need a shrine, something to venerate,' Maire said.

'Maybe, but people who build shrines too often end up by using them as lavatories.'

They called at four hotels before they found one with accommodation to spare. The girl at the reception desk greeted them with a professional smile as they approached, asking Nealis if she could help.

'I'd like a double room,' he said. Maire, standing beside him, showed no sign of having heard.

She watched him fill in the register, calm and untroubled as he claimed her as his wife, only later, when the porter had carried their bags up to the twin-bedded room, he said: 'I hope you didn't think I was taking too much for granted?'

She smiled. There was nothing coy or coquettish in the smile: 'I would have been hurt if you hadn't,' she said.

They unpacked and went down to the reception desk. They were both hungry, but it was mid-afternoon and they were between meals at the hotel. The best offer was a plate of sandwiches and a pot of coffee. In the lounge they sat enjoying their snack, secure in their private world, while two tables away a large German lady was unwittingly giving a public recital of her travels through Ireland.

When they had finished eating Maire said: 'Michael, take me to see it. The lake isle.'

'I'd like that,' he said.

135

They drove down through Magheraboy around the shores of the lough. It was an afternoon that anticipated autumn, for autumn comes early in the West of Ireland. The air was full of brown tints and a lazy sun rolled through high clouds. Seagulls swooped endlessly over the lake, calling out with their tight little voices as they performed their aerial minuets. In counterpoint, a songbird poured forth its hymn in liquefied octaves that rose and fell with startling purity.

Nealis and Maire sat down on the edge of the lake, their hands joined. A slight wind blew over the water, ruffling its calm surface and catching lightly at Maire's hair. There were some men out in small boats playing at fishing. There were good trout and even salmon in these parts. They sat in their boats with the lines dangling over the stern enjoying the sun and the breeze and the water. They were calm, happy fishermen and they did not worry whether they caught fish or not.

Maire studied the reflected patterns of sunlight on the water and looked at the small islands that lay out in the middle of the lough. They looked black and barren.

'Which one is it, Michael?'

He pointed. 'That's it, that dirty black knobble there. With the bushes in the middle.'

'Oh Michael, it is beautiful. It is.'

'Yes. It is.'

They sat there, holding hands on the lake's edge, watching the water gently moving against the banks. Two children, two adolescents discovering love. He squeezed her hand. Love.

'Maire,' he said, 'I love you.'

She was self-possessed, in command of herself, but it broke through. She looked at him, blushing. 'Ooh, Mister Nealis. That's a lovely old-fashioned thing to say.'

'I do,' he said.

She took his other hand: 'And I love you, Michael. The very same way.'

He did not kiss her then, because he knew instinctively that the celluloid cliché of a kiss would have spoiled the moment. Instead he lifted her right hand and gently nuzzled the soft skin of her wrist.

'You know I'm married?'

'Yes,' her voice was quiet.

'It's over, though. It's—'

'Michael.' She cut in, silencing him with eyes that were full and understanding. 'It doesn't matter, Michael ... It wouldn't matter. I love you.' She stopped talking for a moment and then smiled: 'Now there's a confession from a good convent-reared girl, but it's true.' She laughed happily. 'I can fight off conscience and duty, turn my back on my upbringing and throw away everything I was ever taught to think. That's love, I suppose, Michael.'

'That's love, Maire. That poor, overworked word. It sounds so trite and means so much. Most people, poor bastards, never know love in the way that you and I know it.'

She sighed. 'See the lake out there, Michael. That's our lake isle. It belongs to you and me and the dreaming soul of William Butler Yeats.'

'There's something about Yeats. Towards the end of his life Mr Yeats who, as you know, was a man with a fine ear, went to see a famous London physician. He stood in the gentleman's room in Harley Street and the physician examined him very carefully and then said: "I'm sorry Yeats, but I fear I have a bad report to make." "What?" said Yeats, "What the divil?" "You", said the physician, "are an arteriosclerotic."

'Yeats's face lit up and he took the doctor by the hand and shook it. "Thank you," he said, "Thank you. An arteriosclerotic." He rolled the word around his tongue. "Arteriosclerotic. I'd rather be called that than Lord of Lower Egypt".'

Nealis paused: 'Do you think that's sad?'

'No,' she said, 'I think that is very beautiful.'

* * *

They ate dinner back at the hotel and drank a bottle of wine. It was warm in the restaurant and the atmosphere was intimate. Nealis had brandy with his coffee and then left the table to make his daily telephone call to the hospital to find out about Mother Kate. He was looking reflective when he returned.

'How is she?' Maire asked.

'As well as can be expected,' Nealis told her. 'That's what they said at first. They'll tell you nothing. She's been operated on today, but I had to drag it out of them. There was pressure on the brain and they operated to relieve it.' He sighed, suddenly feeling the weight of trouble about him. Then he added: 'She's resting now.'

'I'm glad they've done something, Michael. It must be better.'

Nealis looked at her across the flickering candlelight, smiling slowly as he shook his head: 'You're a funny little creature.'

'Why do you say that?' The glow of the candles on the table emphasized the dimples in her cheeks and illuminated the coppery tints of her hair. Nealis felt suddenly sad and reached out for her hand.

'Because ... because you are. That's all. I love you.'

'Do you, Michael?'

He drew her hand across the table to kiss her finger tips and then, still holding her hand, rose from the table and led her from the dining room. Upstairs he shut the door of their bedroom and looked over to where she was standing against one of the twin beds, looking at him with calm eyes. She stood still as he walked across the room to put his arms around her and kiss her, and as he kissed her she remained, for a moment, motionless and unresponsive. He broke off from the kiss and looked at her: 'What's the matter, Maire?' Her eyes were still calm as she looked at him, but they flickered briefly as they met his gaze.

'Don't rush me, Michael, please. It'll be all right, but don't go too fast.'

Nealis took out his cigarettes and lit two, offering her one, and sat down beside her on the bed, holding her hand and looking at her.

'You're beautiful, Maire,' he said.

She drew on the cigarette, breathing out the smoke gently, waiting for him to go on.

'I need you,' he said. 'Without you I'm only half a man, only half alive. There are no words for it, because all the words have been debased. I love you and I hunger for you. You are my life, here and now and every day onwards.'

Suddenly she was crying, hot salt tears spilled noiselessly down her cheeks. He looked at her, saying nothing until the tears abated and then he smiled: 'Funny one.'

After a while she rose and put out her cigarette. 'Michael, will you go into the bathroom for a few minutes.' She smiled suddenly, 'I'm a little bit shy.'

He went into the bathroom and sat on the edge of the bath, smoking another cigarette and wondering about the strange purity of this child-woman. When he came back she was in the bed, her hair lying in a bronze mass on the pillow. He undressed swiftly and slid into the bed beside her, putting his arm under her head to draw her to him.

Their bodies came together in a total caress as her soft, warm flesh melted into his. He felt the quick tightening of desire within himself, but stayed it as his mouth sought hers.

They lay for a long time, kissing and caressing, as he breathed words of love to her. Slowly the shyness left her and when he put his hand down between her thighs she moaned and clasped him more closely to her.

Beneath the blankets her hand found him, grasping him gently and their bodies began to undulate in passion. Then, with a sudden urgency, she pulled him to her, guiding him to the final consummation. He felt the damp, soft warmth of her thighs enfolding him as their bodies joined. She moved, a tingling, agonizing sweetness beneath him. The frenzy increased within them as they moved until suddenly, in a moment of quaking release, they exploded together.

Afterwards they lay for a minute without speaking, until

the chill of their drying sweat made them seek the warmth of the bedclothes. He lay with his arm cradling her head, and then rose on his elbow to kiss her eyes. Her hands caressed the back of his neck, moving like butterflies, and she pulled him down until his face rested on her breast.

He could feel the warm comfort of it on the side of his face and the hot cloying scent of her body filled his nostrils. He nuzzled his face into her, feeling a sudden need for her warmth and comfort. As his head sank into her breast he closed his eyes and thought of his mother, lying back there in the hospital.

15

There were fewer passengers than usual aboard the Friday afternoon train from Belfast to Armagh and when it arrived only a handful of people scurried down the platform to the ticket barrier. Frank Nealis, keeping pace alongside a small group of businessmen who had been discussing the situation in the Six Counties ever since Belfast, could have wished for a bigger crowd. Throughout his travels in the past few days he had moved with crowds wherever possible, shrinking anonymously into them. His journeys to Belfast, Newry and now the long dogleg across to Armagh had all been made in daylight, by train and public transport. No fast cars through the night, but second class by train and utterly unremarkable. So far, nobody had looked twice at him, which was the way he wanted it.

Frank handed in his ticket—a single, since he would not be leaving Armagh by train the next day. Rinty was waiting for him, discreetly distant from the barrier. They met and shook hands formally, then walked together from the station to catch a bus, passing on the way a newspaper vendor busily unwrapping a bundle of Belfast evening papers and their latest rash of Ulster situation headlines. 'They'll be waiting for you,' Rinty said briefly as they took their seats on the bus.

'Good,' Frank said.

Another meeting. He had been to dozens of them, it seemed, in the last week. In Derry, Belfast, Newry, Portadown, Ballymena, back to Belfast and now Armagh, spreading the word, urging, encouraging and where necessary, kicking. But the euphoria had gone from it now. A week ago the days had been heady. The streets had been stiff with the frantic enthusiasm of dogs slipped from their leashes. Now it was harder work, for although the fervour was still there, so were the British soldiers. It had been easy to get people into the streets; the real problem was keeping them there.

But they'd be in the streets of Armagh tomorrow, right enough.

He felt Rinty nudge him in the ribs. He rose from his seat and followed the other man off the bus. They walked for five minutes, finally arriving at a terraced house indistinguishable from a hundred thousand others. Rinty knocked at the front door and they were admitted by a florid, beefy man with the dark red scab of a split lip disfiguring his mouth. His angry face revealed no flicker of interest as he motioned them inside with a jerk of his arm.

There were seven men in the room. Frank's entrance guillotined the conversation and they stared at him as if at a barely remembered stranger. They shook hands gravely, each man murmuring his name. Except the man with the split lip, who growled his name confidently, almost belligerently.

'I'm Cahil Stevenson,' he said bleakly. 'This is my house. I've brought the lads here to listen to what you have to say.'

It was a barren introduction and Frank would have loved a drink but Stevenson offered him none. Frank was well rehearsed, and without further preamble, he began to review the situation in Ulster as it stood, sketching in the roots of the Civil Rights movement, the first marches, the Protestant opposition, the hostility of the Government, the savagery of the police, the battles of Derry and Belfast and the final introduction of British troops. It was a banal start and he was telling them nothing they did not already know, but it served its purpose, which was to enable him to study the faces around him. Six of them were listening with the respect due to a leader, the man who had been there and seen the action. The seventh, Stevenson, was idly picking at the scab on his lip.

Frank paused for a moment, lighting a cigarette before continuing. 'Well, that brings us to today and tomorrow and all the other tomorrows, because this is a struggle which has got to continue and it will continue. We've begun this fight now, and it will go on until we rid this country of the supremacist bastards who control it.' There was a general murmur of consent. Only Stevenson abstained. 'The most important thing,' Frank went on, 'is that we don't sit on our arses just because we have achieved the first victory— oh, yes, we have won a victory, lads, of a sort. Stormont is already giving ground, but it's not enough. We can't rest now, not until we sweep the bloody lot of them out. We've hit them hard in Derry and Belfast and here in Armagh, too. I'm not forgetting that you lads and people like you were among the first to take to the streets when the chips were down. But it's still not enough. You've got to strike, and strike again. Get out there into the streets again and fight! There's good lads still spilling their blood in Derry and Belfast, aye, and women and children too. They need you! If the Orangemen think they have only Derry and Belfast to deal with, we've got to remind them that they're wrong, show the world that when the victory is won, the men of this city of Armagh were there in the thick of the fight!' Frank was sweating now and he broke off to peel away his jacket and open his collar.

'You've got to fight! There's no other way of winning the freedom we all want. You want proper houses and proper schools for your kids. You want work for your sons and respect for your daughters, an end to the bloody oppression we've had to endure all our lives. Well, I'm telling you, you've got to fight for it and die for it if necessary. Sitting and waiting for it to happen won't win the battle. You've got to fight.'

Stevenson looked up for the first time as Frank spat out the words. His face wore no expression as he listened. 'This isn't just another fight,' Frank continued, more quietly, more intensely. 'This is the start of a revolution! We have in our hands the means and the weapons with which to overthrow the system. This is a revolution of the people, and there's no power on earth can stand in the way of a people determined to be free. Look what happened in Cuba. What Fidel Castro started there is spreading all through South America. Men like Che Guevara were struggling against far bigger odds than us—and dying for it—but they'll succeed in the end. And look what's happening in Vietnam. The biggest, richest, most powerful army in the world can't stop the ordinary people when they rise up and fight for their freedom. That's the lesson we have to learn. Fight, and we'll win. Freedom is ours. Just get out there and take it!'

Frank stopped speaking, leaned forward over the back of a chair and eyed the others fiercely, the sweat trickling down his face and his shirt a damp rag on his back. He wasn't finished with them yet. Stacked up in his brain was the whole catalogue of revolutionary invective; it included thoughts that might be new to them but nonetheless thoughts that they should heed.

Frank was drugged by the words and their effect on his listeners. To most of them, it was all new. They had hated Protestants since birth, for no other reason than that they themselves had been born Catholic, but that kind of hatred could be assuaged in a bottle fight. What Frank brought them were new reasons to hate, new faces to smash, new justifications.

Now, in that smoky room, he licked his lips and prepared to go on. But it was Stevenson who spoke next.

'What has all this got to do with us? What's all this Vietnam? It's the bloody Protestants we're fighting.'

'You're wrong!' Frank replied. 'Dead wrong. It's the system you're fighting, brothers. The social system, the economic system, that's what has got to be smashed. Religion is only a part of it. We've got to set this country alight, by Christ, and cleanse it in the flames.'

'And you think eight thousand police and B-Specials and the British Army are going to stand by and lend us matches? Don't talk silly, man.' Stevenson rose to his feet as he spoke and walked towards the door. With his hand on the door-knob, he glared at Frank. 'I'll go out and fight to rid this country of every last Protestant bastard still breathing, but I'm not going to stand here and listen to a lot of shit from a windbag. I thought you were a man of action.'

Trembling with fury, Frank brushed aside the chair on which he had been leaning, sending it spinning across the room into the fireplace where it scattered a collection of tongs and pokers.

'Action?' Frank snarled. 'I've seen more action than you've had hot dinners, you stupid bastard! Don't you think I'd rather be up there at the Bogside barricades than down here trying to get you up off your backsides?'

'I've not been on my backside,' Stevenson yelled. 'Where do you think I got this.' He jabbed a finger at his gashed mouth. 'That was the butt end of a rifle, mate!'

Heedless of the others, who had backed to the walls of the room, Frank advanced on Stevenson.

'And who was on the other end of the rifle?'

'A B-Special.'

'And what would you do if you got hold of him again?'

'I'd break his bloody neck.'

'You'd fight again?'

'I would, but I can't take on the whole—'

'Never mind that,' Frank said quickly. 'If he came looking for you, you'd fight?'

'I would.'

'Then you had better make up your mind you'll be fighting this time tomorrow.' Frank was close to Stevenson now, and his voice was a hoarse whisper. 'You'd break that B-Special's neck, would you? Well, you'll have your chance tomorrow, my bucko, because him and a thousand like him are going to come looking for you and they'll come with rifle butts and pickaxe handles and tear gas and bullets and

they'll knock the living shit out of you. And you others.'
Frank's voice rose to a scream as he turned on the others.
'They'll beat you to pulp in your own beds!'

There was utter silence in the room as Frank backed away
from Stevenson and encompassed them all with an outstretched finger. 'Unless ...' he continued slowly, measuring
each word. 'Unless you strike first! And you'll have your
chance—the chance to make Armagh the first graveyard of
reaction in the Six Counties.'

'What do you mean, Nealis?' Stevenson demanded.

'I mean this. Tomorrow morning at five o'clock, when
Armagh is in its bed, there's going to be an explosion that
will rattle every window in the city. That'll be your signal to
strike.'

'A bomb? Where? What's going to get it?'

'You'll find out in the morning,' Frank said. 'Anyway, it
doesn't matter. What matters is that you're ready. Arm
yourselves. Guns, petrol bombs, sticks, stones, fists, whatever
you like. But be ready. The shit will hit the fan tomorrow
and those who are ready for it will win the day. Until then,
there's a few ideas I have for you.' Frank retrieved his briefcase from the floor and pulled out a map and a sheaf of typewritten papers. As he put them on the table, he glanced up
at Stevenson.

'You'll have the chance of getting one back at your B-
Special tomorrow, eh?'

For the first time, Stevenson's face creased into a painful
smile. 'Aye,' he said, 'I'd like that.'

Frank unfolded the map and handed out a copy of the
papers to each man in the room. Then he began to talk again.

*   *   *

Rinty drove Frank to Paddy O'Donnell's house on the edge
of Armagh some two hours later, dropping him off at the
corner of the road before driving back into the city. Frank
had known Paddy O'Donnell since childhood, when their
fathers had been friends. He had come to this house then, on

146

rare outings with Me Da' and Mother Kate and Michael and both boys had had to be on their best behaviour. They had been awed in those days by the riches of the house—the chairs that matched, the frilly lace curtains, the fragile teacups.

Frank had loathed it then, disliked the tall, thin Mrs O'Donnell and despised her skinny son. Old man O'Donnell had once been a jovial sort, according to Me Da', who fought in France with him during the First World War, but Frank's memory of old man O'Donnell had been of a hapless old bastard who found solace in the bottom of a bottle whenever he came to visit them in Derry. He had died long ago and they had stopped seeing the O'Donnells.

The house, when Frank entered it, still looked the same and smelled the same, and so did Paddy O'Donnell. He was a small man with a round, mournful face and drooping shoulders accentuated by the loose woollen cardigan he habitually wore. He fussed over Frank as he ushered him into the big, old-fashioned kitchen where he spent most of his time, taking his raincoat and briefcase and offering him a cup of tea all in a smooth flow of obsequious words and movements. Finally, he stopped scurrying and fell silent.

'Where is he?' Frank asked.

'Upstairs now,' O'Donnell said, his voice almost a reverential whisper. 'He drank a cup of tea with me, but he said he had some work to do and preferred to work alone.'

I'll bet he did, Frank thought, then said: 'I'll join him. Bring us up a cup of tea, eh?'

He went up the stairs to the room they always used for meetings. Standing at the window, looking down into the road, was a tall and wiry man with blond hair cropped close to his head, a bony wrinkled face and bright blue eyes. He turned from the window as Frank entered and nodded, holding out a hand in greeting.

'Peadar O'Floin!' Frank said, taking the other man's hand in a warm handshake. O'Floin smiled at him. He always smiled: it was a permanent fixture.

147

'Frank Nealis. I thought you'd got yourself lost.'

Frank laughed. 'Sorry, Peadar. But I got delayed.'

'Sure, you're a busy man. I heard you covered every inch of the Six Counties in the last week. It's a big job you've been doing, Frank.'

Frank shrugged. 'It's my work.'

'I have the stuff, Frank,' O'Floin said abruptly. Frank thought he detected a faint air of uneasiness about the tall IRA man, which was entirely uncharacteristic.

'That's good, Peadar. Where is it?'

'There.' O'Floin nodded in the direction of the door, and Frank turned to look. Previously unnoticed behind the door stood a cheap brown suitcase, its plastic fabric reinforced by two stout leather straps. Frank was aware of the hairs at the back of his neck tingling.

'How much is there?'

'There's fifteen sticks of gelignite there, Frank.'

'Will it be enough?' Frank asked, still looking at the suitcase. O'Floin walked across and lifted the case gently and put it down on the table in the middle of the room and tapped it with his finger.

'If this lot went off now, it would blow the roof off this house and blast this floor right down to the cellar. There'd be nothing much left. It won't do the same with the cathedral because you won't be able to place it in the proper position. But it'll do enough. It'll blow a bloody great hole in the wall, that's for sure.'

'And the fuse?'

'A clockwork mechanism, like an alarm clock. I've just set it for five o'clock.' Instinctively, Frank glanced at his wristwatch. It was now ten minutes past nine. Nearly eight hours to go.

'I suppose it's safe? To carry around, I mean?'

'Gelignite is funny stuff,' O'Floin replied. 'Volatile stuff. If it's kept out of proper storage for too long, it begins to weep—get damp, that is. And then it can go up at any time. But this stuff is new and it's as dry as a bone. It's safe, if you

148

treat it with respect.'

Frank nodded. 'Don't worry. It has my respect.' He strolled over to an armchair and sat down. 'You'll be taking me to church, I take it, at about two?'

O'Floin's face clouded and he turned to stare out of the window before replying. 'I'm afraid I'll not be able to stop with you, Frank. The boys and myself will need to be back across the border when the place goes up. That was the orders from the Commandant. Deliver the stuff and come back, he said. It's too risky in Armagh. You know how it is, Frank, as soon as a man stops for a piss in the street, they close the border tighter than a duck's arse.'

'Well, I'm damned!' Frank leapt to his feet. 'That's bloody marvellous, isn't it?'

'Sorry, Frank. But that's how it has to be.'

'Sorry is it? By God, sorry's a lot of help. How the hell am I going to put all the stuff together and get it to the church, for God's sake?'

'It's all in a suitcase and it's all wired up, Frank. All you have to do is carry the case and put it on the doorstep.'

'Oh, fine,' Frank snorted. 'I'm walking around the street with a caseful of gelignite and you're back across the border sleeping in your beds. That'll make the boys back in Derry laugh, won't it, when I tell them. The IRA were in their beds, lads, while I was strolling through Armagh with a caseful of gelignite all by meself.'

The smile on O'Floin's face had almost gone. 'That's not right, Frank, and you know it. We'll help whenever we—'

'Aye, sure you will,' Frank interrupted. 'Like the pack of brave boyos who came up from Dublin to help us out in Derry. You know fine what happened to them, don't you? They got as far as Dundalk and they headed for the pubs and within the hour they were all as pissed as handcarts, and in the morning they scuttled back to Dublin with hangovers. Agh, you make me ill, so you do.'

'Look, boy, I don't need lectures. There's men of ours have died too. And you've got guns, haven't you? And ammunition and explosives, haven't you, and there's men of ours all over the Six Counties?'

'Sure, and a bloody half-arsed lot they are too.'

A tap at the door interrupted them. They both watched the door open slowly and Paddy O'Donnell slid into the room with a tray bearing a teapot, milk, sugar and teacups.

'There you are, lads,' Paddy breathed. 'A fine cup of tea for you.' Neither of the other men replied, and O'Donnell looked from one to the other worriedly. 'Is everything all right, lads?'

'Sure,' Frank said. 'Sure, everything's bloody fine, Paddy. Away you go now, we've more to do yet.' O'Donnell backed towards the door and closed it behind him. They waited until his footsteps reached the bottom of the stairs.

'What about the IRA support?' Frank demanded.

O'Floin shrugged. 'You're not thinking straight, Frank. There's not a bit of good us coming up here bristling with guns and charging into action like a lot of comic-book heroes. We're doing more good the way we are. Don't you think there are hundreds, thousands, of good men who'd swarm over the border at the drop of a hat? But do you know what would happen to them, Frank? They'd be mowed down like corn. There's not only the RUC and the B-Specials, there's the British Army now, too. And much though we'd like to have a crack at some of them, we haven't the strength. Face the facts, we couldn't do it.'

'Well, it's just as well there's men in the Six Counties willing to try,' Frank said. 'Men who will act for themselves without waiting for promises to come true.'

'I know, Frank, and we all applaud them.'

'Yes, sitting on your arses you do.'

'You're too hard on us all, Frank,' O'Floin said. Frank shrugged irritably and went to the tea tray. He set out the cups and poured the tea.

'Sugar?'

'Aye. Two,' O'Floin said. 'Thanks.' He took the tea and drank it in a gulp. He put the cup down thoughtfully.

'Don't be too impatient, Frank,' he said at last. 'There's a long way to go in this fight and it can't be done overnight. I've been in this game a whole lot longer than you and I know the truth of it.'

Frank made no reply, and O'Floin walked across to the chair over which he had thrown his coat. Picking it up, he walked back to Frank with an outstretched hand.

'It's time. Before I go, though, I want to wish you the best of luck with that.' He indicated the suitcase. 'Take it easy, Frank.'

Frank gripped O'Floin's hand. 'There's not time for taking it easy, Peadar.'

O'Floin shook his head silently and released his hand from Frank's. He went to the door, opened it, and was gone.

Left alone, Frank began pacing the floor, returning each time to the table with the suitcase. He touched it, and felt his heart accelerate. The case was ordinary, so anonymous that it hypnotized him and he had to fight the strong inclination to open it and see for himself the deadly power packed inside it. He lifted it very carefully and was surprised at the weight of it. Then he sat in the armchair and stared at it, deep in thought. He rose an hour later and went downstairs.

The tension was still with him and he felt angry. The waiting was intolerable. 'Got a drink in the house?' he demanded as he came into O'Donnell's room. O'Donnell leapt to his feet in agitation.

'No, Frank. You know there's never liquor in this house.'

'Well, go and get some!' Frank snarled. 'Here.' He peeled a couple of pound notes from the handful in his pocket. 'Pedal down to the corner and buy a bottle of whiskey.'

O'Donnell crossed himself and was about to refuse, but changed his mind. Shaking his head and mumbling invocations he hurried from the room. When he returned, Frank took the bottle and went back upstairs, leaving O'Donnell to his prayer book.

He came down again at midnight with three-quarters of

the bottle inside him, belligerently intoxicated.

'I'm going bloody crazy up there on my own,' he growled, waving the bottle at O'Donnell. 'You'll have a drink with a lonely man, eh, Paddy? You'll join me in a wee drink, eh?'

Nervously, O'Donnell shook his head. 'No, Frank, I'll not take a drink. I'll make myself a cup of tea, perhaps.'

'Tea? Tea? You'll drown in bloody tea. Tea's a drink for old women.'

'I'm sworn off the drink, Frank. You know that,' O'Donnell said, lowering his eyes to avoid Frank's stare.

'Oh yes. I remember. Father Matthew's pledge. By Christ, Paddy, it's terrible what those old monks did to you, isn't it? Those evil old bastards.'

Frank took another swig at the bottle. It was not doing him any good, and he knew it. He could have put away a gallon of the stuff and it would not have done him any good. It only made him more irritable, and the sight of Paddy O'Donnell cringing in front of him made it worse.

'For Christ's sake, man,' he roared suddenly, 'why don't you take a grip on yourself. Start to live.' He began to laugh in a way that made O'Donnell uneasy. 'Look, why don't you and I take a couple of drinks and go on the town. Find ourselves a couple of women and have a good screw. Ever had a good screw, Paddy?'

O'Donnell stared at Frank, his face pale and his lips moving soundlessly.

'Ah, you've not,' Frank said in disgust. 'I'll bet you're still a cock virgin. Sure, you never had it in, did you, Paddy, you poor, misfortunate bastard.'

O'Donnell was looking at him with anguish and fear. Frank watched him through a red haze of bellicosity.

'You'll be saying a prayer tonight, eh?' he said. 'To save the old soul from hell. Is that it? Ah, well now, Paddy, you forget it. Hell is any place you hang your hat, and Christ help us, we're all in it.'

As he took another mouthful of whiskey O'Donnell crossed the room and looked up at him: 'You didn't used to be like this, Frank. You used to pray ...'

'Aye, so I did,' Frank said, 'but that was a while back.' He snarled and advanced on the other man. 'Listen, you can pray yourself into the bloody ground and the only bastards who will hear you are the birds. I've had a gutful of religion. It's the cause of the whole bother. Everybody's too busy rattling their bloody beads to think, let alone act.'

O'Donnell crossed himself. 'That's sacrilege, Frank. That's sacrilege. Don't talk like that.'

'No, I won't talk,' Frank grated, 'I'll act. There's going to be action in this town like you never saw before.'

'What are you going to do, Frank?'

'Ah, piss off!'

'You're under my roof.'

'I am. A good Holy Roman roof. You should get out more, Paddy. Dip your wick a bit. Get to value the feel of a big juicy left tit in your hand, for that's as close as any of us are going to come to heaven.'

'That's enough of that. For God's sake ...' O'Donnell's voice was pleading.

'All right, Paddy,' Frank was smiling, but he was wondering why he was doing this to poor, contemptible Paddy. 'All right, all right. I'll tell you what I'm going to do then.'

'What?'

'I'm going to blow up the Protestant cathedral.'

'The House of God!' O'Donnell breathed the words, backing away from Frank with eyes dilated with shock. Suddenly, he fell to his knees and began to mumble a prayer, his hands held together in front of his closed eyes like a child.

'Get up! Get up, do you hear me?' Frank marched across the room and jerked O'Donnell to his feet by his shirt-front. 'Save your prayers for tomorrow if pray you must. And if you ever breathe a word of this to anyone—anyone at all— I'll break your neck. And don't think I wouldn't, because I would. You'll get yours just the way Ross Simmons is going to get his when the time comes.' He released O'Donnell and went back to the armchair and drank the last of the whiskey.

He sat quite still for several minutes, while O'Donnell moved quietly to the table and sat staring at him.

'You don't understand me,' Frank said in a quiet voice. 'I'm fighting for the freedom of the people, Paddy. I may well die in the fight, but that doesn't matter to me. I'll take a few with me. And the first will be Ross Simmons, d'you know that, Paddy?' Frank was rambling now. 'By Christ, I'll nail the bastard ... I'll wait until he's in full cry ... and then. Bang! All over. The others didn't want to do it. I could see that ... none of them. Well, I saved them the trouble ... saved them the trouble, Paddy ... I saved them the trouble, so I did ... I may die, but I'll take that bastard with me, you'll see....' Frank went on talking a few minutes more, then fell asleep in the armchair.

Rinty came for Frank at one-thirty. Apart from his red eyes, Frank showed no effects from the whiskey.

* * *

After Frank had left with the suitcase, Paddy sat pondering the morality of betrayal. Had Christ, he wondered, ever forgiven Judas? Maybe not. Maybe betrayal was the final, secret, absolute, unforgivable sin. Maybe there could be no redemption for a man who betrayed. But what if the betrayal was in defence of God and in defence of a man's immortal soul? Was it not then justified? Was there not a situation in which it was a duty to betray?

Frank was going to blow up a cathedral, was going to commit scarilege. Was it not a duty to stop him by any means possible, rather than allow him to risk the black sin? And was it not a duty to protect the House of God?

The cathedral was used by Protestants, men who had rejected the True Faith, but the God they worshipped was the one absolute God, the same God that Paddy worshipped. His mind recoiled at the enormity of it. For blowing up a cathedral a man would burn in hell for eternity.

Paddy saw his duty, and it was a penance. For his past

154

sins, for the furtive uncleanliness of his life, God had placed this burden upon him. Then there was Ross Simmons. Did Frank mean to murder him? There was a straight choice here between right and wrong. He, Paddy O'Donnell, who had so often chosen wrong in the past, must now choose right. Or be found wanting in the balance.

This was his personal Calvary, a bitter chance to make expiation for those secret sins that made his life a torment.

There would be men in this town, the same men who had burned down the factory a week ago, men whose faces were so set against right that, if they knew, would misunderstand his action. The factory burners, the Godless street corner boys, would categorize him as an informer, confusing him with those despised spectres of history who had sold their countrymen for far less than thirty pieces of silver. They would not see him as a man impelled to do the Will of God. And afterwards, if Frank was caught and punished, there would always be the pain of betrayal, gnawing at his guts, eating at his heart. That was part of the burden he had to carry, an atonement that might last as long as life itself.

He went out into the yard, collecting his old white raincoat on the way. The raincoat hung down below his knees and he had to pull it out of the way to put the bicycle clips onto his trousers. The streets were dark, with a slight moonglow, and Paddy rode softly and easily down the hill.

At the bottom of the hill there was a telephone box. He looked around the quiet street, his eyes wide and alarmed, and then stepped into the empty box. His left hand reached out to pick up the receiver and as it did so, his right hand travelled to his head and across his body making the sign of the Cross.

16

Armagh is a city perched on a hill. It is an old, old city, washed and hallowed by the tides of history. The oldness is to be seen in the cracking, crumbling fabric of the buildings and the streets and in the air of resignation to be found among its people.

There had been fighting there that August, heavy and bitter fighting in which men had died by gunshot, but unlike other cities there were no barricades and nobody had turned the opposing quarters into insurrectionist camps. There had been comparatively few police and soldiers in Armagh, but now they came in their hundreds, bringing with them guns and barbed-wire rolls and walkie-talkie sets. O'Donnell's telephone call had borne a strange and martial fruit.

As the soldiers came into town they were dropped off in squads to cordon off certain areas. Behind them came armoured cars and scout cars, the full panoply of war with only the air support missing. The police moved in too, subsidiary players in a drama which they felt rightfully to be theirs. Soon, the whole city was ringed with military checkpoints manned by police and soldiers who were equally bewildered and underslept.

Quickly the soldiers got to work, clearing a large area around the cathedral, turning back traffic and sealing off the roads. Citizens were roused from their beds lest they be blown to eternity by staying where they slept.

By first light a motor-cycle escort rushed a team of sappers to the city. They roared through the sleeping streets to where a policeman stood guard over the suitcase bomb. He was a very young policeman and there was a built-in insouciance to his walk when the Royal Engineers major told him to move away.

The major was an owl-like man who wore spectacles and there was a small shadow of beard round his jowls. He looked at the suitcase and blinked. Bloody native squabbles, he thought. Bloody native squabbles. That was the trouble with the Army today. No action. Just squabbling bloody natives all over the place. The major had won the Military Cross in the Second World War, back in the days before his paunch had begun to spread and his hair to thin. Now it was all past and his secret longing was for a well-paid job in the public relations belt, with the opportunity to ease his piles in a well-padded executive chair.

A sergeant came up carrying a case of instruments in one hand, a vacuum flask in the other. He opened the case and handed a stethoscope to the major and then opened the flask.

Beyond the line of police and soldiers a crowd had started to gather. It was early in the morning, but somehow the word had gone round. The ambient eyes that always focus around scenes of disaster or tragedy, or potential disaster or tragedy, had arrived. Among the crowd of flat-hatted, unshaven men there was a tall woman with stringy black hair who stood watching while she fed a baby at her breast.

'Look at that bloody old cow,' the major said.

The sergeant looked. 'Funny people, the Irish, sir. Probably the first bit of excitement she's had since she made the baby.'

The major was bending down, listening through the stethoscope at the side of the suitcase.

'She's ticking all right,' he said. His eyes blinked nervously behind his glasses. 'She could go, sergeant. You never know with these little bastards.'

The sergeant poured coffee from the flask and handed some to the major in a plastic beaker. The major cupped it in his hands, warming his palms. He drank some and handed the beaker back to the sergeant. He knelt down beside the suitcase and ran his fingers along the rim of the lid. His hand was small and pink and delicate and he moved it slowly and carefully. After a while he straightened up.

'Well, I don't think they've boobied it, but you never know.'

At the cordon's edge the growing crowd were pushing forward, trying to break through to where they could see things more clearly.

'I think it's got the usual clockwork timer inside,' the major went on, half to himself. 'You wouldn't expect anything too sophisticated in these parts, I suppose.'

He knelt again and started to work the fastening on the case. His thumbs pushed insistently against the fastening, but it would not move. He peered more closely at it and then stood up, eyes blinking.

'Sergeant,' he said, 'do you know what they've done? They've welded the bloody catch so we can't open the suitcase. I thought it was just locked, but no, it's a solid welding job. Look.'

The sergeant squatted down to see. 'A bit of the old spot welding, sir. Could be nasty, that.'

'Extremely.'

The cordon opened to allow a tall staff officer through. A pack of junior officers cavorted around his heels like attentive beagles.

'Sod my luck,' the major muttered when he saw him. 'Look at this bloody lot.'

The staff officer strode imperiously down on him.

'Good morning, sir,' said the major, saluting.

''Morning,' the staff officer said. 'What's the situation?'

'Under control, so far, sir.'

'Jolly good.'

'But I haven't rendered it safe yet, sir.'

'Oh, really? Well, oughtn't you to ...'

'I've checked it with the stetho, sir.'

'The stetho? Ah yes. The stetho.' He was a little lost, so

close to the groundwork. 'And you've assessed it?'

'Oh yes, sir. Highly volatile, I'd say, sir. Probably won't go just yet though.'

'Probably? Don't you know?'

'No sir.'

'I see. Well, I mean, done this sort of thing before have you ... ?'

'Oh yes, sir ... listen, you can just hear it ticking now. I was in Israel after the war, sir. When the Jews were trying to kick us out. Now the Jews, sir, they really could make a suitcase bomb. It was a pleasure dealing with one of theirs. Can you hear it ticking, sir?'

'Look here, isn't that thing likely to go off at any minute?'

'Yes, sir,' the major was poker-faced.

'Well, get on with it, man. Get on with it.'

As the staff officer disappeared back through the cordon the major grinned evilly and murmured: 'Up your pipe, Algernon.' It was a tenet of his that all staff officers were called Algernon at birth and that they changed their forenames on appointment to the staff to fool everyone. But they weren't fooling him.

'We lost a bit of time, there,' the sergeant said.

'Right,' the major said, 'let's get the damn thing sorted out.'

He rummaged in the case of tools. 'We'll try the hinges,' he said.

He pulled the suitcase flat onto the ground and got a pair of wire cutters in under the lid at the rear. The cutters found something metallic.

'Rivets,' the major said. 'Too round for the cutters to grip.'

He probed again behind the lid with his small, delicate fingers. After a while he said: 'Give me a long knife.' The suitcase was held at the back by two pieces of plastic that held the lid and the case together. The major put the knife on them and sawed through cleanly. Then he lifted the lid up from the rear.

'Here we are. Let's not hang about, sergeant,' he said, 'it

only goes up on you if you twitter.'

There were fifteen sticks of gelignite inside the case wired to a simple clockwork mechanism. The detonator was taped to the side of the suitcase.

'Professionals?' the sergeant asked as he handed the major a pair of watchmakers' pliers.

'Yes, of a sort,' the major said. 'They did all right and then they put in a duff detonator. Old WD stuff, must be twenty or thirty years old. Just as well they screwed it up, it would have made a nice bang.'

'The Lord protecting his own,' the sergeant said.

'What?'

'They say there's an old Irish king, Brian Boru, buried under this cathedral.'

'Oh, really?' The major was examining a bundle of gelignite.

'Yes sir, buried under here he is.'

'Bloody IRA, I suppose,' the major said. 'Bunch of rubbish. Bunglers. No time for them. If you're going to do a job, sergeant, for Christ's sake do it properly. Here.' He handed the bundle of gelignite to the sergeant and turned on his heel.

'I'm going for a smoke. Can't smoke here or we'd have poor Algernon shitting in his breeches. Blasted amateurs. The world's full of them.'

He walked away uneasily, wondering whether Algernon ever suffered from piles. He hoped he did.

*   *   *

Ross Simmons was up and ready for the world before eight o'clock that morning, sitting in the kitchen as his wife moved around preparing his breakfast. After a time he got up and put the wireless on. The news was just beginning.

Something stirred behind Ross Simmons' eyes as he listened to the news reader: 'An Army bomb disposal squad were rushed to Armagh early today after an attempt was made to blow up St Patrick's Church of Ireland Cathedral.

'The bomb, fifteen sticks of gelignite in a suitcase, had been planted on the steps of the cathedral during the night. The cathedral was cordoned off as the bomb disposal squad dismantled the bomb.'

Ross Simmons turned towards the kitchen: 'Sadie, Sadie, come and listen to this.'

The news reader was saying: 'Police and troops sealed off the area and people entering and leaving the city were questioned at checkpoints. Police say they have a strong lead in the case and are seeking a man for questioning in connection with the attempted bombing.'

'What is it?' Sadie asked.

'They tried to blow up the cathedral in Armagh.' Ross Simmons leaned back, frowning. 'Holy God, Sadie, the stupid bastards tried to blow up the Church of Ireland cathedral. The stupid, evil bastards. They'll not get away with this. The whole country will be against them.'

'Maybe it's the time for you,' she said.

'It is. It is indeed.' His face was flushed and he pounded his fist down on the table. 'This is the moment. Everyone will be with us now. There'll be no stopping us now.'

She went back into the kitchen and came back with two bowls of cornflakes.

'A breakfast fit for heroes,' she smiled. 'And there's scrambled eggs to follow. Eat up your breakfast, George.'

* * *

In Armagh Cahil Stevenson had been waiting for the explosion and when it did not come he became angry. There had been a .303 Lee Enfield rifle beneath his mattress. It was cleaned and oiled. He had spent an hour making it ready and counting the ten sharp-nosed clips of ammunition that lay alongside it, preparing himself for action. Now—nothing.

From early morning the activists had been ready and waiting for Armagh to spill over, and now there was a sense of let down. Word had reached Stevenson in the early morning that the police had found a bomb on the cathedral steps.

Dressing quickly he had gone into the pre-dawn blackness to rouse some other men and tell them to stand by with their weapons. Then he had gone home for his rifle. Cradling it in his arms he had gone out again, creeping by back roads towards the cathedral, but as he turned one corner he had come face to face with two members of the RUC.

'Where are you going?' one of them had asked.

Without answering he had turned and fled. Behind, he could hear them calling upon him to stop as heavy boots pounded into the pavement in pursuit. After a long time he had ducked down a back alley and into somebody's yard. While his heart and lungs pumped for life he hid himself in an outside lavatory, sitting on the cracked old pedestal, and listened to the policemen moving up and down the alley looking for him.

Eventually they went away. He sat there, slumped forward with his head touching his knees, as the breath rasped into his lungs. Sweat stood out boldly on his face and trickled down the hollow of his spine. The morning was warm and he excused the clamminess of fear because of it. As his breath came back his bowels began to ache with the need for purging. He leaned his rifle against the wall and let down his trousers. The trousers fell around his ankles and he sat there, one hand on the rifle, as he defecated. He did not hear the woman coming down the yard and she had opened the door before he realized she was there. Her hands were already pulling up her dress when she saw him and backed out screaming.

Stevenson lunged at the door, but she was too quick for him. The old wooden door swung closed and she bolted it from the outside while her screams rent the morning. He stood there in the warm darkness, holding the rifle and feeling foolish.

There was a man's voice outside now, telling her to be quiet, telling her to go into the house. The woman's screams changed to a loud sobbing as the man comforted her. Then he was at the lavatory door.

162

'Who's in there?'

'I'm sorry, mister, if I frightened your woman. I was taken short, that's all. I was taken short and I juked in here.'

There was a rattle as the bolt was pulled back and then the door opened. Stevenson looked out. There was a small, brawny man standing there. His sleeves were rolled up and he wore braces and a wide leather belt around his black serge trousers. He looked familiar.

The man looked at him and said: 'You've got a rifle.'

Now Stevenson recognized him. It was the B-Special who had clubbed him on the mouth with a rifle butt. The B-Special reached in to snatch the rifle away from Stevenson and, in an instinctive reaction, Stevenson pulled the trigger.

The .303 bullet caught the man in the stomach and carried him backwards for about two yards before he fell, still and silent, on the dirty concrete ground. He fell on his back and Stevenson looked at the blood already seeping from his stomach. White intestine was already beginning to debouch from his belly.

As he ran Stevenson felt hobbled. He dropped the rifle, but could move no faster. Something was stopping his legs from working properly. The two RUC men who had chased him earlier came back down the alley, running after him. This time they were gaining on him at a high speed. Sweat streamed down Stevenson's face as panic kept his legs moving.

The police were very close behind now. One of them shouted for him to stop, but Stevenson plunged blindly forward. The policemen had passed the open yard gate, had seen the woman who stood screaming hysterically and taken in the man who lay on the dirty concrete. They shouted again for Stevenson to stop, but he kept going.

He was passing the gates that led into the yards at an incredibly slow rate. A cat sitting on the wall suddenly arched its back and hissed at him. A menacing, hostile cat.

Behind him the voices were louder and more authoritative. There was a note of anger in them which he recognized. That note of anger kept him moving; he was not going to stop for angry men; angry men might hurt him.

Behind him the two policemen stopped and drew their revolvers. They lined them up and supported them on the wrists of their left hands and fired. One of the bullets tore past Stevenson, angry but impotent. The other caught him in the small of the back, just at the base of the spine, severing his locomotive nerves. He pitched forward in the alley and lay still, his hands stretched out above his head.

The two policemen put their guns away and walked towards him. Behind them the woman was screaming at the top of her lungs, strident yells that brought neighbours, bleary-eyed and inquisitive, to their back doors.

One of the policemen nodded down at Stevenson.

He lay there on his face with his trousers swaddled around his ankles. The policeman tapped lightly with his boot at one of the bare buttocks. 'Dignity in death,' he said.

Behind, the woman had stopped screaming. She just stood looking while her fingers tore at the neck of her dress.

17

Nealis awoke suddenly, dreaming that his right arm was trapped, and he was beginning to tug it free when Maire sat upright in their bed and looked at him, puzzled and sleepy-eyed.

'What's up?' she asked, the words distorted by an enormous yawn.

Nealis smiled. 'You were breaking my arm, that's all.'

'Poor darling.' Maire lay back again on the pillow, turning her face to Nealis and smiling softly, rubbing his numb fingers between her hands. She had entwined her naked legs around his and the memory of their lovemaking the previous night stirred her to gentle movement. She watched with growing excitement as Nealis looked into her eyes, detecting the flicker of renewed desire in him. She felt his fingers grip her hand strongly and very slowly he moved his head forward until his lips touched hers.

And then, in the room below, they heard movement, followed by the murmur of a radio. Listening to the radio was part of the pattern of Frank's waking moments ever since he had reappeared in Bogside the previous day. He was deaf to the continuous music but devoured every word of the news bulletins.

Nealis sighed, conscious of resentment replacing the sweet anticipation which had gripped him a moment before. Maire pulled a face and let him go.

Nealis dressed quickly and went down the stairs to the kitchen and washed himself under the cold tap; Maire came downstairs as he towelled himself dry and he forced a smile for her. She had begun to make the tea when he left the kitchen and went to the front room where the radio was playing.

Frank was sitting on the sofa with a tiny coffee table drawn up in front of him. On the table were some papers with diagrams on them, which he gathered up and slipped into his jacket pocket as Nealis walked in.

'Sleep well?' Nealis asked, closing the door behind him.

'Fine. Sofa's a bit small, but I managed fine.' Frank had a cigarette in his fingers and was patting his pockets absently in search of a match. Nealis walked across with his lighter and lit it for his brother. When he spoke it was almost casually.

'You must have been off your head, Frank,' he said. He perched himself on the arm of an easy chair facing Frank. 'What in the name of Christ possessed you to want to go and try it? They've got you fingered now, boy. What the hell did you think you were doing?'

'A lot,' Frank replied with the sharp edge of anger already in his voice. 'I thought it would do a lot of good. I knew it would.'

'But it's so bloody senseless!' Nealis's own anger was a compound of his physical frustration and his resentment at being in a situation that demanded a commitment from him.

'Senseless, is it?' Frank snarled, rising to his feet. 'Well, I suppose it depends on your attitude. I don't know about you, but for me the sense of it is that finally, after bloody miserable years, we are having a go at them.'

'Oh, for God's sake! How is it going to help if you start putting bombs in cathedrals?'

Frank looked across the room at Nealis, slowly stubbing his cigarette out in a plant pot.

'You don't understand, do you?' he said. 'You really do not understand. You've been here in Derry and you've seen the people in the streets and you've seen the machine of supremacist government in action against them, and still you haven't the slightest idea what it's all about, have you?

166

Christ, man, are you blind? Are you deaf?'

'No, I'm not. I can see a damned sight clearer than you can. You don't seem to appreciate that to go on and on and on with this kind of violence will only rebound on you in the end. A civil uprising like this is one thing—it carries a kind of conviction, a kind of truth with it. But your kind of mindless, mechanical bloodshed is something very different. Look, you want to change the system and nobody can argue with you that it needs changing. But the British government in involved now. They've taken their stand, they've forced concessions. What's the point of trying to whip up all the action again, now?'

'Balls. The British government are involved because they're embarrassed that all this should be happening on their own doormat. As soon as the situation quietens they'll be content to turn their backsides on us and let it all go back to square one. If we let them get away with it, there won't be a second chance. That's why it has to be kept going. It's like pulling out half-way when you're having it off. That's where this country is now. What it needs is the orgasm.'

The reference sparked off the frustration inside Nealis and he sprang from the chair. 'And you think blowing up a cathedral is going to achieve that? You think—'

'Yes, a cathedral. So bloody what? It's cheaper than a human life, even though human lives are cheap too if they'll buy us out of this shit-heap.'

'Oh, shut up, Frank. You're talking like a revolutionary pamphlet.'

'I'm not, Michael.' His voice was level and he spoke with controlled intensity. 'I'm not just talking. We have to be prepared to strike first, strike hard, and strike for good and all. Sure, I know you're a copper, you think differently perhaps. But I tell you I'm right, dead right.'

'I don't like to think so, Frank,' Nealis said gently.

Maire came into the room. She was smiling and rosy-cheeked and vital, just like she had been ever since they came back from Sligo.

167

'Could you boys drink a cup of tea?' she asked.

* * *

That morning, less than a mile away from Maire's house but on the other side of the Bogside barricades, five men of the Ulster Volunteers were meeting in the backroom of a tobacconist's shop on The Diamond. They called themselves Task Force Three, one of several groups of men who took their orders directly from George Ross Simmons and who were equally prepared to carry out his orders at any cost with a belief not one whit less passionate than Frank's.

Their leader was a sandy-haired man with almost invisible eyebrows and pale, baleful eyes. They called him Kenny, and the rest looked at him attentively when he spoke.

'These are copies of the passes they issue inside Bogside,' he said, slipping four pieces of printed paper across the table. 'They're pretty good but probably not perfect. Don't let anyone look at them too long or too closely.'

He produced another pass. 'This is the pass needed to get a car in and out, through the soldiers' lines, OK?' The others nodded.

'And finally,' Kenny said, 'this is the man who is going to be our guest.' From the inside pocket of his jacket, he produced a police poster and spread it on the table. Staring up at the five of them was a grim, soot-and-flour photograph of Frank Nealis. 'You've got a little while yet to get used to that face,' Kenny said. 'Then you'll have the pleasure of meeting him face to face. We'll break up now, and meet again at eight o'clock.'

* * *

In the sunshine, Frank Nealis walked through the streets of Bogside, acknowledging the occasional greeting with a tilt of his head. He was in no mood for casual conversation. Inside his rib cage, his heart pounded fiercely with sheer excitement and he felt also a curious sense of content. He had said it all to Michael that morning and now there was no further need for words of explanation to anyone.

He skirted Kilgallen Street with barely a glance at the black bones of the burned houses and the roadway littered with the aftermath of battle. A few minutes later, he entered the headquarters of the Citizens' Defence Association, walked past the man on the desk without a word and mounted the stairs at the rear. Waiting for him in the upstairs room were Bartley Mulholland and Larry Forrester, the monosyllabic American.

*   *   *

By the time Kenny got back to the tobacconist's shop at The Diamond at eight o'clock that evening, he had the information he wanted. The subject of the bomb attempt on Armagh Cathedral and Frank Nealis's part in it were topics easy to broach in casual conversation, even in suspicious Bogside, and he had been able, first, to establish that Nealis was back inside the enclave and, second, that he was staying in the O'Dwyer house in Glenna Street. Skill acquired in the British Army Intelligence Corps allied to Kenny's natural friendly face and easy manner had made the job a simple one. He was nonetheless conscious that the task assigned to his small commando group was dangerous, and he went carefully through all the moves with the other four and only when he was perfectly certain of himself and the others did he give the go-ahead for the operation.

The five men filed out of the shop and climbed into a plain Ford van. Kenny sat in the passenger seat and at the army post barring the way to Bogside, he produced all the passes. It was almost ten o'clock, and Kenny knew that the patrol at the post would be changed on the hour.

The corporal in charge glanced at the passes and looked inside the van without comment, then jerked his thumb in the direction of Bogside. Kenny nodded to the van driver, who drove slowly up Waterloo Street and into the heart of enemy territory. The streets were still busy with people. He continued to direct the driver until he located Glenna Street, where he stopped the vehicle outside Maire's house.

'I'll go to the door,' Kenny said. 'When I go in, you three follow. You'—he turned to the driver—'keep your eyes open.'

Kenny eased himself from the van, crossed the pavement and rapped on the door. Nothing happened for an age, and Kenny felt his gut begin to churn. He pushed on the door and it opened. Kenny entered the house. From the corner of his eye, he saw the other three leave the van by the rear door and follow him.

Frank Nealis was sitting with his feet on the fireplace reading a book when Kenny entered the kitchen.

'Are you Frank Nealis?' Kenny said.

Slowly, Frank put down the book. 'I am.'

'We'd like you to come with us. It's urgent business.'

'Who are you?' Frank asked. 'What business? I don't know of any urgent business.'

'We'd like you to come with us.'

'What's all this about?'

'There's no time,' Kenny said, the smile on his face fading now. 'Come on.' He grabbed Frank by the elbow and pushed him towards the door. The other three were standing there and two of them now produced guns.

'What the hell—'

'Frank Nealis, you are under arrest. You are charged with being an enemy of the state in that you have committed treason, attempted murder and attempted to commit sacrilege at Armagh in the early hours of yesterday.'

He was finishing the recital when Michael Nealis came into the room. One of the men turned a gun on him.

'Who are you?' Kenny asked.

'Who are you?' Nealis countered, still moving until he stood between the men with the guns and the door.

'That's none of your business,' Kenny said.

'What are you doing with him?'

'He's under arrest.'

Nealis's eyes flicked round the room. 'You're not police.'

'There's no time for questions. You come along with us, too.'

One of the armed men stepped forward and pushed his pistol into Frank's side and escorted him towards the door. Kenny nodded at Nealis, indicating he should follow. They left the room and hurried out to the van. It pulled away from the kerb with Frank and Michael in the back facing the guns of their captors.

At the army post on the Bogside perimeter the soldier freshly on duty had a good look inside the van and then waved them on. He had not seen their guns, hidden but menacing below the folds of the men's raincoats.

The vehicle headed out of Derry and up into the hills that slumbered beyond the rim of the city.

18

The place where they had been brought had once been a mill. It had stout stone walls and a stone floor and not far away they could hear the rush of water from one of the hill streams. Nealis had had no idea where the van had been heading, except that it had been mainly uphill, and there had been little chance to get bearings in the darkness as they were rushed out of the vehicle and into the room. The room itself was on two levels, one half being a raised stone plat-form probably used in its milling days as a storage area. On the platform stood a trestle table and a few kitchen chairs. The lower level contained a large refectory table and more chairs. There were two paraffin heaters on the floor and unshaded electric bulbs hung from the rafters. The only open-ings in the room were a large wooden door, a smaller door at the far end and half a dozen narrow windows, all of them barred on the outside. There had been plenty of time to take in the scene, for both Nealis and his brother had been sitting for over an hour in different corners of the room while the man named Kenny and his four accomplices sat around the big table, watchful and talking sporadically in low voices. One of them had boiled water on one of the paraffin heaters and made tea for them all, but it had long since been drunk and they were still waiting. Nealis had, at first, tried to question the others, trying to find out what the hell was happening, but his questions drew no response and he had given up. In the far corner, he could see Frank. He was sitting back-to-front on his chair with his arms folded across the chair back, his chin resting on his arms and his eyes staring at the floor.

172

Nealis judged it to be between two and three o'clock when they heard the sound of a car labouring up the steep path to the mill. Kenny and the others rose to their feet and Kenny went to the door and opened it, peering into the darkness. Car doors slammed and footsteps approached. Nealis was mystified to see Kenny suddenly snap to attention and execute a smart military salute. It was returned by a burly man who appeared on the threshold wearing a trench coat. For a moment, the shadow of the portal obscured his face, but as he stepped into the light, Nealis recognized him. Ross Simmons had arrived.

He screwed up his eyes against the light and slowly peeled off his coat. 'Why are there two?' he asked.

'The other one was with him when we took him,' Kenny said. 'I thought it best to bring the other one along, too.'

Ross Simmons nodded and walked across to Frank and stood looking down at him while Frank glared back. They remained in that position for several seconds, until Ross Simmons suddenly turned on his heel.

'We'll begin right away,' he said. Two men who had arrived with him had already jumped onto the platform at the end of the room and as he strode towards the platform, he approached Nealis's chair. Nealis rose, slowly.

'Would you mind telling me what the hell this is all about?' he said. Ross Simmons had stopped and one of Kenny's men moved close to cover Nealis with his gun.

'You?' Ross Simmons said, momentarily puzzled. 'Corporal Nealis? Are you ...?' He half-turned towards Frank.

'Frank's my brother,' Nealis said. 'But I'd still like to know what this is all about.'

'Are you mixed up in all this?' Ross Simmons asked.

'Not yet.'

'What is that supposed to mean?'

'It means I'm not mixed up in anything yet,' Nealis replied. 'But if this circus is anything like what I think it is, I might well be mixed up in it, and I'm warning you—'

'Warning me?' Ross Simmons' voice took on a harsh note.

'Warning me, Mister Nealis? Nobody warns me any more!'
He turned abruptly from Nealis and strode to the platform.
'We'll begin immediately. Bring the prisoner Frank Nealis
forward.'

Two of Kenny's men hustled Frank towards the platform
and stood either side of him. Ross Simmons took a seat at
the centre of the table on the platform, flanked by the two
other men. One of them handed him a sheaf of papers and
laid other papers in front of him.

'This is a military court martial,' Ross Simmons said loudly.
'The prisoner Frank Nealis has been brought here to answer
a number of serious charges. The Provost-Marshal will now
read them.'

The man on Ross Simmons' left began to read. Nealis could
hardly believe his ears. The charges alleged acts of treason,
acts of sacrilege and a handful of lesser charges, all phrased
exactly in the terminology of military justice. It should
have been laughable, but Nealis was becoming increasingly
alarmed at the seriousness of the whole charade.

'How do you plead?' Ross Simmons' voice cut through his
thoughts, and he watched as Frank was prodded in the ribs
by one of his escorts. 'How do you plead?'

'Go and fuck yourself, you bloody madman.' Frank spat
the words out, his face crimson with rage. There was a silence
and the whole assembly stood still for a second or two. Then
Frank sprang forward and leapt onto the platform in one
graceful movement and threw himself at Ross Simmons, over-
turning the table and sending the other two men scattering
to the stone floor. Kenny was the first to react. He fired a shot
into the roof and the suddenness of the earsplitting noise
froze the action for just long enough. As Frank rose from the
ground to lunge at the prone figure of Ross Simmons, they
hit him with their gun butts, dragged him across the platform and threw him down to the lower level. Frank hit the
floor and rolled over twice and then lay still with blood
welling from his nose and forehead.

Nealis, who had moved to the platform, took the full weight

of one of Kenny's men on his back as he hit the edge, and collapsed, gasping for breath. The blood pounded in his ears, but above it he could hear the noise he was making as he forced his paralysed muscles to draw air down into his lungs. Above him, he could see Ross Simmons standing at the edge of the platform and then jump to the ground and walk over to where Frank lay. Ross Simmons' feet were close to him and he watched as they kicked viciously at Frank's body. Nealis tried to struggle up, but he could only make it to his knees. He reached out for Ross Simmons' arm but the other man had moved on and Nealis fell close to his brother. He could see the blood on his face clearly now. If he could have reached Ross Simmons, he would have killed him, and he felt himself trembling with frustration as he began to retch.

An excited din of voices echoed around him and then slowly subsided as Ross Simmons' authoritative tones cut through it. Nealis saw two of Kenny's men come across to Frank and drag him away to the far end of the room where they disappeared from his view. He remained on his knees with his throbbing head bowed in grateful supplication on the cold stone floor until the breathing grew easier and then he gradually uncoiled and stood up. Apart from the regular stabs of pain in his gut when he breathed, he felt recovered.

Ross Simmons had also regained his composure and was sitting at the refectory table.

'Come here, lad,' he said.

'Don't patronize me, you murderous bastard,' Nealis snarled. 'I'll see you sent down for a long stretch for this.'

'Still the policeman, Nealis?' Ross Simmons said. 'If you are, you're a long way from your beat. I'm the law here.'

Nealis forced a smile. 'You call that pantomime law? You must be off your head. In fact, I'd have been prepared to see you go to the madhouse until you began to put the boot in on Frank. You'll answer for that one day, Simmons, believe me.'

'I'll answer for nothing to the like of you,' Simmons roared. 'You think I'm playing games or something?' As he spoke, he got up from the table and came to stand close to Nealis, speaking more loudly than was necessary. 'I'm not playing, lad, believe me.'

'You're a bloody nut,' Nealis said.

Ross Simmons looked at him coldly.

'You should be locked up,' Nealis said.

'You be careful now, boy,' Ross Simmons said. 'You're flying in the face of the Lord. There is evil stalking this land and I mean to weed it out. I mean to purge this land of its sins. Hallelujah, the Lord has chosen me to be the instrument of his justice.'

'You're off your bloody head,' Nealis said.

Ross Simmons trembled with anger. Abruptly and without warning, his mood changed.

'You must have respect,' he shouted. 'You know what I am. I've told you. You must treat me with respect.'

'You nut,' Nealis said contemptuously.

'Hit him, please,' Ross Simmons said.

One of the men came across, a big man with big hands. He punched Nealis violently and suddenly in the kidneys. As Nealis slumped to his knees Ross Simmons said: 'I'm taking over the government of Ulster very soon. We're going to get rid of all the traitors and I'm taking over.' He smiled softly. 'Your brother will go on trial for treason,' he said at last. 'And so will many others. The penalty for treason is death. You see, lad, I'm really not playing games. I was never more serious in my life.'

Nealis gazed at Simmons for some seconds before he replied.

'I think you are certifiable.'

'You're a bit of a problem,' Simmons said. 'I'm not quite certain what to do with you, but you can keep your brother company. By the time we meet again, I think it very likely that I shall have the power I need. Goodbye.' He marched to the door, followed by the two men who had arrived with him. Kenny went out with them, but returned after a few minutes and muttered an order to two of his men. They lifted Nealis from the chair into which he had

176

slumped and walked him across to the door at the far end of the room. Inside, Frank was lying on a carpet of straw scattered over the floor. Nealis was pushed in, the door closed and bolts were drawn. Nealis knelt by Frank and, in the dim light of a single bulb, examined him. There were cuts on his forehead and bruises had spread darkly over his cheek and his jaw, but he was breathing regularly and as Nealis struggled to drag him to a sitting position, he regained consciousness.

'You all right?' Nealis whispered.

'I'm still alive,' Frank said softly.

'OK, now, you'd better rest up. There's just about fuck-all we can do for the moment except sleep.'

Frank nodded, touching his bruised face tenderly before curling up in the straw.

Nealis kicked a bundle of it together and sat down, deep in thought. He remembered he still had cigarettes and his lighter and he lit one gratefully, reflecting on the events of the past twenty-four hours, dwelling on the conflicting values he had seen in that time, remembering the things he had seen and heard and experienced since his return to Ireland eighteen days before.

It was daylight before he lay down to sleep, covering himself with straw and cloaking his mind in the sweet memory of Maire.

*   *   *

He was awakened by the noise of the bolt on the door being rattled. He had not meant to sleep so deeply, had intended to be alert when the men on the other side of the door made their move. Now, he burst from his bed of straw and waved silently to Frank, who had already risen to his knees. Urgently, Nealis motioned his brother to lie down again and keep quiet. Frowning, Frank obeyed him.

The door swung open. For a few seconds, nobody appeared, but then one of Kenny's men advanced cautiously to the threshold. Behind him, another man held a pistol in readiness. The first man held two steaming mugs of tea and he advanced warily into the little room, putting the mugs down on the floor without taking his eyes from Nealis and Frank.

Nealis walked slowly to the door, stopping to pick up one of the cups. 'I won't be needing this one,' he said. 'My brother is dead.' Nealis slumped against the doorpost, a picture of dejection. The two men exchanged quick glances, both revealing a hint of fear. The man with the gun was the first to react. In a sudden movement, he stepped forward to the doorway. Nealis threw the scalding tea in his face when he was a yard away. The gunman had no chance. As Nealis locked his arm and propelled him into the room, Frank emerged like a bull and bent him double with a battering-ram punch. The pistol spun to the floor and as Nealis scrabbled for it, he saw the other man running out.

'Wait here,' Nealis yelled, and leapt across the mill room in pursuit. Outside, his quarry was opening the door of the van in frantic haste. Nealis yelled at him to stop, keeping the pistol pointed at the vehicle. Ten yards away, he could see the other man at the wheel and he realized that if the van moved, it would need to travel no more than three feet before the driving cab was hidden behind a stone wall.

Suddenly, the van door opened and the man sat there with his hands in the air. Suspicious, Nealis backed against the wall to his right, covering the man with the pistol. Slowly, still with his arms aloft, the man slipped from the van and walked towards Nealis and stopped.

'I haven't got the fucking key,' he said. There was just a tinge of humour in his voice, and Nealis grinned.

'Tough,' he said. 'Now move inside.'

Frank had already torn the electrical flex from one of the light fittings and had bound the arms of the unconscious gunman. After tying up the second man, he and Nealis searched the gunman and found an ignition key. Leaving their former captors, the brothers took the van and headed away from the mill.

Frank's face was badly bruised and the cuts on his head

had congealed but his nose was bleeding again. Nealis, at the wheel, glanced across at him.

'How are you feeling now?'

'Fine.' He watched the road for a while, then added: 'That was a pretty smart thing you did back there.'

'Maybe I'm not so dumb as I look.'

'Maybe not,' Frank almost smiled.

'Anyway, it was lucky. We might both have been killed.'

'Oh, no,' Frank said. 'Not me. It'll take more than those bastards to kill me. I'd have crawled back somehow. I've something to settle with Ross Simmons.'

They relapsed into silence. The signposts ticked off the mileage to Londonderry. They would be back within the hour.

19

The soldiers sitting behind their sandbagged barricades were conscious of the hostility in the air, but they could not tell where it was coming from, or if it meant anything. Then, on a Saturday night after the bars closed, the hostility fused together into a solid wall of hatred. Some people saw what was happening and went home to their beds, but others turned the other way and set out to allay their rage in action.

At the Bogside barricades a group of Protestant youths assembled and began hurling taunts across the wire. For a while the soldiers looked on in silence. Then, by the time they decided to disperse the crowd, there were too many people and the mood had built up into one of unrelenting, vigorous aggression.

The Protestants felt that their government had been humbled by these people in the Bogside, and they had stood out against the constitutional forces of law and order. Inside their papist ghetto they were paying no allegiance to the Crown, and their attitude towards the historical fact of Protestant Ulster was one of contempt. They should have been crushed ruthlessly, as traitors and revolutionaries, but they had not. Instead the government had brought British soldiers in to safeguard them in their open defiance of authority. If the government could not subdue them somebody else had to do it.

The people at the front were jostling the soldiers, trying to push their way through. A corporal who was in charge of the detachment saw what was going to happen and spoke urgently into his walkie-talkie, asking for reinforcements, but now the crowd was powerful and implacable. With a giant surge they pushed their way forward, skeltering the soldiers like so many ninepins. Within yards they were in the enemy territory.

With the first rush over there was indecision. There was no leader and the crowd swayed to a stop, tangled and disorganized only ten paces within the Bogside area. Men looked at each other, whispering and asking what was the next thing to do, but nobody was quite sure. They remained like that for a short time, then somebody shouted: 'Come on, you Fenian bastards. Come on out.'

On the opposite side of the road there was a small group of Bogsiders. They had been standing, taking the night air and talking of the events which had so rudely brought drama to their lives. In silence they watched as the invaders pressed against the barricades, and then in horror as they saw them break through. Several of them had been dispatched to pass the word, and even as the challenge rang out across the wasted no-man's-land, the streets behind were already beginning to fill with men, summoned from their homes by this new threat. Many of them were in shirtsleeves and one man, on his way to bed when the summons came, wore a pyjama jacket with denim trousers.

As they approached, somebody in the front rank of the invaders charged forward and the Bogside men quickened their pace. Seconds later they came together in a vast swirl of fists and clubs, yells and screams.

The fighting had been going on for no more than minutes when the army reinforcements arrived. They drove into the crowd, singling out the ringleaders and hauling them away.

The khaki line wedged itself between the battling factions and drove the men who had come down from The Fountain back out through the barricades. Then the medical orderlies moved in to pick up the wounded.

There was a jumble of men on the ground, men with cracked skulls and broken bones. The orderlies went about their work methodically, picking them up on stretchers and taking them to military ambulances. Some of those who were conscious and capable of movement rose at the approach of the soldiers and scuttled away into the night.

As they reached each man the orderlies bent down to feel his pulse. After a time one of the orderlies paused at one man and called: 'Sergeant.'

The sergeant came across and looked.

'This one's dead, sarge.'

The sergeant bent to examine the body. 'Poor old sod. Kicked to death, most likely.'

The man had been about fifty. His sparse, greying hair was embedded in his skull, covered with deep, red coagulating blood. His face had been battered out of shape, his features pulped.

'Have a look, lad, see if there's any identification.'

The soldier crouched beside the body, going through the pockets of the shabby serge suit. After a while he straightened up: 'Nothing, sarge.'

'Well, we'll have to get some sort of identification. Put him in the ambulance.'

A large, muted crowd of Bogsiders stood across the road from the ambulance, watching the soldiers taking away the injured. Suddenly there was a commotion at the barricade. A small woman of middle age was standing there, arguing with the soldiers.

'I want to see if he's in there,' she was saying. 'Will you not let me through? Please. You'll have to let me through.'

There were two vigilantes standing among the Bogside crowd. Now they walked forward to the barricade. They looked at the soldiers and at the woman. Then one of them asked: 'What is it you want, missus?'

'My man, he was in there. He hasn't come out. I want to know what you've done to him.'

'We haven't done anything to him, missus.'

'You've done something. He hasn't come out.' The woman's voice rose an octave in anguish.

'Come on and see then.' One of the vigilantes nodded to

the soldier who held her back. The soldier moved out of the way and the woman slipped round him and into the alien area.

They walked back to the ambulance and as they did so the woman paused to peer at each of the men who lay on the ground. There were only a few left now, but the man she was looking for was not among them. Two orderlies marched up with a stretcher bearing the dead man. The woman looked at the stretcher, disbelief etched on her face. Then she moved forward, walking alongside the orderlies, saying nothing as she looked at the body they were carrying. They were about to put the body in the ambulance when she stopped them. 'No, put him on the ground.' Her voice was steady.

The sergeant bustled over. 'Can you identify ... ?'

'He's my husband,' she said. She raised a hand to her head, patting her hair into place, then she turned back to the sergeant: 'What's wrong with him?'

One of the vigilantes looked across at his companion, then turned and walked quietly away. The other stood there, watching the woman and the sergeant.

'What's wrong with him?' she asked again.

The sergeant looked away, shaking his head. 'Please, what's wrong with him?' the woman said again.

The vigilante moved towards her: 'He's dead, missus.'

'Ah, look at his poor face. What have they done to his poor face?'

'Come over here and sit down, missus.' There were some women standing by. The vigilante turned to them and said: 'Go and get a cup of tea for this woman.' One of the women hurried away.

'Ah, Jesus, the poor cratur,' the widow moaned. 'He only came in to look for the young feller.' She was crying now, the slow tears running down her face. 'He didn't want any trouble, but he thought the young feller was in here. He only came in to look for the young feller.'

She looked at the vigilante accusingly. 'How did they do that to his face? It was boots that done that, no fists ever done that. The filthy swine.'

A woman approached her with the tea. She had got out her best china and she proffered the tea in a dainty cup with roses on the side. The woman from The Fountain looked at it for a moment: 'Take that away. I want nothing from you people. Take it away.'

The woman with the tea stood looking around, embarrassed, but when the vigilante nodded to her she moved back among the crowd.

'So you killed him,' the woman said. 'Ah, so you killed him.' She rose and turned to the army sergeant. 'Would you bring him up for me? Up to my house. It isn't far.'

'Yes, ma'am.'

They put the body in the ambulance and let the woman into the passenger seat and the ambulance moved away into the night. The crowd watched as its tail lights went through the barricade and disappeared up the hill to The Fountain.

20

Mother Kate died of a compound fracture of the skull and because a sharp piece of broken rib speared its way through her lung. The doctor in charge of her case was not surprised that she died, only surprised that she had lived so long.

Maire heard the news over the telephone.

She went to the telephone box at the corner of her street, put in her money and dialled the hospital. There was a wait while they put her through to the ward sister.

'Are you a relative?'

'Yes, I am.'

'Well, I'm sorry to tell you that Mrs Nealis passed away in the early hours of this morning. It was in her sleep, and there was no pain.' The voice was cool, efficient and oddly comforting.

'Can I come up?'

'Yes, please do. You might like to know she saw the Father before she died.'

'Oh good, good. Thank you.'

Maire pushed herself out of the phone box and leaned against the wall, tears misting her eyes. After a while she straightened herself up, wiping her eyes with a handkerchief, and walked around the corner to the church. She waited in the cold, bare ante-room to the presbytery, looking at the oilcloth that smelled of disinfectant, until the priest came. It was not the parish priest, but a curate newly arrived from Maynooth seminary.

'I'd like to make arrangements for a funeral, Father,' she said.

'Somebody belonging to you, Maire?' he asked. He was a young, fresh-faced priest whose shoulders looked uncomfortably large in his black soutane.

'Mrs Nealis,' she said.

'Ah, poor Mrs Nealis. When did she go?'

Maire told him about the telephone call to the hospital. 'I'd like a Requiem Mass for her,' she said.

The priest looked puzzled. 'Tell me, Maire. Why are you doing this? Mrs Nealis has a family, has she not?'

The sudden tears were in her eyes again: 'Her sons have disappeared, Father,' she said. 'Frank and Michael. They just disappeared. I don't know where they are. Somebody has to do this.'

'Are they taken by the police, do you think?'

'God alone knows.' Her manner was defeated and resigned. 'Well ... well, I'll look after this now. I'll arrange for the Requiem and all that, but what about the funeral arrangements? Can you do all that?'

'Don't worry, Father, I'll manage.'

At the Free Derry Citizens' Defence Association there were the usual clutch of men standing around. Maire walked through them and up to the desk, which Festy was manning.

'Mrs Nealis is dead,' she said.

'Ah, God in heaven, isn't that terrible,' he said. The sympathy was apparent.

'That's not all,' Maire said, 'her two sons have disappeared. There's no relative to claim her.'

'Now that's a problem,' said Festy. 'It is indeed.'

'We'll get over that somehow, but there's other problems. She'll have an insurance policy, no doubt, and nobody can claim that but either Michael or Frank. God knows what's happened to them. I think the Bogside should bury her. Every man and woman here should put in something for her funeral.'

'You're right there,' Festy said. 'One of our own undertakers will do it in grand style.'

'Yes, they might. Thank you, Festy. I'm going up to the

hospital to make the arrangements there. Can you get some-one here to make the funeral arrangements? I've already been to the church about the Requiem, but the priest will need to know when the funeral is to be. Can that be done?'

'Ah, sure I'll do that myself,' Festy said.

As Maire went out, Bartley Mulholland, who had been standing with the men near the door, fell into step alongside her. 'I'll walk a wee piece of the way with you,' he said.

She felt a vague sense of annoyance. 'All right. If you want.'

When they had walked about twenty yards in silence Mulholland suddenly said: 'I found out what happened to the Nealises.' The way he said it was deliberately casual.

Maire stopped in mid-stride. 'What?'

'I found out what happened to them.'

'Where are they? How do you know?'

'Oh, I have my sources of information too. I hear things. Ross Simmons's bullyboys took them.'

'What? Here in the Bogside?'

'That's right. Here in the Bogside. They came in and snatched them away as clean as you like.'

'But why should they do that?'

'Ah, well ... who can say? They may have come in after Frank and taken the other fellow to make up the weight.'

'Christ alive! What will they do to them?' Fear and per-plexity mingled in Maire's face. 'Where are they? What's happening?'

'I don't know that, and what they'll do is anybody's guess. They're not the only two to go missing. Mr Ross Simmons is up to something.'

'God curse him. He should be stopped, that man,' she said.

'Ah now, he will be. When the time comes.' He paused, looking at her. 'You might be able to help, Maire.'

'Me?'

'You're a pretty girl, Maire.' Mulholland gave one of his characteristic nicotine smiles.

'Is that a compliment?'

187

'It is. And a general observation. Female beauty is a great weapon, if it's used right. Ah, but no doubt you know that.' He chuckled.

'What is all this, Bartley?'

'Ah now, think of Mata Hari.'

'What the hell do you mean, Mata Hari? What do you want?'

'I'm just thinking, if the time came would you be the girl who'd give us a hand?'

She thought for a moment. 'Sure, I'll help with the Civil Rights, but I'm not sure about you. I don't know what you are up to. You're playing some game of your own.'

He looked at her, candour in his eyes: 'Now that's true, Maire. To an extent that's true. You see, the marching is one thing, but what I believe in is another. After the marching and the speechifying the situation will always return to where it was before, unless something stops it. There's very little that's as solid as the status quo. If it is to be budged then things have to be expedited.' He grinned again: 'You can call me an expeditor.'

'What do you want me to do?'

The candour was back in his eyes. 'Maire, child, I don't know yet. But if you have the heart for it I'm sure there'll be some work for you before long. Valuable work that will put an end to this supremacist nonsense for all time. Are you on?'

'Try me,' she said.

Leaving Mulholland, Maire took the bus that climbed steeply across the face of Derry to the hospital. There was a brisk nurse, all starch and white uniform, beside the almoner's office, which was a small glass cubicle set in the middle of the casualty reception unit. Maire walked up to it, looking at the battered debris of a city's life sitting around on benches waiting for attention. The almoner was a quizzical girl with rimless spectacles. She kept nodding in agreement as Maire explained what she was there for.

It took some time to fill in the hospital form. Little things

188

like the details of when Mrs Nealis had been born defeated her, but eventually the almoner was finished. The nurse who had been standing by the office smiled at her. 'I'll take you down,' she said.

They walked down to the basement and along endless corridors that smelt of soap and anaesthetics to get to the mortuary. There was a little man at the door wearing a black uniform and a hat that was half a size too large for him.

'Mrs Nealis,' Maire said quietly.

They went in to where the dead were filed away in decency and order in long sliding drawers that moved silently and smoothly on oiled castors. The drawers were green and impartial, but the little man led her to one on the second tier that said 'Nealis' on a piece of white paper smaller than a postcard. No 'Katherine', no 'Mrs', just the surname.

The little man was pulling open the drawer and she watched in silent fascination and sorrow. The dead woman, Nealis, was laid out neatly in a long white shroud that covered her from neck to toe. The hands were loosely folded across the chest and somebody had closed her eyes.

The face was lined and waxen, peaceful and set in the lines of a last repose, but around her head she wore a thick swathe of bandage.

'She looks like an Egyptian mummy,' Maire said. It was not what she meant to say, but that is how it came out.

'Aye, that's thon bandage,' the little man said. 'She'll be right as rain when the undertaker gets at her. Sure he'll take that off and comb up her hair all nice and neat. Thon's no trouble.'

'I suppose not.'

'Naw, the undertaker'll have her fixed up in no time. Sure I've seen these head cases, aw, far worse than thon, but when your man the undertaker has done with them sure they look absolutely beautiful.'

'Yes,' Maire said, feeling the emptiness all around and inside.

'Aye, miracles they can perform. Your mother was she?'

'She was my mother-in-law.' The statement came out unthinkingly.

'Aye, it's powerful sad. A fine woman, and her no age at all. What was it—car crash?'

'No, she was murdered.'

'Christ almighty. Murdered? Where was that?'

'Down in the Bogside.'

'Who murdered her? I didn't hear anything about no murder.'

'No,' Maire said, 'you wouldn't. They're trying to keep this one a secret.'

* * *

She carried the picture of the pale corpse back to the Bogside with her, and as she thought of the still form that lay alone in the hospital, a feeling of utter isolation took hold of her. Life was for protecting the ones you love from hurt. She remembered the words, and grimaced now at their futility. Nobody can save anybody from anything, she thought. In the end, everybody's got to take it, take it where it hurts most, and take it alone.

That woman, Mrs Nealis, Mother Kate, lying there dead, had asked little of life, and even then, got less than she asked. And after it, the end had come for her mindlessly and without discrimination. She had two sons, Michael and Frank, but when the hurt came they could not do anything about it, they could offer no protection. She was a woman on her own, as ultimately everybody is on their own. Nothing could alter that. And nothing the sons could do or say or think could alter that. The pain and the hurt were hers, and hers alone.

Back in the Bogside she met Bartley Mulholland again. He was leaning against the boarded-up window of a bar and as she came along he raised a hand in salute.

'We meet again, Maire. The luck is with me today.'

'Bartley.' She moved to step around him.

'What's the matter, Maire? You look down. Are you

190

pining for that English policeman, maybe?' There was a sly, insinuating smile on his face.

'And what if I am? What's that to you?'

'Well now, say I'm jealous as ever man must be to see an Englishman, and a policeman to boot, coming in and getting the best-looking girl in Bogside under the noses of everybody.'

'Oh,' she said, her voice cracking with ice, 'I didn't think you were interested. In any case he's not an Englishman, he's as Irish as you and then some, and you can forget the cracks about him being a policeman.'

She paused, remembering the conversation she and Michael had had when they had discussed going away together.

'I'll have to make some changes in my life,' he had said.

'I'm the change,' she had replied, happy and in love.

'More than that, Maire. I'm going to finish with the police.'

'But Michael, that's your job, your career. Are you sure..?'

'I'm sure,' he had cut in on her. 'Maybe even if I hadn't met you I would have decided that I'd had enough. I have my thoughts about it.' Suddenly he had laughed. He had picked her up by the waist and pivoted round till her skirt billowed out behind her. He had been slightly out of breath when he had put her down, saying: 'Maire, I have you now. I don't need the police force, I'm not going back when my leave runs out. I don't need any God damn thing.'

Mulholland was still smiling at her: 'All right, Maire. No cracks. You know me, I can't resist a bit of a laugh.'

Suddenly she could no longer bear to stand talking to him: 'Well, go and laugh some place else, you silly bastard.'

He grinned disarmingly: 'Silly bastard is it? All right, Maire. But don't forget there may be work for you yet.' He walked off down the street, big and confident and whistling an old Irish rebel tune.

And there goes Bartley Mulholland, she thought. Bartley Mulholland who whistles and laughs, and drinks and enjoys a laugh and who does not know pain. Christ help you, Bartley. Christ help you.

While back there in the hospital the old woman, dead and stiffening with the huge white bandage like a rajah's turban sticking up on her head, waited for the undertaker to take it off to restore her to a semblance of life so that some of the pain of her death could be spared the living who saw her. Christ help you, Mother Kate. And Christ help the poor dead man from The Fountain, who had been looking for his son and meaning no harm, or in there fighting savagely with oaths on his lips, according to whom you believed. It did not matter now, for he was dead and there was pain too up in The Fountain, in the breast of his widow and the hearts of his children and friends. Christ help them all.

And Christ help Michael. Wherever he was and whatever he was doing.

Suddenly she realized that she was crying for the third time that day. She stopped and dried her eyes with the small, linen handkerchief that was hardly dry from the last time she had used it.

She walked on up the road, graceful and girlish, and the young men lounging at the street corners turned their heads and whistled after her as she thought: And Christ help me.

21

They abandoned the van on the edge of the Bogside and walked towards the barricades. A few yards in both men became aware of the subtle change in the atmosphere of the city. The hangover of the previous night's foray hung in the air along with the Union Jacks and the orange favours with which Protestant taunted Catholic across the flimsy barriers dividing them. The soldiers were more numerous than they had been for a week, and their bayonets were once more fixed and the clips on their gas mask carriers unbuckled in readiness. At the barricades, the troops were stopping and searching everyone who attempted to cross the line. Frank took Nealis's arm and directed him into a side street running parallel with the Bogside boundary. There, he led the way through an alleyway between two houses, scaled a fence, crossed a patch of waste land. On the other side, they were back in Bogside.

They hurried past the shifting groups on the street corners and past the open doors and the doorsteps where the mothers stood and the children played bizarre games and re-enacted the violence with innocent laughter.

Nealis broke into a run as they reached the corner of Glenna Street and arrived at the door of Maire's house ahead of Frank.

She was standing in the kitchen watching the kettle beginning to boil on the blue gas jets and didn't hear him arrive. Nealis stopped on the threshold and indulged himself in the unobserved sight of her.

'Maire,' he said softly. She turned, startled and dumb and

remained rooted for seconds. There were tears on her cheeks and her lips trembled as she struggled for words which could not be spoken. And then she ran into his arms and hugged him with frantic fervour while he stroked her head and whispered to her, pacifying her and soothing her. Frank entered as they kissed and she broke off at the sight of him, shaking her head in an attitude of disbelief as she saw the bruises on his face and the congealed blood caked around his cuts. She busied herself around them with unnatural energy and spoke now in a verbal cascade, blinking back tears which Nealis thought were tears of joy. She questioned them and they answered with the barest details while she tended Frank's injuries. He submitted to the hot water and iodine without protest. He offered to leave her and Nealis, but she pounced on him and insisted he take tea which she was going to make anyway. In a high, welcoming-nervous voice she told what details she knew of the previous night and the single death which had already assumed a significance beyond its intrinsic importance. All the time, she talked. Only when she had given them tea did she pause for a few moments and sit down at the table. Suddenly, she stood up.

'Mother Kate's dead.'

'What?' Frank's low growl was an automatic response to which Maire did not reply.

'I'm sorry,' she said. 'She went peacefully. I couldn't do any more ...' Her voice trailed off inaudibly.

Nealis remained perfectly still, riding the impact of the news. Frank had buried his head in his hands. Maire reached out a tentative hand to touch Nealis's shoulder.

'I'm sorry,' she said. He kissed her fingers absently and shook his head, absolving her but lost in the quicksand thoughts inside him. Poor Mother Kate. The victim. Always the victim. How typical of fate to let her die alone.

'That bastard!' Frank had barely moved as he spoke. 'That bastard. We should have been there, shouldn't we? And we would have been, but for that bastard.'

'Easy, Frank,' Nealis said.

'Easy?' He got up from the chair and went to stand by the fireplace, lighting a cigarette with hands that shook slightly. 'How can I be easy? Me Ma died all on her own, didn't she? All on her bloody own, when we should have been there with her.'

'Frank, you mustn't torture yourself,' Maire said. 'You mustn't do that.'

'I'm not torturing myself,' Frank snapped. 'It's too late for that, but I'm going to settle this score with Ross Simmons, by God I am. And I'm going to settle it soon.'

'Oh Christ, Frank, do we have to go through all that again?' Nealis felt sick in his gut. 'Isn't it enough that she's dead?'

'It may be enough for you. You can sit on your arse and let the world walk over you, but I'm not. My mother is dead. Alone in a bloody hospital bed ... not a soul in the world to care about it, while I was being held prisoner by a maniac—'

'She was my mother too,' Nealis said. 'And I was in the hands of the same maniac at the same time, but for God's sake let's think about one thing at a time. Do what you like with Ross Simmons. If someone shoots him it can only be an act of kindness to the rest of the world, but don't use her body as a barricade, Frank.'

'OK, OK. I'm sorry. It's just ... Oh, Christ, me poor Ma. That poor old woman lying there and dying all on her own.' He sank into an armchair and rested his head on his arms. He was crying.

Nealis had never seen Frank cry before, even when they had been kids. They had had private worlds of their own then, of course, separated by the chasm of three years. He had only known Frank as a defiant, unyielding boy, a loner with a toughness that was unique in that it appeared to have no weakness at the core of it. Nothing made Frank cry, but now he was crying. For the first time in his life, Nealis felt the tug of the unfathomable bonds which linked him to his brother.

Frank slowly uncoiled and stood up. He averted his face from Nealis and Maire and started for the door.

'Where are you off to?' Nealis asked.

'I'm going to see her.'

'Frank!' Nealis sprang across the room, blocking the doorway. 'You can't go, Frank. That place is crawling with police. They'll pick you up for sure, the moment you go inside.'

'Let them try,' Frank said hoarsely.

'They will.'

'I don't give a stuff. I'm going. I want to see Mother Kate and nobody is going to stop me.'

'But—'

'Not even you, Michael. I'm going. Out the way.'

'Look, Frank. Wait. Just wait. I'm coming with you. Please.' He held his brother by both arms in his urgency. 'We'll make it all right, but together, Frank. We'll go there together.'

Frank stood impassive, then nodded and leaned back against the kitchen wall with his head thrown back, staring at the ceiling.

'Fine,' Nealis said. 'We'll wait until evening. Visiting hours are at seven. We'll go in with the crowds and in case there is any trouble at all, I'll have my warrant card with me. We'd both better get into some decent clothes, too. And when we get there, do as I say. But the main thing is to get in and pay our last respects in peace and then get out again.'

'Do you think there'll be many police there?' Maire said.

'I don't know. I hope they've been too busy elsewhere, but if I knew that the mother of a wanted man had died in hospital, I'd stake the place out round the clock. What we have to bank on is their not knowing or at least, not tying the two things together.'

Later, upstairs in Maire's bedroom where he had gone to change into a suit, Nealis stared at the worn old photograph of Mother Kate which he kept in his wallet. It was a rough sepia print with the word 'Proof' stamped across it. She had had it taken at a photographer's studio in Derry and had never managed to afford the price of a proper print. As she had prophesied, with an optimistic shrug, the ink from the rubber stamp had almost worn away and although the cardboard was bent and cracked, the handsome, long-ago features of the woman who had been Katherine Holloran stared out with the same fortitude with which she had lived her life.

The tingle of imminent tears made him blink and the picture blurred. Nealis turned away from it, depressed and empty inside. Slowly, he undressed and pulled on the trousers of his suit, glad of these few moments to himself. He had been glad that the problem of Frank had arisen. It had given him something to think about, something to do. He pulled on his jacket and picked up his wallet. His warrant card was in there, and the last of his cash, about thirty pounds. He wondered, half-thinking, where he would get more and the train of thought reached back to Liverpool and the tangle of his former life, and then the thought petered out. He walked downstairs to where Maire and Frank had been talking sporadically.

'Ready?' Frank said. He too had changed.

'Yes, let's go.' Nealis turned to Maire and kissed her once on the cheek. 'We'll be back.'

'Yes,' she said. 'You said that before. I'd almost forgotten to be glad you're back. It's ...'

'Sure. We'll talk all about it later.'

'You're always going away.'

'And coming back.' Nealis kissed her again and made for the door. Frank followed, and they walked out into the street and the mellow gloom of a summer evening.

They negotiated the barricades without difficulty and walked together across the city, skirting The Diamond and heading for the Foyle Bridge. They walked quickly and said little.

At the Isolation Hospital on the Waterside, they found a squad of soldiers standing at the main gates in the wall surrounding the building. They showed no interest in the thin stream of people entering and leaving, however, and Nealis walked past them with Frank a pace behind him. Now Nealis was fully alert, watching for uniforms and assessing every man for the chance that he might be a detective in plain clothes. They went through the main entrance of the hospital. Nealis hesitated for a moment, deciding whether to go to the ward and enquire there or whether to ask at the reception window. He elected to go to the ward. The fewer who knew why they were there, the better. The corridor leading to the ward was empty and their footsteps squeaked on the plastic-covered floor. A nurse was walking slowly round the ward, pausing here and there for a word. It took several minutes for her to complete her round before she made for the door.

Outside, Nealis spoke to her: 'I would like to see the body of Mrs Katherine Nealis.'

'May I ask who you are?' the nurse countered.

'I'm her son.'

'Will you wait here?'

As she spoke, Nealis recognized the almost imperceptible dilation of her pupils. He had seen it before, a thousand and one times, when questioning suspects. The nervous system responds to the impulses of the brain and the effects show in the eyes. Alarm, surprise, shock, they all register as they had just done in the nurse's eyes. Nealis knew then that they had been expected.

The nurse excused herself and opened the door of an office adjacent to the ward and shut it behind her quickly, but not fast enough to prevent Nealis catching a glimpse of a uniformed policeman sitting inside.

'Get out, Frank. Quick!'

Frank stared at him for a second too long, and the moment was past. The door of the office opened and a young policeman stepped into the corridor, adjusting his peaked cap and then dropping his hand to his hip, near to the holster on his belt.

'Just a moment,' he said. 'I believe you are Mister Nealis.'

Nealis caught a glimpse of the nurse standing just inside

the office, watching. She probably had no idea.

'Yes, I am,' Nealis said. Frank had kept his back to the RUC man, and Nealis moved in, still talking. 'I am Detective Inspector Nealis. My mother died this afternoon.' He took out his wallet and waved the warrant card in front of the policeman. Out of the corner of his eye, he saw Frank begin walking slowly down the corridor.

'There are two of you?'

'Yes, this—'

'Hey, you! Wait a minute there.' The policeman brushed past Nealis and walked towards Frank, who stopped but kept his back to them. 'Nurse! Call the others,' the RUC man shouted over his shoulder as he advanced on Frank.

Nealis motioned quickly to the girl. 'Don't do that,' he commanded her. She glanced briefly at the policeman and didn't move. Nealis ran, and thrust himself between his brother and the other man.

'Listen, you get back into that office and wait there. That's an order!' For a split second, the RUC man hesitated.

'That's Frank Nealis,' he said. 'I have orders to ...'

'I'm giving you new ones!'

'That's Frank Nealis,' the policeman repeated. He was reaching for his gun. Farther down the corridor, an orderly backed out of a lift door, pulling on a wheeled stretcher. It was half out the door when he saw the three of them, and he stopped. The feet of the still body on the stretcher stood out under the white sheet.

'Go back!' Nealis ordered, but the policeman only backed away from him and now the gun was in his hand.

'Frank Nealis,' he shouted. The sweat was pouring down his face. The orderly with the stretcher had moved, pulling the trolley into the corridor. The white sheet covered the body entirely, and Frank saw it.

'Me Ma!' he yelled, and began to run down the corridor.

The policeman suddenly crouched with his gun arm outstretched, screwing up his eyes in readiness for the shock of firing.

'Frank!'

Nealis bellowed the warning but it was drowned in the thunderous noise of the pistol firing. Rigid with shock, Nealis watched Frank still running while the sound crashed and banged down the corridor. The orderly had thrown himself to the floor and the stretcher free-wheeled along only a few paces ahead of Frank. Another shot blasted Nealis's ear and then a third. Frank staggered forward, down on one knee, but recovered and reached out for the trolley, now slowly skewing across the corridor. Frank got to it, but stumbled clumsily and only managed to snatch at the sheet. He fell, skidded a foot or two and then lay still. In a sickening slow motion, the sheet was dragged from the trolley, which stopped laterally across the corridor. The RUC man was on his knees, looking helplessly at his gun and the smoke seeping from the barrel and breech.

Nealis stood looking at the body of his brother lying in the shadow of the stretcher. Down the corridor a nurse stood frozen against the wall, small trembling noises of fear breaking from her lips. Nealis walked slowly along to the stretcher and glanced down at the dead woman, wondering idly who she was and what she had died of.

22

A blackness had enveloped Nealis, driving all feeling from him save for a dark, murderous hate. It showed in the way he moved, hunched up and aggressive, fists balled against the world, and the way he looked at people. There was no warmth in his eyes now, only a challenging hostility. He made no conversation and sat for hours, huddled to himself while the pressures built up inside him.

Maire tried to break him out of it, but he was too far gone, the dejection was too complete. Yet there were practical matters to talk about. She came back into the house, her red hair tossed by the wind into an iridescent halo, and saw him sitting as she had left him, crouched forward in a chair and looking out through eyes which saw nothing. She walked across to him.

'Michael.' He sat, not moving, only nodding his head to acknowledge her presence. 'Michael, you've got to listen.'

They had picked up the broken body that had been his brother and put it away in the mortuary. After a time, in the first few hours, he had roused himself from his inertia and gone with Maire to make arrangements with undertakers and policemen and hospital officials for the release of Frank's body. He and Mother Kate were to be buried together in the same carefully kept plot that already held his father.

'Michael, look. Will you listen to me, please? I've seen about a Requiem Mass for them both. The whole of Bogside will be there. The whole of Bogside, Michael.'

'God curse them,' he said.

She fell silent, not sure to whom he was referring. He sat there, still as a statue, feeling the gnawing in his gut. Suddenly Maire had had enough. He had been sitting there for too long, there was no time for sitting. Arrangements had to be made. The anguish and frustration erupted.

'Michael, for Christ's sake, will you snap out of it.' Her voice was harsh, an edge of tension and desperation to it.

He looked at her without interest, saying nothing.

'What's wrong with you? For Christ's sake, what's the matter with you? Stand up to it, for God's sake, stand up to it.' The tears came abruptly and she stood there, not caring that she cried.

Michael got up quickly, putting his arms around her. 'Now Maire ... Maire, darling, don't.'

He pulled her into him and stood there stroking her hair and saying nothing while the sobs subsided. When she had stopped he patted her cheek gently. 'Come on, we have to get ready for the wake,' he said.

The bodies were being brought back that afternoon and they were to be laid out in their coffins on trestles in Maire's front room so that the neighbours could come and pay their last respects. It was an old custom and some who came would get drunk while others cried, but behind all the outward formalities or indiscretions there was always the knowledge that a grief was being shared. Maire began to move about the room, adjusting the tall candlesticks that were to lie around the coffins, laying out the crucifixes ready for the undertaker's men when they arrived. Michael helped her for a while, then sat down, watching her. From the corner of her eye, she caught the expression of distaste on his face.

At last, he spoke to her. 'I've been thinking, Maire,' he said.

'Yes, I noticed.'

'I've been thinking and what I thought was that Frank was right. This is a stinking, lousy, rotten country and it needs a bloody good shake-out.'

'Yes, we all know that.'

'Do you? Do you, Maire? I wonder whether you do. The sort of purging I'm talking about won't be done by a bunch of do-gooders getting out on the streets and shouting that they want equality. It needs more than that. We want a force here, a dedicated force whose only allegiance is to the human race.' She was still moving about the room. 'Come here and sit down,' he said, 'I've been thinking all this and it's all crammed up inside me so I think I'll burst if I keep it in any longer. Sit down.'

She moved over and sat beside him on the settee, looking into his face.

'What we should do is burn down all the fucking churches and shoot any bastard who tries to stop us. Banish the priests and the ministers and the clergymen or forbid them to practise their religion and jail them for life if they do. That would be a start.'

'Michael,' she began, feeling a pang of alarm deep inside her. He ignored the interruption.

'I'd do it. By Christ I would. Register every child as an agnostic at birth and banish the God of the Catholics and the God of the Protestants to some country that can support them. They shouldn't be allowed a God in this country because they don't know how to handle Him. He's supposed to be gentle and loving, but the Irish use the cross as a weapon to crack heads with.'

'Banish the churches? Could anyone do that?'

'I could, and would, if I had the men and the weapons. I wouldn't discriminate, I'd have the whole bloody lot out. Frank was right, you know. Total destruction, that's what this country needs. Religion, government—the lot.'

'Michael, what's got into you?' Maire said, shaking her head in wonder. 'Why do you talk like this? It's not you.'

'It is me. It's Michael Nealis, who's stood on the sidelines too long. It's me that's going to do something at last.' With a final savagery, he added: 'I've got nothing else to lose, anyway.'

Maire rode the sudden deep hurt of that remark and said nothing.

'This sounds melodramatic,' he continued, 'but it's true. I spent the whole of my adult life building up a belief in a system. It was the best I had seen and the best I could imagine. In a way, I had a mystical belief in that system, the sort of belief that lets you overlook the little imperfections and anomalies. But by Christ, those bastards have destroyed it. There's nothing left to believe in now. Unless violence. A month ago, that wouldn't have been true, but by Christ I've seen it working—against me. Now I believe in it, and I'm going to hit back.'

She felt the wild, unforgiving hate that pulsed through him and sorrow settled on her: 'You're upset, Michael. That's no way, you can't believe that. It's one thing to agree that violence may be sometimes necessary, but that's not what you're saying. You're building a whole creed based on violence. It won't do.'

'It will do, Maire,' his voice was steady and controlled and he spoke with the hard certainty of conviction. 'The whole of this society, this lousy bigot-ridden society, has been based on violence. The Orange Lodges, the police, Ross Simmons, every stinking one of them are hanging together in a violent alliance. It's time there was some real violence in return.'

'I'm not sure I believe that, now,' she said.

'Well I am. Jesus, every time there's been violence it was the Orangemen who started it. In Derry, Belfast, Armagh—everywhere. They struck the first blow and the reason they struck the first blow is that they felt secure. The police and the authorities provided that for them. Look Maire, it's fifteen years since I was in this country, and I'd forgotten what it was. Or maybe I never knew what it was, but I know now. They got my father, and then they got my mother and after that they got my brother. You think I can go on sitting back watching it happen?'

'Michael, there's nothing you can do. You're out of it. You're not involved.' There was pleading in her voice now. 'Please, Michael—'

He turned a tight face upon her: 'I was out of it, but I'm back in it now. Whether I like it or not, or you like it

204

or not, I'm back in it and something's going to be done before I'm out of it again.'

There was a knock at the door and Maire went to open it. The hearse had arrived bearing the bodies of Frank and Mother Kate. Michael watched in silence as the deferential undertakers carried the coffins in and laid them on the trestle tables. Maire moved around the room lighting candles.

The lids had been screwed loosely onto the coffins and Michael watched one of the undertaker's men releasing the brass screws from the light, pine wood. Mother Kate's coffin about eight inches shorter than her son's, was opened first. Nealis walked over to it and stood looking down. The undertaker had done a good job on the face. It was peaceful. But when Frank's coffin had been opened and Michael went across to look he saw the face was twisted. All the undertaker's skills had not been able to erase the last grimace of pain.

Neighbours had crowded around the door outside and they started coming in now. They entered, shy and intrusive in little groups of two and three, mainly women at first. The women carried wreaths and flowers which they put down inside the door before going across to look into the coffins. They were followed by the men, shambling and embarrassed in the presence of death, but with their bottles of liquor clutched tight in their hands. They formed a mournful queue past the coffins, shuffling slowly along, each of them crossing themselves and muttering a prayer as they looked into the faces of death.

The room filled quickly and the air was heavy with respect. The people stood around in little groups, remembering the actions, the words and the voices of the two dead people, and telling each other what they remembered. Maire went out into the kitchen to fetch plates of sandwiches, and when she came back she found them all kneeling in prayer.

It was customary to pray, so they knelt there murmuring the De Profundis, the traditional prayer for the dead. The voices rose in a mumble of invocation and somewhere amongst them a woman wept.

After the prayer they rose and started coming to Nealis, singly and in twos.

'I knew your mother, son. God rest her soul.'

'Ah yes, a fine woman, she'll be sadly missed.'

'And God help us, your poor brother. A great man he was.'

Maire watched as he stood there accepting their tributes with an expression that registered little interest in what they had to say. This was the form, the traditional form that things had to pass through, but she could see that his grief was tight and private and that only a sense of loyalty to his mother kept him standing there, civil but distant, as he listened to the sincere, hackneyed tributes.

Pogue Mahone came in, taking the cap from his head and thrusting it into the side pocket of his jacket. There was a rip down the shoulder of his coat where the sleeve joined the back and the padding was hanging out in a white fringe. His face was red and sweaty, as though he had been drinking heavily, which he had. He nodded to Michael and then went across to the coffins to stare blankly into them. Then he came back: 'I'm sorry for your trouble,' he said.

'Thanks, Pogue.'

'Listen, I've something to tell you.' He looked around the room to see if anyone was listening to him and moved Nealis away from the others by pushing at his elbow.

'Mulholland wants you.'

'What for? I'm in the middle of waking my mother and my brother, for Christ's sake. What does he want me for?'

'Jaziz, you wouldn't expect him to be telling the likes of me what he wants you for, would you? Cute as a snake's belly that fellow is. He said to tell you that he would have come over, but it's something important and private that he wants to talk to you about. Will you come?'

'All right.' Nealis turned and followed Pogue from the house, walking down the darkening street, vaguely conscious of the reel that one of the mourners had started to play on an old, whining fiddle.

23

It was quaint, Mulholland was thinking as he watched the American carefully filing his fingernails, that the fellow should be so meticulous when he lived in such a shithouse. He had never been to the place before. They had always met at Pogue's place or sometimes at the Free Derry headquarters or at some other house, but never before at Forrester's. What made it more quaint was that he lodged in the back room of a bar and he never, ever took a drop of the stuff. But then, the American was a peculiar man in many ways. Nevertheless, Mulholland was realist enough to recognize how well they complemented each other. The American had an educated brain and organizing ability: Mulholland had instinct and the gift of communication at any level. The one could plan, the other persuade. It was a powerful combination.

'We've got work to do,' Forrester said suddenly

'That we have,' Mulholland said.

'Right, then, let's get down to it.' Swiftly, he cleared the table, throwing newspapers, books and pamphlets onto the camp bed already strewn with papers. From beneath the bed he retrieved an elegant dispatch case, unlocked it and brought out several sheets of paper.

'I was up at first light this morning,' he went on. 'And I think I've covered most of the angles in this problem, which is when and how to take out Ross Simmons, right?'

Mulholland snorted. 'Take him out? You've a quair way of putting things. I want to blow the bastard's head off.'

'It's the same thing.' Forrester didn't smile. 'Anyway, I believe I have the answers. They're going to lay on a big production for this funeral of the Protestant guy tomorrow. Right?'

'Right.'

'And Ross Simmons will be there. So that's when we take him.'

'Wait a minute, me bucko. Ross Simmons will be there, surely, but they're going to walk in procession from the middle of the city right up to the cemetery beyond Waterside and there will be thousands of police there too, and soldiers. They'll be looking for something like this. Expecting it.'

'I plan to hit when they don't expect it.'

'Go on.'

'We'll make the hit at the last minute. In fact, when Ross Simmons and all the rest are right there at the graveside.'

'Can it be done?' Mulholland felt a shiver of excitement. It was brilliant. The effect would be shattering. If it could be done.

'Yes,' Forrester continued. 'It can be done, this way.' He beckoned Mulholland to the table and spread out a map of Derry and two sketch maps he had drawn himself.

'The funeral is at eleven. The procession will form up and begin to move off from the city centre at about nine, OK? So we have our man, whoever he is, right in there with the cortège but well back so he can trail the whole thing right to the cemetery. I checked out the location this morning and got hold of the schedule. The procession is going to move into the cemetery and up this path here.' He traced the dotted line on the map.

'Now, this pathway leads slightly uphill to the chapel of rest at the top. Inside there, they will hold a service which will be attended by the relatives and the big wheels of the day. Our man will remain outside with the rest of the crowd. At the end of the service, the coffin will be carried out again and down this path here. It leads downhill and about fifty yards down, the procession will leave the path and turn off onto the grass to the grave, about ten yards from the path. We couldn't have been luckier with the choice of the patch, either, I tell you.'

'How?'

'Well, there's a tree almost in line with the chapel and the grave. Almost in line, but not quite. Which means that our man will have a shelter, but a good field of fire.'

'From the chapel?'

'Sure.'

It was Mulholland's turn to laugh. 'You're a bastard. A lovely, devious wee bastard.' He laughed and smacked his fist into his hand. 'Shoot him at the graveside and fire the shot from the chapel! Bejesus, that's good, that is. Bloody good.'

'Fine, but there are some problems yet. Number one is the gun. Our man cannot carry it with him, even if we break it down. Too much could go wrong. That means somebody else has to take it to him when he is inside the chapel and while the rest of the crowd are gathering around the graveside. So we need someone as reliable as the gunman himself to take the weapon to the spot. I'll leave that part of it to you, right?'

'Right.' Mulholland pursed his lips in thought for a few seconds, then snapped his fingers. 'Got it! I know just the person. She'll do it.'

'Who will?'

'The O'Dwyer girl.'

'A woman? You think that's worth the risk?'

'There's no risk about it. She'll do it all right.'

'But you'll have to tell her what it's about. I'm not so sure—'

'See her yourself, then. Go around to Glenna Street yourself and see her. Tell her I want her to run a message for me. She'll do it. That girl's got a lot of nerve—she's got a lot of everything as a matter of fact, but that's neither here nor there. You see, she's just what we want. Don't tell her too much, mind. Just enough to let her know it's important.'

'Fine. I'll do that. But the next problem is something I haven't figured yet. I'd like to know what you think.'

'Ask me.'

'Well, it's this. We can make the hit easily enough, providing we have the right team and they follow the plan. What may not be easy is to get them out from the scene after the event.'

Mulholland shrugged. 'Maybe we should leave it to the man to make his own arrangements. Maybe we can suggest some way.'

'Or maybe we'd be better not to mention it at all?' Forrester was looking directly at Mulholland, silently emphasizing the full message in his words. Mulholland got the point.

'You mean, leave him to fry?'

'If necessary. Of course, there's a chance he'll make it, but ...'

'But there's a good chance he won't.'

'OK, but this is the time for being realistic, isn't it? Does it really matter if he gets away with it, so long as he does it? The point of this operation is to kill Ross Simmons, and the purpose of that is to light a bonfire under this country. What's one man against the chance to create something new right here and now?'

Mulholland had lit a cigarette while Forrester had been talking and now he blew a cloud of smoke to the ceiling and leaned back in his chair. 'You're talking as if you're trying to convince me,' he said. 'And that's a pure waste of your breath because I don't need to be convinced. I'm with you.' Mulholland took another drink. 'But while I agree with the sentiment, there's the practicality. We've got to find a way to get our man out of there because if he's nabbed by the police or whoever there's always the chance he'll start talking too much. And that's no good. No good at all. I've got to stay clean and pure and white if there is to be any advantage in this thing. It's not going to be everybody who'll clap their hands with joy at this thing, you know, even those on our side. When the blood is running we still have to think of the politics and in politics there's always a wee bit of running with the devil. No, we shall have to put our minds to it and make sure our man gets away.'

Forrester's face creased into a frown. 'Maybe you're right. I'll think of something.'

'On the other hand there's no lack of folk who'd give themselves for the cause, as they call it. You've heard those bloody boneheads down at the Free Derry place, haven't you, all wind and piss shouting their stupid heads off? The pity of it is they don't know what it's all about. They haven't got the slightest wee sniff of a notion of what is happening. You know something? Some of them think we've got what we've been fighting for already. They hear the B-Specials are going to be disbanded and they all leap to their little feet and jig around the room. Ah, Christ, it makes me puke. Do you have a beer here?'

'There's a barful out there. Go get one if you want.'

Mulholland ambled out in search of a Guinness, leaving Larry Forrester staring thoughtfully after him. When he returned, he held the uncapped bottle in his hand and he stood to take a swig.

'That's better,' he said, and burped loudly.

'I don't quite figure you,' Forrester said. 'Even now, I can't figure you.'

'And I can't see to the bottom of you either,' Mulholland replied, taking another drink. 'Does it matter?'

'Maybe not. But I don't understand what you are aiming to get out of all this. You personally, I mean, at the end of it all?'

Mulholland shrugged his shoulders. 'I'm a practical man, me bucko. I can't say what the end of it will be. I know what I think it will be, what it ought to be, but I have the habit of taking it all bit by bit, you know. Step by step.

'Things have been getting quiet—too quiet. It's time they started up again and maybe we'll get them started. If we do it right the whole place will fall apart. Then maybe I can help put the bits together again, but in the right way this time. Ah, well, if it comes to that, I don't know what you're about. You're a good man to have on our side, but I don't believe you really care a stuff about us or this country, do you?'

'I'm a strategist,' Forrester replied. 'And a strategist takes the global view of all life and does what he thinks is necessary where he can, catalysing events. But when he's done that, he doesn't belong any more. Then it's the turn of others to figure out the tactics.'

'Like in a war,' Mulholland said. 'With long term objectives and short run aims. I've read the manuals too, you know.'

'I'd say you were an effective son of a bitch,' Forrester said.

'Yes,' Mulholland said. 'Perhaps that's why we work so well with each other. Anyway, screw the chat.' He took a last mouthful from the bottle and lobbed it neatly into a wastebin in the corner of the room. 'There's still things to be sorted.'

'OK, so now we come to the sixty-four-dollar question. Who is going to pull the trigger on Ross Simmons tomorrow with Nealis gone?'

Mulholland smiled slyly. 'Now, it's a funny thing you should be asking that at this time, for the very man is on his way here.'

'Who is it?'

'Just you wait and see.' Mulholland began to hum a tune to himself. 'You know, I think I'll have another Guinness while we're waiting, eh?'

24

There were men standing around the bar, quiet and moody men who drank with an earnest sense of quiet desperation. They did not indulge in the usual bar-room banter, but just stood there silently, too close and too involved in the events that swirled around them to be bothered talking. Pogue elbowed his way through them and led Nealis into the back room where Mulholland was waiting.

Forrester was sitting on the camp bed, still manicuring his fingernails. As Nealis entered he looked at him, then shot a questioning glance at Mulholland.

'Is this your man?'

'Could be.'

'That's an inspired choice.' He rose as he spoke, and it was impossible to tell from his tone of voice whether he was being derisory or complimentary. He stood there, inspecting his fingernails for a moment, hand outstretched and fingers splayed, and then said: 'I'll leave you guys to it. I'm going to split.' He went out still looking at his fingernails.

Nealis stood there, looking down at Mulholland, waiting for him to speak.

'Sit down, Michael.' Mulholland's tone and smile were friendly. Nealis sat on the camp bed which Forrester had just vacated.

Mulholland reached into his jacket pocket and drew out a tobacco tin and some cigarette papers. He put some tobacco in the centre of one of the papers and began rolling it back and forward to get the shape right before putting the paper to his mouth to lick the gum.

213

When he had lit the cigarette he drew on it deeply and turned to Nealis. 'Did you know that your brother was going to kill Ross Simmons?' he asked.

Nealis looked back at him stolidly. 'Was he?'

'He didn't breathe it to you?'

'I'd like you to tell me.'

Mulholland smiled easily, drawing on his cigarette. 'That Ross Simmons is a dangerous man, you know.'

'I know that.'

'Well.' An expansive spread of the arms, another smile. 'That's why Frank volunteered to kill him.'

'Volunteered?'

'Oh yes, volunteered all right, like the great-hearted man that he was. He didn't need to be asked to step forward when there was a job to be done. This country is going to miss men like your brother Frank.'

'How was he going to do it?'

'Well, that had not been settled. We were looking for a way. But he was the man for it when the time came.'

'The time will never come now,' Nealis said.

Mulholland smiled again, amiably and disarmingly. He felt like an angler with a fish on the end of his line, playing the catch until he was able to ground it. At the moment he was slackening his line. It was not yet time to reel in and land the fish. 'No, that's right. At least, the time won't come for Frank.'

'What are you telling me this for?' There was an edge of impatience to Nealis's voice.

'Be easy, man, be easy.' Mulholland struck a match to relight his cigarette before going on. 'I've watched you since you came over here. I'll admit that. I'll admit that I thought you were some sort of English instigator, a plant, but I changed my mind.' He waved his cigarette in the air. 'Michael, your heart's in the right place. Sure I know that. I know that now.'

Nealis did not reply. He sat there waiting for something he could understand, conscious that Mulholland was giving him a build up. A suspicion of what Mulholland might want flitted through his mind. If he was right, well, it would depend on the circumstances. And if the circumstances were right?

'How much do you know about Ross Simmons?' The question cut into his thoughts.

'I know a hell of a lot about Ross Simmons. I was in the Army with him. He saved my life one time. I was grateful to him for that, but now he's taken the lives of my mother and my brother. I'd say that leaves me level.'

'In the Army with him, were you? I didn't know that,' Mulholland said. 'Boys, oh boys, it's a small world now, and that's a fact. He'll have changed a lot since you knew him, of course. No, he wouldn't be the same man at all.'

'He's changed all right,' Nealis said.

'Do you know, Michael, I think there are some men who are not fit to live. Ross Simmons is one of them.'

'How are you going to do it?' Nealis asked abruptly.

'We're going to shoot him, that's how. At least, I hope we are. If Frank had been spared there would have been no difficulty ...' He spread his arms again in resignation.

Nealis waited.

'By Christ, Michael, I'd do it myself, but I'm no hand with a rifle and that Pogue Mahone is so bad with the drink that he'd never be able to hold the rifle long enough to get a shot in. There's nobody else we can rely on.'

'Nobody else?' Nealis said. 'You mean nobody else but me?'

'Yes. Michael, that's exactly what I mean.' Mulholland took a deep breath. 'Would you? For your brother and your mother's sake, Michael. Would you?'

'I might. Then again, I might do it just for myself.' His voice was sharp and bitter.

Mulholland left him then and walked out into the bar. Minutes later he came back with a bottle of whiskey and two glasses. He poured a good measure into each of the glasses and gave one to Nealis.

'You'd have your own reasons of course, but there are others. I think I should tell you about them.' While Nealis waited he took a swig at his whiskey and topped the glass up before offering the bottle to Nealis.

'You know there's a hard-core bunch of Orangemen in the government who are in favour of UDI? They want to cut adrift from Britain, like Rhodesia, and go it alone with their own little fascist state, backed up by the police and the B-Specials? If that happened, Christ help the Catholics in Ulster.'

'Is that likely?' Nealis asked.

'By God man, it could be a fact. It's the Protestant extremists who caused all the fighting.' His voice went soft: 'It was the same people who killed your mother. And Ross Simmons is their leader.'

There was a long silence, and then Nealis said: 'Tell me how it can be done.'

Mulholland throttled back his jubilation and moved closer. From among the papers on the floor he picked up the rough diagram which the American had made. He began talking, softly and persuasively, pointing at the diagram as he did so. Nealis sat back, listening.

*   *   *

Larry wondered whether Mulholland had been right in his choice of man, but after some thought, concluded that he probably had. In clinical terms, this man Nealis had been suffering from a loss of identity during the past weeks. Add to that the traumatic shocks administered by the death of his mother and brother and it was obvious that the character disintegration had gone pretty far. Then, he was a naturally aggressive man, as policemen are, and the only way such a man can take pressure is by exploding. Just so long as Mulholland channelled the explosion in the right direction everything would be all right.

Nealis would be looking for some way to express himself because he was psychologically ready to hit back. The trick was to focus his hate on the subject, beam it all in on Ross Simmons, and then he would be right, then he would take him out. And, after that, the holocaust. When that bullet struck down Ross Simmons the old hatreds would be instantly polarized, and blood would follow.

There was music coming from the house in Glenna Street, and the wild whoops of half-drunken people. Larry entered the house through the open street door.

There was a fat woman dancing in the middle of the floor in the front room and a crowd of people around applauding her. He looked distastefully at the fat woman, massive mammaries jiggling as she leapt up and down on the floor with her face red and sweating to the music of the traditional dance. There was a small, vacant-looking man playing a fiddle in the corner. He wore a shirt without a collar and his Adam's apple bobbed behind his shirt stud in a frenzy of musical appreciation. The incongruous coffins lay isolated amidst the revelry around them.

Somebody pushed a drink at him, but he refused.

'Come on, boy, you've got to drink to the dead.'

'I don't drink.'

'Well, you're a quair old sobersides. Give us a song then.'

At that moment he saw Maire, flushed and pretty, watching it all from the other side of the room. He circled around the dancing woman to reach her: 'Hello, Miss O'Dwyer.'

'Oh, hello.' She wondered what he was doing there.

'I've a message for you. Bartley Mulholland says will you be at his house at nine o'clock tomorrow morning. He has something he'd like you to help with. He said you'd understand.'

'Understand? Well, yes.'

'You'll be there?'

'All right,' she said. 'Tell him I'll be there.'

Forrester walked out into the night, glad to be away from the obscene ritual of death.

25

Twenty thousand people were on the move in Derry that grey, damp day in September. They had come from all over the Six Counties to pay their respects to a poor old man whose life had been a cypher but who, in death, had been discovered as a symbol of Protestant martyrdom. They had filed past his open coffin throughout the night and the wreaths which were tossed to him bore the inscriptions of Orange Lodges, clubs, movements and loyalist organizations from the length and breadth of Ulster. A guard of honour had spent the night in vigil round the bier, changing frequently to accommodate the mass of volunteers and to revive their circulations with generous toasts to the soul of the dead man.

Now it was nine o'clock in the morning and they were preparing to carry the coffin and its Union Jack through the city to the cemetery on the hill.

In the place of rest, four men stooped low to get their backs under the coffin and strained as they lifted it aloft. They had more than three miles to carry their burden and the dead lie heavy on the backs of the living.

Others trooped into line to pick up the mass of wreaths and flowered tributes. A word of command was whispered and the coffin moved rhythmically forward as the pall-bearers, with the smell of the fresh linen flag in their nostrils, took their first steps.

When they emerged, the thick crowds standing silently on the kerbs lowed softly in sympathy. Billowing out behind the coffin, like a multi-coloured cloak, came the wreath bearers and then the widow, a straight little figure swathed in black and supported on one side by a clergyman and on the other by one of her menfolk. In her train came the men for whom this was more than a funeral. Grimly solemn, they had wrung the widow's hand and murmured words of solace, words of encouragement, words of sorrow, brave words, but reserving to themselves the thoughts that she would not have understood.

Across the city the four men trudged with their load and they dragged behind them an ever-growing multitude. Those who had stood and watched them pass now fell into place to swell the cortège.

Through The Diamond, draped in red, white and blue flags, and across the Foyle Bridge where a squad of British soldiers watched and came to attention as the cortège passed. There was no noise at all save for the feet and the ripple of conversation which echoed in the wake. The weight of the body and its wooden envelope bit deeply into the shoulders of its bearers. Later, they would find blood on their shirts where their blisters had burst and they would be proud of it, but now they gritted their teeth and carefully kept pace, each with the others. Uphill, leg muscles straining, twenty thousand people walking towards the cemetery. The leaders were approaching the gates when the rearguard was still crossing the Foyle and, further back, the traffic began to move again in Derry.

The procession filed through the cemetery gates and up the path to the chapel, hung with yet more flowers. There, it stopped and the long orderly line began to spill and spread like an inkstain among the gravestones until the flow of humanity was shut off by the closing of the gates and the great mass outside congealed around the entrance.

*   *   *

It was ten o'clock and quiet outside. Larry Forrester moved slowly around the little room that served him as an office, study and bedroom. He was packing a holdall with a vague air of absent-mindedness and welcoming the quiet outside which so exactly matched his mood. After the bustling anguish that had filled the street an hour before there was now almost an air of let-down. In many ways that was how he felt. He had experienced the same feeling that morning in Paris when the students took to the streets and tore up the pavements in the Sorbonne while they waited for the riot police to charge.

He had gone to his room, then, empty and hollowed out while he waited for the vicarious thrill of having his ideas confirmed in action. It was the same now, but different and the difference, he knew, lay within himself. He stopped and peered into a looking glass, examining his face and finding in it tinges of sadness. The sadness was there for a very strong and cogent reason. At the age of thirty-one, Larry Forrester had lost his faith.

It was impossible for him to pinpoint the exact moment at which his faith had crumbled and collapsed, because it had been suffering from a gradual erosion for some time, but Paris was one of the catalysts.

After the barricades had gone up and the students had invested the Sorbonne there had been a heightened sense of fulfilment within him, for here was the real stuff of revolution. For a time it was a great moment, but then Forrester walked up to the Sorbonne to see the revolution that the students had wrought. He was met at the gate by a student policeman and taken to an office for documentation. Then he was issued with a pass and told of the ordered regime which the students had imposed on the anarchistic structure of the new Sorbonne. In a moment of blinding disgust he realized that they had reimposed all the old, bourgeois formulae, and from that moment things had started to go sour.

Without thinking, Forrester picked up the dark green folder on the table and looked at his passport photograph, flicking through the visas and customs stamps that partially told the story of his life during the past five or six years.

Forrester, Lawrence Leclair, born 1937 in Albany, New

York. There was the picture, a lean, dark-haired young man with intense eyes. Only he knew he had betrayed those eyes and that the fires were going out. He enjoyed only the mechanics now, and even then the joys were getting a little ragged around the edges. And, in the back of the folder, the final betrayal ... the first-class air ticket, open-dated, from London to New York.

He had made the decision now. It was no good any more. He looked at the airline ticket thinking that when it was no good any more a man had to go somewhere, but he wondered if he would ever again fit in to the Ivy League pattern of his former life.

*   *   *

Bartley Mulholland sat beside the telephone, watching it happily and waiting for the message that would set things moving. Pogue was up there somewhere in the cemetery, watching and waiting. As soon as the bullet hit Ross Simmons he would rush to a call box and telephone Mulholland.

In his hand Mulholland held a list of numbers for various towns throughout Northern Ireland. There were men waiting beside the telephones at each of those numbers. All he had to do was telephone them and say: 'Obliteration completed' and hang up. They would understand, and throughout the Six Counties the activists would be out in the streets, rallying and herding the mob forward into the awful, bloody confrontation.

'Obliteration completed.' It was a fine, rolling, melodramatic phrase, entirely suitable for the occasion.

*   *   *

Ross Simmons walked tall and straight this morning, absorbing the solid sympathy of the huge crowd. A feeling of pride welled up within him as his eyes took in the long line of God-fearing, compassionate people who stood along the route. These were good people, men and women of his own kind. This was his Ulster, a geographical area which defined a metaphysical entity that could not be properly known or appreciated by those who were not born into it.

The man ahead of him was either drunk or stupid, he decided suddenly. He was a small, thin man and he seemed to be having difficulty in walking, for he kept changing pace as his legs got out of step with the rest of the marchers. His constant agitation began to grate on Ross Simmons, intruding upon his thoughts. Deep in his mind he was delivering the speech he would have made at the graveside, if an interfering and subservient authority had not banned him from doing so. It would have been a marvellous oration, stirring up the memories and glories of the past and strengthening the spirit of those who heard it for now and for the future.

He stole a glance backwards down the hill as he turned into the gates of the cemetery. There was a line of people, six abreast, stretching back as far as he could see. Twenty thousand people in need of his message of comfort and hope. Poor, frightened bewildered people, needing the leadership that only he could give them. They were his people, and by the living God, he would protect them.

* * *

Maire had to move quickly to get into the cemetery before they shut the gates. Yet, once inside, she almost wished that the gates had closed in her face, barring her way. She knew now what was in the heavy bag. Marching along with the mourners she had raised it and looked inside. Then she had closed it quickly, her heart pounding as she looked around to see if any of the marchers had seen what was inside.

She was disquieted by the morality of what she was doing now and since she had looked into the bag her whole being had been a battleground on which moral strictures fought against gleaming little arguments of expediency. Could some acts be considered amoral, totally outside the sphere of primitive rights and wrongs, because of the results they achieved? she wondered. But no. That was a sophistry, a bromide for the conscience. The whole thing was morally wrong, but sometimes people had to do bad things so that good things could flower from them. If that was the case she would do it and face the moral judgements later.

There were loudspeakers set up outside the chapel of repose and the mourners who had not been able to get inside clustered around them, listening to the funeral service which echoed, brazen and metallic, across the funeral field. Slowly, politely, with many whispered apologies, she edged her way through the crowd towards the chapel. It was still a long way off and she could see nothing of what was going on there and she was not listening to the service. This thing had to be done and she wanted it done quickly. Everyone owes a debt to their mother country, she thought. Everyone would pay this one and then it would be finished. Then it would be herself and Michael. Maire and Michael. It would not be an idyll among the orange blossoms, she thought, but she would not have wanted it that way. If people want happiness they have to work at it, and she was prepared for that with him. Any time, any place. Maire and Michael, and the strengthening dependence of love.

This thing must be done first, though. She worked her way closer in towards the chapel, thinking of peace and happiness and a kiss that could bathe the whole world in tranquillity.

*　　*　　*

I'm off to make some last arrangement about the funeral, he had told Maire. He had thought later of this ambiguity, wondering if it had been unconsciously deliberate. He had left Glenna Street before eight and gone down into the city to watch the funeral procession form up and move off. He had chosen his place with care, so as to be not too near the man he was going to kill, but near enough to watch him. As a shadowing job, it was all too easy.

He had walked the three miles with his head bowed deep between the wings of his raincoat collar, concentrating on the thing he had to do. He had been remembering the sequence of events Mulholland had outlined to him, visualizing the interior of the chapel and the sight-line from the choir gallery window, running through once more the assembly of the rifle and recalling its surprising lightness.

When he had done that, he did it again, successfully damming up the flood of deeper thoughts which threatened to confuse him. Of those which did spill over into his full consciousness, he retained only the ones he wanted. The picture of Mother Kate and the sight of Frank dead on the floor. The sight of Ross Simmons in the mill and the things he had said and done. The bloody savagery of Bogside and the naked hatred of the RUC that day in Kilgallen Street. Those were the things he would purge today. Those were the scores he was levelling with the gun. And more than that, he was about to do something about the bloody mess of Ireland.

He reached the top of the gentle hill near the chapel but remained in the crowd, waiting until the chapel emptied. In the interval, he began to sift carefully through the crowd for the sight of anyone he knew who might be the man bringing the gun. But he saw nobody he knew, and he settled himself to wait in the rain.

It took half an hour before the service ended and the congregation spilled out behind the coffin. The crowd surged forward in an amoebic mass, sliding down the slope towards the graveside. Nealis edged towards the chapel doors and waited for the moment to slip inside. It was as Mulholland described it and the steps leading to the choir gallery were where he said they would be. He walked down the aisle and waited in the shadow of the lectern and near the foot of the wooden steps.

The doors of the chapel remained shut. He was dying for a cigarette.

26

Nealis climbed to the top of the bare wooden stairs and stopped. The ache in his gut had made it an effort. There was a risk in lighting a cigarette, but the craving within him made the risk worth taking, and he drew on the tobacco with the intensity of a man at the execution post. While he smoked, he looked down at the plain, whitewashed chapel, marvelling at its lack of ornamentation, and austerity. There were no pictures on the walls, no crucifixes, none of the pageantry of his own, discarded, faith.

The choir gallery ran laterally across the end of the chapel. There was a tiny space for the choir, two long benches crammed against the pipes of the organ. Nealis shuffled along between the benches to the side of the gallery, where a window of mottled glass gave out over the cemetery. The handle moved reluctantly, unused for decades, but Nealis bore on it and pushed the window outwards an inch or two with strong, blunt fingers.

He looked down on the backs of a thousand heads spread out between him and the nucleus of the scene—the slow, sad procession led by the coffin. It was shuffling gradually towards the centre of the cemetery, where an open grave gaped vacantly beside the mound of fresh, soft earth thrown up by the gravediggers.

A few miles away, at another cemetery, another grave lay open-mouthed, ready to receive the bodies of Frank and Mother Kate. Ashes to ashes, dust to dust. He shook his head grimly. A hell of a thing that.

The rain was lancing down diagonally across the cemetery

and as it fell a sudden gust of wind took hold of it and sent it driving into the faces of the people. Some of it came through the window, stinging clean and wet into Nealis's face. Some umbrellas began to appear among the crowd and as his eyes narrowed in on Ross Simmons he wondered whether they would provide an obstruction to his shot. Ross Simmons was standing there, large and important and surrounded by his entourage. Nealis assessed the distance at less than two hundred yards, a good easy shot with a telescopic rifle. He took a piece of blank white paper from his pocket and threw it out of the window, watching it move as he assessed the wind direction and velocity. He knew that over two hundred yards the wind would hardly make any difference, but he was leaving nothing to chance.

The crowd was standing silent now, hushed by the approach of the coffin and the dead man's family. The widow was there leading the family mourners, her small, grieving body wrapped in black clothing. She walked steadily and slowly, not looking at anyone, keeping her eyes straight ahead and clutching a wreath of flowers to her middle. As the coffin approached, women wept and men bared their heads. Ross Simmons was standing about ten yards to the left of the open grave. He took off his bowler hat and stood with the rain pattering on his unprotected head.

There was a noise in the chapel below him. A creaking noise of a door opening uncertainly. Nealis moved swiftly and silently away from the window and crouched near the top of the wooden stairs to watch. The chapel door swung open gradually and then Maire appeared. She was holding a soft leather bag in her hand and she peered hesitantly into the gloom. Nealis was perplexed, uncertain, nervous. He raised himself from his hiding place and began to walk down the little staircase. She had stopped in the middle of the aisle and was watching him, wide-eyed with surprise. She cast a quick glance around the chapel as if searching for someone else, and then stared at him again as he approached.

'Maire! What the hell are you doing here?' There was a

degree of irritation in his voice, which reflected the feeling inside him. He didn't want her here. He didn't want complications. Not now. Maire shook her head, saying nothing, shifting the weight of the bag in her hands. He caught the movement and looked down at the bag. 'Are you the messenger? Did Mulholland send you with this?'

'Yes,' she said.

'Fuck him. The bastard.'

'I know what's in the bag, Michael.'

'The bastard,' Nealis repeated.

'What are you going to do, Michael?'

'Don't you know?'

'No. I didn't know I had a gun. He didn't tell me. I had a look.'

'Give me the bag, Maire,' Nealis said. His voice was calm and level. 'I want you to go away from here. Go home and wait for me.'

'I will not.' Sadness and defiance mingled in her eyes.

'Maire, for Christ's sake, will you go?'

'No. I want to know what you are doing. Tell me, Michael. Why are you having a gun brought up here. What are you going to do?'

'It doesn't matter. You shouldn't have been involved. I'll kill Mulholland for this.'

'Will you, Michael? And who else are you going to kill?'

'Go home, Maire. Please. Get out of here and go home.'

'I know.' Maire's face was white. 'It's Ross Simmons, isn't it? Him out there.'

Nealis snatched the bag from her and walked away to the stairs. He mounted them and began moving across the gallery to the window. Maire followed him like an accusing finger. He began unzipping the bag, the sweat beading on his forehead.

'Go home!' he said suddenly, savagely.

'Don't worry, Michael,' she said. 'I'll not stop you. I can't, can I? Go ahead if you want to.'

Outside, the silence between them was broken by the low

227

chanting of a group of youths congregated below the window. Nealis peered out carefully. They were boys of about fifteen or sixteen and they were just audible in their insistent chant.

'Hell roast the Pope. Hell roast the Pope.' The old tribal chant droned on, repeated and mindless.

Nealis moved back quietly and said: 'Do you hear that, Maire?'

She nodded: 'I hear it.'

'Do you know what they are? Fodder for Ross Simmons. What can you do with a country where attitudes like that are bred in the bones of the people? What can you do?' His face was pleading for an answer and there was agony in it.

'I don't know, Michael.' She shook her head again, sad that she did not know, because he needed an answer.

'Nobody knows, that's the tragedy. But those fellows there, Ross Simmons is waiting for them. He's ready to pounce on them and put their training in mindless bigotry to good use. His use. Do you know, Maire, he's ready to take over the country. He's just waiting his chance.'

'Does he matter? If it wasn't him it'd be somebody else.'

'No, Maire, he's the one. He is the one.'

There was a line of armed soldiers and police around the edge of the cemetery. They had been deployed to keep a watching brief on the crowd and they were relaxed and assured in the rain. Nothing was going to happen here, they felt. There was no antagonism among these people, not towards their own.

Nealis lifted the rifle out and started assembling it. The stock fitted neatly together in two parts and the firing mechanism screwed into the side. The barrel, a deep metallic blue and shiny with gun oil, screwed into the front of the stock. There was a slot for the magazine. He fitted it in and then slid the bolt home and began clamping the telescopic sight on.

'You're going to do it, then?'

'Yes.' The answer was flat and final.

Outside they had the coffin at the graveside now and they were fixing ropes underneath it, so that the dead man could be lowered into the ground. A clergyman stood by, Bible in hand, as the crowd crushed closer into the graveside.

Nealis brought the rifle up and laid it along the line of the window, resting it on the sill, but rested like that it did not lie right. He walked across the gallery and down into the chapel looking for some padded kneelers in the pews. He found two and came back up the stairs with them, looking over to where the rifle lay.

Maire had stood up to let him pass and as he returned and busied himself at the window, she said: 'You do realize you're throwing it all away, don't you? You do realize that?'

Nealis didn't answer while he placed the hassocks down by the window and knelt on them, testing the rifle for height and position.

'What do you mean, throwing it away?'

'I mean us, Michael.'

'Us? What difference does it make to us? We're all right, Maire. We're together.'

'Are we? I'm not so sure.'

'I'm sure.' Nealis's voice was flat and hard.

'You've thought it all out, then, have you? You've thought beyond this, have you? You're just about to kill a man. Someone else might be able to do that and forget about it, but you won't, Michael.'

'Won't I?' Nealis's fingers were moving restlessly up and down the steel-blue sleekness of the gun barrel.

'How can you, Michael? You're not built that way.'

'It's not the first time I've shot a man,' he said slowly. 'I've shot a man before, and all he was doing was fighting for what he believed in. He thought he was fighting for freedom, but I had to shoot him.'

'You were a soldier then. It was different.'

'Was it?' he said. 'Was it different? A man gets himself into a situation where the choice is no longer his. I had no choice about shooting the man in Cyprus. I have no choice now.'

'All right,' she said, 'all right. Destroy yourself if you like. If that's what you must do, then do it. But I'm afraid for you, Michael.'

The boys beneath the window had stopped their chanting, but now they were laughing together. While sorrow settled over the rest of the people they sought refuge in jokes, but when the jokes ran out they started their *sotto voce* chant again.

For them it was a gesture of defiance against a baffling and ruthless enemy and, at the same time, a cry of solidarity with their fellows. The chant had an almost hypnotic effect on them, filling them with the confidence of heroes and assuring them of the rightness of their place in the universe. They were among friends, enjoying a friendship that was woven out of something deeper and more permanent than the mere happy inter-relation of human beings. There was a common goal and a communion of thought. They belonged, and those who belong need never know the dread of insufficiency.

'*Hell roast the Pope. Hell roast the Pope.*'

In sudden irritation, Nealis swore. 'For Christ's sake stop those kids!'

'I can't. You can't. Nobody can.'

The coffin was being lowered into the grave and the only other movement was the falling of the rain. The only sound was the solemn, indistinct tone of the clergyman. That, and the mindless chant below.

'They'll hear you if you fire,' Maire said. It was a comment, detached and unemotional.

'I'll take the chance.'

'They'll know where you are.'

'I'll be all right. I'll get away in the confusion. Now go, Maire. Get away before it all starts.'

'No. I'm staying with you.'

Nealis was taking sight now. The hairline tracery of the

telescopic sight crossed on the breast of Ross Simmons' over-coat and hovered over his heart. Nealis steadied the gun. One squeeze of the trigger, now, and it was over.

'Go, for Christ's sake.' Nealis tore his eye from the sight and snarled the words over his shoulder.

'I won't, Michael.'

Nealis trembled and let go the stack of anger inside his head. 'In the name of Christ, won't you go. I don't want you here.'

Maire flinched and then looked down at him. Disbelief. Sorrow. They made her eyes liquid, but she said nothing and turned abruptly from him. Still at the window, Nealis heard her footsteps receding down the stairs, along the aisle and out the door. He listened, straining his ears for the last sound of her, then turned back to the gunsight.

He settled himself on the kneeling pads, moving his legs around until there were no bumps beneath his knees, nothing to distract him, and shoved the rifle out through the window, looking out along the length of its barrel. He scanned around for Ross Simmons and found him easily. He was standing big and bluff and through the telescopic sights Nealis could see the whiteness of his teeth as he sang.

Nealis lined the rifle up, finding again the exact spot on Ross Simmons's breast that he had found before. The target was a little more than twelve inches down the trunk of the body, centred but slightly left. They had called it musketry practice in the army, quaint and old fashioned like that. Well, here he was and here was his trusty musket. Had Sergeant Simmons called it musketry practice? he wondered. Rough, tough Sergeant Simmons. Simmons the life saver and Ross Simmons the bringer of death.

Goodbye, Sergeant Simmons, you've had your chips ...

He took first pressure on the trigger, feeling it move easily and then met some slight resistance as the firing pin was engaged. Through the telescopic sight the nap on Ross Sim-mons's coat stood out, the fibres plainly showing. Down there they were still singing.

His tongue darted out of his mouth, licking his lips, and he pulled the stock of the rifle more tightly into his shoulder and prepared to fire.

Suddenly there was movement in the telescopic sight, the black cloth of Ross Simmons's coat swirled through his vision and then came to rest again. He lowered the rifle and looked out, searching through the density of the crowd with his naked eyes, and then he found Ross Simmons.

He was standing now with his back turned to Nealis, talking to some men who had been standing behind him. The back was big and broad and provided a perfect target.

'Turn around,' he whispered, 'for Christ's sake, turn around.' The deadly cross in the telescopic sight trembled a little.

Ross Simmons was deep in conversation with the men. The singing had stopped now and the mourners were beginning to leave, a slow, labyrinthine procession that shuffled slowly and solidly through the huge iron gates.

'Turn around,' Nealis pleaded. 'Please turn around.'

The people were walking more easily now, the duty done and all the tributes paid. They walked in groups, talking with their friends, smiling and being friendly with each other. They had come to bury their dead and they had done that. Now the mood of reverential sadness was passing from them, for it had been a duty well done, and it was time for the terrible burden to lift from them. They talked easily and happily and some of them even smiled. The reverence in the damp air was subsiding and as it did so, the youths standing below the window were emboldened. Their voices became louder. Nealis heard the voices of a man telling them to shut up, but they were unstoppable now.

'Hell roast the Pope. Hell roast the Pope.'

Ross Simmons still had his back turned. The perfect target. The bloody fool. Never turn your back on the bastards, that was your advice, Sergeant Simmons. Nealis shifted and re-aligned the sights. And then Ross Simmons turned. The telescopic sight became a brief kaleidoscope, then settled. He had him now.

'Hell roast the Pope.'

Nealis closed his eyes for a moment, driving the sound from his head. But it returned, insistent and insidious, a song of hatred which could never be erased.

He sighted along the barrel again and held the rifle firm. After a time, the nerves in his left arm began to quiver and the cross-hairs wavered and soon he was no longer focussing on them. Little by little, he lowered the rifle.

The chanting went on, taken up by some of the others farther away, as Nealis began to strip the rifle.

He took a last look out the window. Ross Simmons was still there, waving his arms around him and talking noiselessly. There was a group gathered about him, listening intently, transfixed, it seemed, by the word of the prophet.

Nealis picked up the bag and slipped away. Down the stairs. Along the aisle. He opened the door and stepped out. They were streaming past now, talking and jabbering and with their heads no longer bowed. The chanting was still going on around him and some of the youths were drifting past the chapel to the gates of the cemetery.

'Hell roast the Pope.' One of the lads brushed past Nealis, repeating the formula to himself, unaware, committed now and until the moment he died.

Maire was a few yards away and now she hurried to him.

'Michael! Have you—'

'No,' he said.

'Thank God.'

'It's no use, Maire. You can't stop them.'

'Who?'

Nealis grimaced. 'None of them.'

'I thought ... You frightened me, Michael.'

'I'm sorry, allanah.' The old Gaelic endearment came out more softly. He took her arm. 'Let's go, Maire. We've our own dead to bury.'

They put their heads down into the wind and walked

slowly away, engulfed by the tide of mourners that flowed downhill.

'You can get lost in a crowd like this,' he said.

'What?'

'Never mind.' They walked on, holding tightly to each other while the wind blew up from the lough, driving the rain into their faces. 'Come on,' he said, 'let's stay with the crowd.'